Robert Nicholas Barrett

Child of the Ganges

A tale of the Judson Mission

Robert Nicholas Barrett

Child of the Ganges
A tale of the Judson Mission

ISBN/EAN: 9783337088880

Printed in Europe, USA, Canada, Australia, Japan

Cover: Foto ©Andreas Hilbeck / pixelio.de

More available books at **www.hansebooks.com**

THE

CHILD OF THE GANGES

A TALE OF THE JUDSON MISSION

BY

REV. ROBT. N. BARRETT

FLEMING H. REVELL COMPANY

NEW YORK | CHICAGO

30 UNION SQUARE: EAST | 148 AND 150 MADISON ST.

Publishers of Evangelical Literature

TABLE OF CONTENTS.

CONTENTS.

BOOK FIFTH.

BOOK SIXTH.

THE CHILD OF THE GANGES.

BOOK FIRST.

CHAPTER I.

"Northward soared
The stainless ramps of huge Himalaya's wall
Ranged in white ranks against the blue untrod,
Infinite, wonderful, whose uplands vast,
And lifted universe of crest and crag,
Shoulder and shelf, green slope and icy horn,
Riven, ravine, and splintered precipice,
Led climbing thought higher and higher until
It seemed to stand in Heaven and speak with gods."
—*Light of Asia: Edwin Arnold.*

"GANGA! Ganga!" cries the sinful Brahmin who rushes for cleansing into the purifying stream. "Ganga! Ganga!" gasps the fainting pilgrim, as from a distant mountain top he hails the gleaming plain on whose billowy bosom is cradled the divine Mother of all. More sacred than the Jordan to the Israelite is the Ganges to the Hindu; for its waters are believed to cleanse from sin all who bathe in its tide. Pilgrims who come annually from afar bear back to their homes quantities of the precious fluid in their brass lotas to be used when bodily weakness detains them; and thousands who are unable to attend the great feasts absolve their souls by simply crying the mystic word, " Ganga !" From the dark depths of shady dells, from the burning wastes of arid plains, and from the busy streets of crowded cities, five hundred million voices cry " Ganga !" Within the curtained zenana, hidden from sight by the purdah's fringe, the little child in its swinging punka is taught to cry to Ganga as to its own mother.

The Ganges is the impersonation of the goddess Ganga, the daughter of the Himalaya. It is believed to be a gift from heaven sent in answer to sixty thousand years of prayer and severe austerities. Siva was required to catch the descending stream upon his head lest its sudden fall should tear the earth asunder.

Nor is the myth of its divine origin so incredible as it may first appear. The Himalayas are the highest points on the earth's surface. On their vast world of crags and snow is believed to be the home of Indra, the god of storms. Extending far above the surrounding range, with their summits lifted to the sky and covered with perpetual snow, are the two peaks, Gungootree and Jumnootree, respectively the sources of the Ganges and the Jumna. It seems that the god, extending his frozen arms to heaven, had caught in his icy fingers the congealed drops from the clouds, and sent them rushing in crystal streams down the mountain sides to refresh the burning plains below. The Ganges is, in one sense, the mother of the Hindu people; because, with its many tributaries and divisions, it irrigates the great plain of Hindustan, from the spontaneous products of which the indolent people derive their sustenance. All junctures of other streams and the Ganges are held sacred; but where it is joined by the sacred Jumna is especially so, and the sanctity of this place has been perpetuated by the founding of Allahabad, the City of God.

On the western bank of the Ganges, midway between Allahabad and Hurdwar, where the stream rushes from the gate of the mountain, is a noted grove, the favorite resort of religious ascetics. The river-bed at this point is more narrow, and its waters purer than below where they are continually defiled by the offal of the cities and the ashes of the dead. A landing *ghaut* of stone steps leads from the water up the very steep bank to the plain. Here the scene is something remarkable even for India. The plain, open for about a mile square, is covered with a carpet of green, variegated with flowers of the most gorgeous hue. Below, and facing the river is a small village with its ever present *pagoda* gleaming above the branches of the *tamarind* trees which shelter the village tank. Above is a background of dense forest, whose sombre shade, in contrast to the lovely view without, is the haunt of *fakirs* and *devotees* who seek such lonely and secluded spots where they may practice unmolested their deeds of self-torture and thus free the soul from its burden of guilt. At the entrance to the wood is a noble *banyan* tree which extends its main body, like a tall pagoda-spire, two hundred or three hundred feet in the air, and, with gently sloping sides and cloistered columns stretching out on either side and far within, presents the appearance of a vast natural temple, not unsuited to the presence of gods and those who desire to spend a life in solemn meditation. Most prominent on the western border of the plain, and from which the whole neighborhood derives its unusual sanctity, is a natural tower or unnatural mountain of solid granite. It rises abruptly from the plain, and is entirely bare, save where the rock has crumbled to decay, forming little patches of soil which support some scanty vegetation. Half way to the summit on one side is a level place furnished with a tank, shade trees, and a *mundapam* for the accommodation of pilgrims who visit the shrine on top by hundreds every morning before sunrise. The perpendicular shaft above is ascended by means of steps cut into the solid rock leading directly to the portico of a small temple on top dedicated to the worship of the elephant-headed god, *Ganesha*. The base of the temple is formed by the smoothed summit of the crag itself from which natural projections were left ranged around the idol and used as altars for the reception of the offerings, rice and *ghee* (melted butter), which are left in great quantities by the pilgrims. After these have all performed their worship and returned to their homes the *Brahmins*, who are the representatives of the gods, ascend and bear away the offerings for their own use. Every night a *pandarum*, or religious ascetic, absolves his soul from the sins of the day by lighting a lamp before the shrine which serves as a reminder to the sleeping villagers that their god is watching over them.

Our story opens at the close of a hot and sultry day in the month of August, 1808. The sun was just setting behind the dim blue hills in the distance, kissing "good-night" the gilded pagoda-spire, and darting its parting glances beneath the dense foliage of the forest; and, for the first time since morning, revealing the miserable forms that languished there. As the shadows were deepening on the landscape, and all nature's voices lulled to silence, a gentle dip of oars was heard in the river, and a gilded boat glided noiselessly up the stream to the ghaut. A man arose and lifted a woman and child from the boat to the steps, and the boatman having received his accustomed *backsheesh* rowed rapidly back down the stream, as the man, woman and child appeared on the plain. The fading light, though dim, served to reveal that they were not natives. The man appeared to be about thirty years of age, stalwart and handsome; and, though his dress and accent as he spoke to the boatman, showed him to be a stranger, there was a certain dignity about his bearing that betrayed his noble, if not royal descent. His head was covered with a luxuriant growth of glossy black hair, which, thrown back, revealed a peculiarly intellectual brow and a pleasant though serious face. His complexion was a deep brown, and his eyes, dark and lustrous, revealed a strong soul within.

He was simply but becomingly clad. The *in-gie*, a jacket of white linen, covered his body, and the *put-so* wrapped around his waist fell in heavy folds to his ankles, while the simplest form of sandals protected his feet.

The woman's apparel consisted of a rich saffron vest, open in front, disclosing folds of crimson beneath, and a skirt of embroidered silk wrapped closely about her waist and falling gracefully to her feet. Her physical features were mainly the same as her husband's, though more softened and less serious. It was only when she

looked at her child or its father that her countenance
betrayed any depth of expression. The child was a
girl of eight months, sweet and winsome; and like its
parents, bearing in its face the distinctive marks of
their *Burman* nationality.

They stood on the border of the plain for some
moments as if hesitating in which direction to go;
then, the father taking the child on his shoulder, and
the mother bearing on her arm a basket containing
their baggage, they proceeded toward the forest.

The full moon was just rising and making more
gloomy the shadows within as they reached the main
entrance of the banyan temple. They had come thus
far in silence, but as they entered the shadow the child
clung timidly to its father's neck and the woman shivered with fear, complaining that wild beasts would be
sure to devour them. The man placed the child on the
ground, and still holding her by the hand, he looked out
on the moon-lit plain so lovely and still; then, as if
inspired by the enchanting scene, replied:

"Mahdri, the very air is holy. No harm can come
to us here. Did not the priests in the Holy City assure
us that we should be perfectly secure? Be content. I
know there is a Supreme Being somewhere, and though
unable to see him, I am willing to trust myself in his
hands. Let us make here our couch and rest till morning, when some holy man will show us what we must
do further."

The woman, thus assured by his fearless manner and
confident words, said no more, but placing the basket
on the ground removed all its contents except a cushion in the bottom. On this she laid the child and

covered the basket with a light veil to protect the little sleeper from mosquitoes. The man then hung the basket from a branch above and tied to it a long cord reaching to the ground with which to rock the bird's-nest cradle if the little one should become restless through the night. In the meanwhile his wife had spread a blanket between the projecting roots of a column, on which they reclined to rest, the father holding the cord in his hand and gently swaying the basket to and fro. The mother and child fatigued with the journey of the day, soon fell into a deep restful slumber; but the man's stronger nature, harassed by con. flicting doubts and hopes, could not rest, and for hours he lay against the tree looking out on the soft Indian night and vainly trying to solve the problem of his future destiny. The *pundarum* had long since placed his lighted lamp before the shrine of *Ganesha* on the mountain, where it gleamed like a beacon to guide the feet of pilgrims to their destination, but, alas! it was a false beacon luring to destruction thousands of human souls who trusted in its god. The moon, shining through the hazy atmosphere, had a soft crimson hue; and its mellow radiance seemed to pour a flood of glory upon the plain, bathing surrounding objects with the glimmer of Fairy Land. An almost imperceptible breeze stirred the branches above and set in motion the many little silver bells on the pagoda whose distant chimes seemed to ripple and dance on the air, play hide-and-seek among the leaves and speak in a thousand piping voices from the dew-laden flowers of the plain, filling the heart with thought and memories sweet, or speaking to the soul in anticipation of a scene

of perfect rest beyond the sunset's gate of gold. Still
the man in the shadow of the banyan lay as if unconscious of anything. His eyes gazed vacantly upon the
plain or watched the glittering fire-flies darting like
meteors through the gloomy vaults above his couch.
Two young gazelles chased each other playfully in the
moon-light for awhile and then lay down under the
same tree with himself, but he saw them as in a dream.
In fact, all was a dream. What reality could there be
in all that loveliness when all within was a raging sea?
Ah! he had yet to learn that though in "a land where
every prospect pleases," true happiness cannot come
where "man is vile." Ever and anon a sigh escaped
his lips, and then he heard in response the wail of the
self-inflicted devotee as he held his lonely vigil far
within the wood.

"When, oh! when," he inwardly cried, "will I find
that rest and peace for which I long?"

Again the mournful wail echoed from the gloomy
depths, so distant and sad, he was fain to believe it
came from the troubled chambers of his own heart.
Thus thinking and praying, he fell into a troubled,
half-waking slumber.

Such, O reader, is a soul without a God!

CHAPTER II.

—Arnold.

NEXT morning at sunrise the little family arose, and having replaced their impromptu couch in the basket, took their way to the river to bathe. Returning to the grove after their ablutions a strange sight met their gaze approaching in the direction of the mountain shrine. A human being it was, but so bent and misshapen with age as scarcely to be recognized as such. His back was bent below the shoulders in such a manner that his trunk was horizontal, and his chin, when his head was not lifted by force, on a level with his waist. His brown, sun-burned skin clung about him in tough, wrinkled folds. A pair of linen trousers, once white, but now stained and yellow, reached like suspended sacks to his waist, leaving the remainder of his body entirely bare. On his brow, shoulders and breast were painted the peculiar marks, emblematic of the worship of Vishnu, while over his left shoulder, down to his right hip, hung the sacred cord of one hundred and eight threads, testifying his Brahmin caste. The single tuft of gray hair allowed to grow from his crown had attained a wondrous length ; and parting on each side hung down in front of his ears, mingling

(13)

with his snow-white beard, which extended almost to
his knees. His right hand held a short, stubby bamboo cane, with which to support his crooked trunk ; in his
left he held the customary brass lota, in which he carried
food. He walked with wonderful briskness considering
his aged appearance, and as he approached, his eyes
bent upon the ground, his perspiring back gleaming
unflinchingly beneath the rays of the tropical sun, his
smooth head bobbing up and down to the motion of his
feet and cane, and his enormous beard dangling about
his knees or flowing around his back in the breeze, he
presented the appearance of a most strange and picturesque being. Had he appeared by night, instead of
open day, he might have been mistaken for a hobgoblin,
or something worse.

Entering the shade of the banyan tree he became
conscious of the presence of strangers. He paused,
and lifting with his hand the long, over-hanging brows,
he peered with his keen black eyes into the face of the
stranger.

"Who art thou?" he demanded.

With perfect composure the other replied, "I am
Prince Mekara, son of the Golden Face, the Great King
of Burmah."

"What doest thou here?"

"In company with my wife, Mahdri, and infant
daughter, Manohara, I left my father's royal palace in
the Golden City, Ava, in search of rest for my soul,
which the religion of Buddha and all the splendors of
my father's court, with even the companionship of my
beloved wife and child, could not afford me. I have
journeyed far, visiting many sacred shrines and bathing

BURMESE NOBLES.

in holy waters, but still unrelieved. I have been directed to this place where I may live an ascetic. I wish to be guided in the way of truth, and before taking upon myself the vows of a devotee, I want full instruction as to the nature of the duties I am to perform and the reward to be gained thereby. If I mistake not, thou art a Brahmin. May I ask thy name?"

"Thou hast rightly judged," replied the old man. "I am a Brahmin, and my name is Asita." Then, as if pleased with the story of the prince, or desiring to further show his importance, he continued: "My race sprung from the mouth of Brahma, the Almighty Creator. We are by birth pure and holy, priests and guides of men, even superior to lords and kings. We are the medium of blessings from heaven to men. Without us the world would be a desert. By our prayers misfortunes are averted, the sick are healed, and curses removed. Though beggars, we are more powerful than the kings of the earth; yea, the gods are subject to our prayers. My mission is to guide men, and if thou wilt follow my directions thou mayest attain to the greatest happiness in this life, and dwell with the gods in the next. But before I can prescribe for thee a course of life I must first know all the deeds thou hast already done, the shrines thou hast visited, and the vows thou hast paid. But I warn thee that thou must surrender all earthly enjoyment before becoming an ascetic." As he spoke the last words he darted a sharp glance at Mahdri and the child. The woman saw the snapping of his glittering black eyes and a momentary chill of suspicion caused her to tremble from head to foot; but all was lost on her husband except the question as to his former life.

Mekara invited the old Brahmin to rest on his own blanket, and having dispatched Mahdri to the village in search of food for their morning meal, he proceeded to relate the circumstance of his leaving his father's court and his life afterwards. Old Asita, reclining on the ground with the crook of his back supported by a column of the tree in order to face the speaker, gave attention to his story told in Sanscrit, the only language common to both.

CHAPTER III.

—Arnold.

AVA, the Golden City, under the rule of the renowned
statesman, King Minder-a-gee Praw, attained the highest magnificence of almost any city of the Orient. The
Irrawaddy, at this point four thousand feet broad, and its
two affluents connected by a canal, entirely surround the
walls, which are seven miles in circumference. The
streets are broad, straight and clean, dividing the city
into square blocks. The squares are surrounded by
tenement houses enclosing within green plats laid out in
flower gardens, and in the centre of which stand the
sumptuous palaces of the nobility, built of brick and
trimmed with gold. Numerous pagodas towering above
the tree-tops like great inverted bells, their snow-white
sides and golden spires glittering in the sunlight, present a most imposing spectacle. The life within is
equally as pompous as the splendor from without. The
luxurious carts of the nobility, ingeniously wrought of
bamboo and furnished with mats and cushions of silk,
are drawn by white bullocks in a brisk trot, the chains
of bells around their necks keeping merry time to the
motion of their feet. Fat, burly lords, arrayed in their
white linen jackets, flowing robes and gaudy turbans,
stalk about the streets beneath immense silken umbrel-

(19)

las borne by slaves from behind. Each step is taken as if its tread would shake the earth, and each word spoken by them in the name of the king, "Lord of Life and Death," is expected to carry with it conviction of supreme authority, temporal and religious. The canals and rivers, fringed with luxuriant vegetation, are fairly a-glitter with the royal boats and barges, which are entirely covered with gold even to the oars. Some are gorgeously striped, and as they dart rapidly about under the control of the skillful boatmen they present a most dazzling appearance. The various buildings composing the king's palace cover an area of a quarter of a mile square. The great audience hall stands in the centre, and its roof, supported by immense pillars, is nearly two hundred feet in height, rising like a steeple and sloping in many successive stages to the outer buildings, which are the lowest. Every stage is variously adorned with handsome carvings in wood richly inlaid with gold; every spire, projection, or cornice is covered with gold.

Within, the scene is awe-inspiring beyond description. Beneath the great vault in the audience hall is the throne of the king, curiously carved and overlaid with gold, rivaling in splendor the famous "Peacock Throne" of India. It is raised upon a high platform approached by successive flights of steps. The pillars supporting the lofty ceiling are magnificent in proportion and inconceivable in number. Forming a square around the throne, they extend in long colonnades and winding labyrinths in every direction; as in a forest, the eye cannot see where they end. Though of such immense size, so high, and so many in number, each is delicately carved, entirely overlaid with gold, and inwrought with filigree of silver. The ceiling is also of fretted gold, and the floor of polished marble reflects as in a mirror the dazzling scene above.

In this hall thousands had gathered and made the echoing vaults ring with their shouts at the coronation of the king, and the same roof had reverberated often since with the stern voice of the Golden Face as some poor criminal cowered before the throne. A command to the executioner and a wave of the hand was all. The condemned man is dead even if innocent. No one remonstrates. The king is autocrat. The religion of the heart, the thoughts of the head, the words of the mouth, the deeds of the hand, the babes of the household, the fields and their crops, all are subject to the "Lord of Heaven and Earth," the Golden Face.

In this hall a few months before the opening of our story was enacted a decree, which for paternal severity might well compare with the deed of the patriotic Brutus of legendary renown.

A thrill of surprise and fear rushed through the apartments of the palace. The noble and well-beloved heir to the throne had been seized and ordered before the judgment seat. One by one the attendants of the king crept in between the pillars and ranged in a circle around the throne. Their eyes were dilated and their cheeks ashy with fear and grief. Not a word was whispered. Suddenly their keen ears heard in the distance a stately tread on the marble floor, though no form appeared. Every head was bowed to the floor. At the eastern extremity of the colonnade appeared His Majesty, followed by his private minister, Moung Zah.

His stately form, now much magnified by the fear of the beholders, was carried with that commanding and haughty air which only an eastern monarch can assume. He was magnificently clad in the native garment made of linen and silk, elegantly embroidered, and fringed with gold. His turban was of purple and red, and a blue sash fastened about his waist served as a belt, in which was thrust a short gold and jewel-hilted sword used in the room of a sceptre. In silence he ascended the steps and took his seat upon the throne. Moung Zah, endeavoring to restrain a feeling of anxiety betrayed in his face, stood by the throne holding over the king a plume of peacock feathers. A death-like silence pervaded. The attendants could almost hear their own hearts beat as they throbbed with dread. Presently from the opposite end of the hall footsteps were heard, slow and measured. They drew nearer and nearer. The attendants looked up. Prince Mekara, between two officers, stood before the king.

His Majesty, placing his hand on the hilt of his sword, demanded:

"Thou rebellious son, is it true that thou hast refused to bow before the shrine of Buddha and worship in his holy temple?"

Moung Zah looked eagerly into the face of the prince as if his own life depended on the answer that should be made. Mekara, without evincing any fear, but with the utmost respect, replied:

"The report is true, O king, my father."

"What reason canst thou give for thus disobeying the command of the king and trampling under foot the religion of thy fathers?"

"My father," replied the prince, "I have worshiped at the shrine of Buddha since I was a child, even at the most sacred pagoda which contains his tooth, but all my vows, offerings, and prayers to his image have failed to bring relief to my hungry soul; and, indeed, what could be expected from an image of stone representing only a man who is dead? Something within me whispers of a greater Being, One who never dies, is not seen nor heard, and yet controls the worlds. I have no knowledge of Him beyond the consciousness of my own heart, nevertheless I will search for Him in the hope that I may have a clearer light. For that reason, O king, I can no longer worship a senseless stone."

The countenance of the king was gloomy and threatening. Clutching his sword he arose to his feet and said:

"No more! Thou hast said enough. Death is the penalty for those who disobey the king's commands. Nevertheless, for the sake of thy wife and child whom I love, I spare thy life, and not because thou art my son, for such thou shalt be no longer. I disown thee. Let me not find thee in my palace at sunset. Thou art dead to me. The king hath spoken."

With one impressive sweep of his hand he pointed to the entrance and retired, leaving Moung Zah behind.

CHAPTER IV.

—Arnold.

THE reader may have wondered at the trepidation of Moung Zah, and why he exhibited so much interest in the proceedings. The reason is easily seen. The Minister had often conversed with the prince, and together they had arrived at the conclusion related by the latter to his father, though without involving any one except himself. Moung Zah was firmly convinced of the foolishness of worshiping idols, and believed that there was a Supreme, Personal God. But his conviction was not so deep, nor his courage so strong as that of the prince, who boldly refused to sacrifice his principles to what he conscientiously believed to be wrong; and in the sentence of the prince, Moung Zah derived some conclusion as to what would be his own fate if his views should be exposed.

In contrast to the severity of his father, Mekara had always been characterized by a gentle disposition which had won for him the universal favor of the people; and the knowledge of this fact, rather than the reason given, induced the king to make a show of clemency in delivering the sentence of his punishment.

After the king had left the chamber, Moung Zah descended from the platform, and extending his hands, while the pent-up tears flowed down his cheeks, embraced the prince, and expressed a desire that he might be successful in his search of the True God and send him word in return. Mekara was now thronged by the attendants, who, with repeated glances toward the entrance where the king had made his exit, expressed their love for him, and their desire for his welfare. Bidding a hasty and affectionate farewell to all in the chamber the prince turned and walked rapidly toward the woman's apartment where his wife and child were enjoying themselves, blissfully unconscious of the cloud overhanging them.

In times of distress, or when conscious of pending danger, the mind often comes to conclusions with marvelous rapidity. While the last words of the king were yet thundering among the massive pillars and re-echoing from the vaulted arches above, the prince had already determined upon what course he would pursue. From a copy of the Veda, the holy book of the Hindus, which he had procured from his Sanscrit teacher, he learned that the religion of the Brahmins in India recognized the existence of a Personal God, the knowledge of whom he was seeking. He determined that, after placing his wife and child temporarily under the charge of Moung Zah until he could further provide for them, he would depart immediately to Benares, the holy city of India, and apply for instruction to the learned Brahmins who dwelt there in great numbers.

Reaching his wife's apartments, he stood for a moment at the door unobserved, holding aside with his hands the silken curtains, and feasting his eyes on the happy domestic scene before him, having scarcely the heart to break it. Seated on a many-colored woolen rug, imported from the famous vale of Cashmere, in the midst of her maidens, was the lovely princess, bewitchingly dressed in her rich Oriental costume, and playing with their infant daughter, Manohara, who sat on her lap, laughing and crowing as babies of all nations do, and reaching delightedly to catch the sparkling jewels that dangled from her mother's ears and throat. On her own chubby arms gleamed a pair of golden bracelets of the most delicate workmanship, and having her name inscribed with inlaid pearls and rubies, the gift of the king, her grandfather. The child was the first to observe her father, and reaching her arms toward him, begged to be taken. The mother looked up with a smiling welcome in her face, but seeing his troubled expression, her countenance changed, and seating the child on the floor she sprang hurriedly to meet him.

"Pray, my lord, what has happened that thou art so sad?" and then with a woman's quick intuition, guessing the cause, a deathly pallor overspread her face, and she continued breathlessly, "hast thou offended the Golden Face?"

"Thou hast rightly guessed, my princess," he replied, laying his hands tenderly on her shoulders and gazing into the tearful depths of her eyes, "I am no longer a king's son, but an exile in disgrace, forbidden my father's house. And oh! I could gladly go on my long search were it not for parting with thee and Manohara, whom I must leave behind until I have found a place in keeping with your present surroundings."

"But why must thou go away?" she asked, "may not the king be reconciled to thee?"

"Impossible. I have steadfastly refused to worship longer at the shrine of Buddha, and for that I must leave. My mind is fixed. I cannot conscientiously engage in a worship which to me seems folly, and my father will allow no other."

Mahdri knew nothing of deep religious conviction, the only worship she paid being to husband and child. She took part in the gorgeous ritual of Buddhist worship more on account of its gaudy show and entertainment to her child than from any motive of principle. The condition of her soul had never given her the least distress. In religion, as in everything else, she was led only by her husband's wishes. Not realizing the importance to be attached to the performance of religious duties she was unable to sympathize with him as she wished. After hearing his decision she stood for a moment looking at the floor, while she, for the first time, thought seriously upon the subject. Raising her eyes to his face she asked:

"Hast thou not perhaps acted too hastily? Would it not have been better for thee to retain the Buddhist faith until thou hadst found a better? The hope which thou hast now may be vain after all."

"No, Mahdri," he replied, "I was not rash. For years my soul has been hungering for something that lies beyond this vain idolatry, the superstitious incantations and ceremonies of men. All is dark to me, and while I grope in darkness I cannot expect to find light. I am resolved to search every land and inquire of every nation until I find that for which I seek, or until I am convinced it does not exist. Thou hast here no want, the king loves thee and the child, and no harm can befall you. Moung Zah will care for you as for his own household. Do not provoke the king to anger, but remain in peace until I can send for thee, for I must now be going. Yonder sun is now dropping behind the great pagoda, and its departure marks my own."

Passing her he walked into the room, and taking the child from the arms of the nurse caressed her tenderly. The little one seemed to understand his sorrow for she ceased her laughter and clasped him lovingly about the neck; then, drawing back in his arms, she noticed the tears flowing down his cheeks, and laying her dimpled hands over his eyes, besought him not to cry so. Turning at length to bid his wife adieu he was astonished to find her standing by the door, her head dress on, and a hastily gathered bundle in her hands.

"Why, Mahdri!" he exclaimed, "what meanest thou by that?"

"We are going, too," she replied, with a pleading determination in her tone, "why should we remain here when the only one we love is gone? Oh, please do not ask us again to stay!"

"But, my love, think of the hardships we must endure, and the dangers we must encounter before I may find that for which I seek. Nothing is lacking to thee here. Surely thou hast not considered."

"I have considered everything," she said, "life without thee would be worse than death. Have not our souls passed together through a thousand states of existence, and is it right that we shall be separated now? Where is my place but at thy side? I fear not the dangers, and will gladly endure the hardships for thy sake; and little Manohara shall gladden the journey when we are sad. I shall care no longer for shrines, pagodas and temples, nor for the pomp of royalty. Do take us with thee!"

Mekara had never had occasion before to test the devotion that is in the heart of woman, even though she be a heathen. Clasping her to his bosom while tears of joy streamed down his cheeks, he cried:

"Now do I love thee more than ever, my princess, my jewel! And though I never would have been so selfish as to demand it, together will we go out into the great world on a holy pilgrimage, and may the Great Being favor our quest. The sun is now setting, let us be gone."

So, with the child, they departed in silence from the golden palace, BUT NOT FOREVER.

CHAPTER V.

"Yet will I leave a remnant, that ye may have some that shall escape the sword among the nations, when ye shall be scattered through the countries. And they that shall escape of you SHALL REMEMBER ME AMONG THE NATIONS whither they shall be carried captives."—*Ezek. vi: 8, 9.*

KNOWING, as he did, the minds of the people, and expecting an uproar would be raised when they heard of his banishment, Mekara endeavored to retire unobserved from the palace to the river where his own boat was always in readiness. Bearing the child in his arms and followed by Mahdri, he passed quietly into a back street through a private way and proceeded rapidly toward the river. Having seen no one, he was congratulating himself that he had escaped a friendly mob, but on reaching the gate of the city, great was his mortification to see the wharf swarming with almost the whole population of the city. The news had spread like magic, and this was to be his parting salute. The people overcame for a moment their dread of the king, and with great shouting, and vehement gesticulations, proclaimed Mekara as their sovereign, and, with uplifted hands crowding around him, implored that he would return and be their ruler, promising to depose the king if he would only accept the throne and relieve them from the grievous bondage imposed upon them by the "Lord of Life and Death."

Much grieved at this meeting, which he would gladly have avoided, the prince mounted the steps of a pagoda and, addressing them as brethren and friends, besought

them to remain faithful and obedient subjects of the
king, his father. "For," he said, "you are all laboring
under a worse bondage than that, and if I should remain, though made a king, I should be in greater bondage than all. There is a better way of ruling than by
fear, and a more efficient means of subduing than the
sword. I go in search of greater light and knowledge
than that which came to Buddha under the bo-tree
when he saw the streams of his existence down through
the past. More important to us are the concerns of the
future. I can do you greater good by finding and communicating to you the true knowledge of the soul and
its destiny than by sitting on a throne. My going may
secure to you peace and happiness; my staying is certain to produce war and confusion without end. Therefore, O, my people, return in content to your homes
and allow me to depart that I may aid in bringing to
us all inward peace. Till then, O, my people, farewell!'

The crowd no longer forcibly interfering, the prince
proceeded to his golden boat at the wharf, and taking
his little family on board, bade the boatman to row
them quickly down the stream. The people stood
watching the little craft as long as it could be seen,
waving their turbans and calling entreatingly to the
prince.

Mekara viewed with unutterable sadness this parting
scene. The Golden City never appeared more beautiful.
The palatial residences of the nobility, embowered
within their groves of mango trees, the gleaming white
pagodas, and the glittering turrets of the king's palace,
all against a back-ground of crimson-and-gold sunset

sky, fading gradually away into the approaching twilight, formed a picture never to be forgotten. By degrees the songs of the laboring boatmen died away on the evening air, and the Golden City with its haughty king and oppressed people disappeared from sight as the boat glided into the shadow beneath the banks of the Irrawaddy.

They had come thus far in silence, the prince too much occupied with his thoughts to give attention to anything else. At length, arousing himself, he said:

"Boatman, canst thou land us at Rangoon within a fortnight?"

"By the help of Jehovah, I can, my Lord," replied the man at the oar with a low salute.

Mekara started visibly at the name of "Jehovah." "By the help of whom?" he asked, as if the language of the slave was not familiar.

"Of Jehovah, Master, the God of our fathers."

The countenance of the prince, hitherto dull with sadness and pain, was now filled with an eager light of joy and hope, and delighted to find the God of his imagination spoken of as a reality by another, even though a bond-servant, he cried:

"Listen! Mahdri, did I not tell thee that there was a Supreme Being who ruled the destinies of the human race? Tell me, boatman," he continued, "where is his dwelling place, what is his nature, and how may I obtain a knowledge of him? Draw in the oars and let the boat drift with the current till thou canst tell me of this the object of my search."

The man drew the glittering paddles from the water and crossed them in front of him, then sat thoughtfully in the stern, his arms folded and his eyes fixed on the feet of the prince.

"Ah! master," he said, "thou hast demanded much. I know not the dwelling place of God, but our fathers teach us that he is everywhere. Of his nature we know but little, save that he is a pure spirit, visible only to the soul of man. How thou mayest obtain a correct knowledge of him, alas! I know not. The light we once had is gone out, and only a passing glimmer can be seen. Tradition says the light will return. For that good time I am watching and longing. Till then, O, prince, thy question must go unanswered."

Mekara was not satisfied. Interested in his boatman, he desired to learn more of him and the "God of his fathers." "Tell me thy name," he said. "I judge thee to be a Karen, one of a despised and rejected race. How, then, did this knowledge first come to thy people in preference to the nobler Burmans, and how did they lose the knowledge once revealed to them?"

"My name, O, prince, is Ko Tha-By-u, and thou hast rightly judged my nationality. I am a Karen, for many years past a bond-servant in the royal household of thy father, the king. My people, despised and down-troddened by the nobility, are banished from the cities and compelled to seek refuge in the mountains and jungles, where some of them have become as wild and free as the beasts that surround them. Though oppressed in body they have an inward hope that gives them strength to live on in anticipation of deliverance some day. It was not always thus. Centuries before the throne of the Golden Face had ever been reared, our people were the rulers of Burmah. Happy and pros-

3

porous, they were renowned across the seas, but thy people came upon us with great power and cruel weapons of warfare, taking possession of our peaceful homes and driving us to the jungles.

"Why God revealed himself first to our people I know not. The memories of our fathers run back to a time when, far beyond the seas, their ancestors lived in a beauteous land flowing with milk and honey. They worshiped God with great splendor in a temple covered with gold, more costly than the noted shrine of Buddha. Their king was the richest and the wisest the world has ever seen. The voice of God spoke from the sanctuary of the temple, and was written by holy men in books of parchment to be afterwards referred to as the divine Oracles. After the death of the great king the people were divided into factions, and because of their transgressions, were allowed to be smitten by their enemies. Some were driven away in captivity, but the remnants of ten tribes escaped hither, where the king had found the gold, ivory, and precious stones used in building his palace and the house of God. Here they founded a colony, and, becoming owners of the fertile soil, lived in great happiness and prosperity for many centuries.

"The sacred roll containing the revelations from Jehovah was preserved and brought over by a priest; but, through carelessness, while the workmen were building their houses, it was left lying upon a log, where it was torn by swine into many fragments, which were swallowed by the fowls; hence, they are looked upon as being the repositories of the Word of God, and no one is allowed to harm them under any circumstances. Thus we lost our knowledge of Jehovah, and all we know now is through dim traditions handed down through two thousand years of suffering. But our prophets tell us that a white man from the West will come some day and restore to us the book, and tell us all its wonderful meaning. Herein lies our strength, and to this we are looking forward with great hope. More, O, prince, I can tell thee nothing."

Mekara's eyes were filled with a strange light and his bosom heaved as he followed the slave through his narrative. Hearing the last he spoke not a word but sat in deep thought, too full for utterance.

By this time the boat had drifted far below the steep banks that first concealed their retreat, and they were fast nearing a village by the river side. Taking his oars in hand once more, Ko Tha turned the boat from its course in the mid-stream and approached the bank As the boat touched the sedge that fringed the border, he stopped and gave a shrill whistle.

Startled from his reverie and surprised at the sudden stop, Mekara looked up inquiringly. "What is the meaning of this?" he asked.

"Pardon, master, I am only waiting for a boy whom I always take on here to aid me in rowing over the rapids as I return."

Soon a rustling was heard in the sedge, and parting the leaves, a boy with deep brown skin, and half naked, stood on the bank staring like a startled fawn at the unexpected sight of the prince and his family.

"Haste, Quala," said the boatman impatiently, "step on board and let's be going, for our master must not be delayed."

Thus admonished, the lad crept timidly into the boat and sat crouching like a dog in the bow.

"Why dost thou call him Quala (hope)?" inquired the prince. "What does that indicate?"

"It may seem superstitious, my Lord," replied Ko Tha, "but at the time of his birth his parents were living in daily hope of the coming of the white man from the West, bringing the lost book of God; and so strong was that expectation that they gave him the name of San Quala, which signifies hope, and we fully expect the coming of the white man to be in his day."

"Hope, hope, hope!" echoed in the brain of Mekara. "Look up, O, my soul! Light will yet dawn upon thee."

Ko Tha-By-u now gave himself vigorously to the oars, and the long gilded shell darted like a flash down the swift current of the stream, leaving the moonbeams dancing in long, glimmering streaks in the wake behind, as if they slipped from the golden sides of the vessel itsef. Mekara sat in deep thought musing with himself.

"Why is it that my soul lingered so long in darkness while in the palace of my father, and then the first light, though dim, cometh from a poor bond-slave who is considered unworthy to kiss the feet of a Burman? Can it be that the Great Being revealeth himself to the poor and simple in preference to the rich and powerful? Oh! that I knew more of him! Why delayeth the white man his coming? I will go to Rangoon, thence embark for India, where I will seek instruction from the Brahmins. If I find no rest I shall return, by which time, perhaps, the white man will be here. O, boat, glide swiftly and bear me away from all that recalls the sweet, sad memories of the ignorance of my childhood!"

Mahdri sat quietly by his side, holding the babe in her arms; speaking never a word and taking no interest in the conversation, except as it seemed to affect her husband; her tender, affectionate eyes gazed fondly from the face of the sleeping child to that of the troubled father, one of whose hands she held clasped in her own as if to assure him of her sympathy. Thus sitting in silence, the soft, hazy sky above them and the perfume-laden air shimmering around them, they passed through the land of the Golden Face.

.   .   .   .

The story of Ko Tha-By-u, though simple and mixed with superstition, is both suggestive and interesting to a Bible reader.

Solomon, in building the magnificent temple at Jerusalem, overlaid it with pure gold, garnished with precious stones brought from the famous mines of Ophir, which is believed to be Burmah. Here the wise king and his prosperous vassal, Hiram, king of Tyre, had established trading posts and planted flourishing colonies to aid in the easy transportation to Jerusalem of the great cargoes of gold and rich products of the soil.

After the destruction of the temple and capture of Jerusalem, when pursued by enemies and rejected by friends, who knows but that the ten missing tribes escaped in remnants to the colonies in Ophir, and there became the owners of the soil as related by the Karens? There, as Ko Tha said, they lived for centuries, prosperous and happy. Certain peculiar traits of character among the Karens, their traditions, and the form of certain words pertaining to the worship of Jehovah, all testify to their Hebrew origin, which is now no longer a matter of dispute, but an accepted fact among eminent scholars.

Before leaving their own country the temple service had fallen into disuse and the Scripture readings neglected. In the confusion and terror of flight the sacred roll containing the Law and the Prophets was lost, and with it all knowledge of God, except through tradition mixed with error.

Jerusalem was again besieged and destroyed on account of her rejection of the Messiah. The curse of God was visited upon the wretched inhabitants, who were driven homeless into every land, a "curse and a by-word" in every nation. The same punishment was also inflicted upon their brethren in Ophir, who, given to money-making and the quiet and peaceful occupations of life, were unable to withstand the attack of the lordly and more warlike Burmans, who drove them from their quiet possessions like beasts into the jungles. Because of their determined refusal to engage in the idolatry of the surrounding nations they were hated and abused, driven from society, and cursed by the lowest outcasts.

For two thousand years have they groped in darkness, clinging to the faint light within their bosoms, waiting for the restoration of the Holy Book, and vainly trying to recall the Songs of Zion in their wild mountain homes. Look forward, O, reader, to the wonderful providence of God manifest toward his people. Of a surety he has reserved unto himself a remnant who "escaped the sword," and who remember him "among the nations" whither they were carried captive.

"This is the Lord's doings, and it is marvelous in our eyes."

CHAPTER VI.

"That sweet Indian land,
Whose air is balm ; whose ocean spreads
O'er coral rocks and amber beds ;
Whose mountains, pregnant by the beams
Of the warm sun, with diamonds teem ;
Whose rivulets are like rich brides,
Lovely, with gold beneath their tides ;
Whose sandal groves and bowers of spice
Might be a Peri's Paradise !"

—Thomas Moore.

THE story of " THAT DELIGHTFUL PROVINCE OF THE
SUN " would be the most interesting and fascinating ever
written. Its legendary lore, recording the marvelous
exploits of gods and god-like men, embraces in its scope
millions of years, extending far beyond the creation of
the world, and, in comparison to which, the most extravagant mythologies of classic Greece and Rome are
but nursery tales.

Centuries . before wandering outlaws founded the
Eternal City on the banks of the yellow Tiber; the
sacred Ganges, in its majestic course, washed with its
saving tide the crowded ghauts leading to many a
teeming city. When ancient Greece had not yet
dreamed of her Golden Days of Athenian Glory, nor
listened with rapt attention to the thrilling tale of her
blind old bard, these favored children of the sun
dwelt in luxurious splendor; and yellow-robed priests
recited in Sanscrit the wonderful Epos, Ramayana.
When Jerusalem, The Golden, had not yet been conceived in the mind of The Sweet Psalmist of Israel,

(39)

Benares, the Holy City, offered daily sanctification, through its six thousand shrines, to the eager millions who crowded thither.

With an origin veiled in the misty shroud of the Ages, with a modern Past burning with the recollection of foreign royalty waving triumphantly over a suffering land made fertile by the warm, gushing life-blood of its slaughtered inhabitants, and with a Future that bids fair to lift them far above their present benighted condition under the blessed rule of the Prince of Peace, the Indian people invoke the attention of the present generation.

Their sacred books, the Shasters, teach the doctrine of One Supreme Being, Brahm, whose pure spirit, pervading all space, is the origin of every human soul. And into this Great Soul they are all to be once more absorbed when freed from the stains of earth and the defilements of the flesh. Brahm is without beginning or end, without form or attributes, a purely negative character. Nevertheless, in order to the creation of the world he laid aside his negative nature and took upon himself form; as spirit could not create matter without being united with it. Says the Veda: "Brahm awoke and said, 'Let me be many!'" And he immediately took upon himself material form and became, for a time, Brahma, the creator.

The germs of the universe were in the shape of an egg, into which Brahma retired to perfect his work. During one year of creation, equal to three hundred millions of our years, this egg, shining with the brightness of a thousand suns, floated on the waters of chaos. At length the shell burst and Brahma leaped forth, a being of terrible appearance, having a thousand heads, a thousand eyes and a thousand arms. From his body sprang the four castes in order. From his mouth the Brahmins, who are the highest of all and expounders of the Vedas; from his arms and breast, the Kshatryas, who are the kings and warriors; from his loins, the Vaisyas, merchants and farmers; and from his feet, the Sudras, slaves to all the others.

The material universe also escaped from this luminous egg in the form of Sargan, a monstrous creature, whose "hairs were the trees and shrubs of the forest; his head the clouds; his beard the lightning; his voice the thunder; his breath the atmosphere; his eyes the sun and moon; his nails the rocks; and his bones the mountains of the earth."

Brahma now becomes Brahm again, and retires to eternal slumber, leaving the government of the world to his representatives, Vishnu and Shiva, the second and third members of the triad composed of Brahma, the creator; Vishnu, the preserver; and Shiva, the destroyer.

Brahm is everything and everything is Brahm. In thus multiplying himself in giving birth to the universe he "became many," the soul inhabiting every material form, high or low; and authorized the worship of the three hundred and thirty millions of deities representing him to the eye.

The human soul, unable to absolve itself entirely from the stains of earth, during this life, passes, at death, into the body of a higher or lower order of being, according to the degree of merit attained during its former existence. If it degenerates it passes into the body of a lower animal, and is doomed to undergo thousands of transmigrations before released. If, on the other hand, the deeds of this life are sufficiently meritorious, the soul of a person of lower caste may next inhabit the body of a Brahmin, after which the next death releases him from the shackles of mortality and his soul is lost in the Great Soul of the universe, like the upward soaring of the lark that is lost to view in the bosom of the sky. Humanity becomes divinity. This state of blessed annihilation may be merited in three ways: By works, as bathing in holy waters, doing penance, and feeding Brahmins; by the worship of the gods through their images and temples; and by solemn meditation and mental worship without visible demonstration. Religion is altogether ceremonial. He who neglects these ceremonies, even though his heart may be pure, is counted the vilest of sinners; while the most wicked morally, by keeping these observances, becomes pure and holy.

The great wealth and power of India formerly belonged to the Kshatrya caste, composed of the warlike heroes and princes or rajahs. Then was the poetic period of India, when the exploits of famous Maharajahs afforded abundant material for the songs of the bards, and when their lovely zenanas, filled with the fairest of the land, evoked the strongest passion of the emotional southern soul. But under the tyrannical tread of foreign oppression, crushed successively beneath the heels of invading Moslem and Mogul conquerors, we find the downtrodden people, at the opening of our story, servilely giving allegiance to a handful of British merchants; ambition gone, the fountains of literature dried up, and only religious zeal remaining.

India had, for centuries, furnished to the world her jewels, tapestry, spices and drugs. After the discovery of America, when a new way was opened to the East around the "Cape of Storms," great competition in trade was raised by the various nations—the Portuguese establishing trading posts and monopolizing the traffic.

Under the reign of Queen Elizabeth the merchants of London, realizing the great financial gain to be acquired by trading with the wealthy Hindus, sent agents to Calcutta and Madras to establish trading posts for the purpose of exchanging with the natives English wares in return for their natural products, fabrics, etc. This trade became so profitable that a company was formed and procuring a charter from the English Government they settled permanently in India, bearing the name of "The East India Company." This was destined to become not only one of the greatest commercial, but also one of the leading political and military powers of the world, and its achievements are everywhere viewed with wonder. By ingenious manipulations they soon became possessed of the principal cities, and in a few years nearly all of Central and Southern India was under their control.

The movements of this great power soon attracted the attention of the civilized world and revealed to its sympathizing gaze the distressing moral condition of the people, and opened a way for their enlightenment. The company objected to the preaching of missionaries because they were under promise to the people not to interfere with their religion. Nevertheless, the undaunted William Carey, with his associates, Marshman, Ward and others, succeeded, after years of indefatigable industry, in establishing a mission at Serampore, a village on the banks of the Hoogly, fifteen miles from Calcutta. Here, on the 22nd day of December, 1800, Krishna Pal, the first Hindu convert, renounced caste, and, with his family, sat at a table with the despised missionaries, and a few days after Mr. Carey enjoyed the exquisite pleasure of " desecrating " the sacred Ganges for the first time by the baptism of the now out-cast Krishna and his own son Felix. In rapture of joy Mr. Ward was led to exclaim : " Now the chain of caste is broken, and who shall be able to mend it ? " Krishna became an efficient minister of the Gospel and co-laborer with the missionaries. Felix Carey also became a missionary, but was much given to wandering, as we shall afterwards have occasion to notice.

"THE CHAIN OF CASTE IS BROKEN, AND WHO SHALL BE ABLE TO MEND IT ? "

CHAPTER VII.

" The painted streets alive with hum of noon,
   The traders, cross-legged 'mid their spice and grain,
   The buyers with their money in the cloth,
   The war of words to cheapen this or that,
   The shout to clear the road, the huge stone wheels,
   The strong, slow oxen and their rustling loads,
   The singing bearers with their palanquins,
   The broad-necked hamals sweating in the sun,
   The housewives bearing water from the wells
   With balanced chatties, and athwart their hips
   The black-eyed babes."

—Arnold.

GAUTAMA sat alone under the bo-tree after days and nights of anxious waiting and fasting, birds singing around him, and the Himalayan crests glittering beyond and above him. Night came, gloomy and terrible, with stormy clouds. Dark forms of all the sins that beset mankind passed in horrible procession before him. One by one he conquered them, and as the first roseate hues of the morning gilded the Eastern sky, light dawned upon his mind. His soul opened and unfolded like a rose, and he became Buddha, " the one who knows." The streams of his past existence appeared to him from the beginning; as when a traveler pauses on the mountain slope and looks back through surrounding mists to see the winding path over which he came, stretching far away in the valley below. There was also revealed to him the cause of human sorrow and its remedy. Lifting his now clarified vision toward Benares, the Holy City, his heart was filled with pity to see the mad strife and suffering of its inhabitants as they sought release from sin. "I will go first to that queenly city," he said, "and preach the doctrine of the soul's progression."

Benares is the heart of India; daily sending forth, and receiving, countless streams of humanity to and from every province between the Himalayas and the Bay of Bengal. Five hundred millions of people speak with awe the dread name, "Benares," the home of the Hindu faith. To die within its walls secures eternal happiness. Litters bearing the dead are continually swarming the shores of the sacred river, and the smoke ascending from burning funeral pyres darkens the sky.

The city is in the shape of a crescent and fits like a cap on a great bend of the river. It is three miles in front, from horn to horn, and one mile in depth. A vast amphitheatre bordering, with stone ghauts, the bank of the river, and rising, in successive stages, to the lofty temples crowning the cliffs beyond, it fills the eye with wonder and delight.

Its history can be traced back through three thousand years. The Brahmins assert it to be coeval with creation, and that it does not stand with the rest of the earth upon the back of the great tortoise; but is upheld on the point of Shiva's trident, on account of which circumstance it is believed to be indestructible. Nevertheless, with all its magnificence and reputed sanctity, it is only a faint picture, a dim reflection of the true Benares, which stands on a vast plain midway between Earth and Heaven.

Benares is the city of a thousand temples; temples on the river; temples on the outskirts, temples in the center, temples crowning the heights. And the great golden temple, built of dark-red sandstone, capped with a tall golden spire surrounded by a cluster of smaller ones, gives the appearance of a great gilded pine-apple, in the center of which is inclosed the shrine of the god. Innumerable hordes of mischievous monkeys are worshiped as gods, and every house is a monkey-temple, on the roof of which are built the little cots in which they live, and from which they sally to descend upon the streets and commit all manner of depredations unmolested. An insult offered to a monkey thus engaged is punishable with death.

Great white bulls, also held as sacred, infest the narrow streets, perfectly at home in the crowded throngs, among whom they force their way by the unscrupulous use of their broad horns. The grain merchant's store is not allowed to be closed against them, and they stand contentedly munching the most costly food while the owner looks on, flattered that the gods thus notice his stock. They even enter dwellings, and, ascending the stairs, air themselves on the house-tops, looking out over the city and the green fields across the river as if the authority of the Great Mogul belonged to them.

The shops and bazaars are open to the street, and display in rich profusion all kinds of quaint oriental wares; brilliant tapestry, exquisitely carved vases, handsomely engraved brass lotas, always brightly burnished, grotesque figures supporting lamps, grinning little gods, and stern-looking big gods, curious incense burners, and mysterious boxes, and inlaid plates without number. Everything bright and attractive that is kept for sale is displayed to view and adds to the general decoration.

Many of the streets are so narrow that passing
elephants touch the houses on either side, some so narrow, in fact, that only the tonjaun, carried by natives
after the manner of a palanquin, can be admitted. The
houses are built of stone, with ornamentally carved
fronts, some six or seven stories high, with projecting
balconies of dark red wood literally meeting overhead,
and shutting out the sun, so that, only here and there,
can be seen a spot of blue sky.

Great quantities of birds blacken the sky and fill the
air with their cries. Kites and crows, the scavengers
of the land, walk about the streets, mixing with the
multitude with as much an air of importance as any
citizen of the place. Flocks of pigeons whirr through
the long passages, or huddle under the tall over-hanging eaves, and green-and-purple paroquets flit from
roof to roof, their glossy plumage glittering in the sunlight.

The streets are thronged with a thousand incongru-
ous scenes. Tall, handsome men and beautifully clad
women from Cashmere; pilgrims from the Decean and
from the Punjaub; yellow-robed priests, white-clad
Brahmins, sweating coolies, veiled and jeweled women,
rich Parsees, and long-bearded Mohammedans—all are
mixed in indescribable confusion. The clamor is dreadful. The traders crying their wares; priests and
mendicants, one demanding, the other craving, "backsheesh"; the ox-driver shouting to his laboring team;
Brahmins expounding the Vedas; the driver on the
royal elephant shouting, "Clear the way for the Maha-
rajah!" fakirs yelling; monkeys chattering above and
mimicing the crowds below; devotees trying to repeat

all the names of the thirty-three million gods; deafening gongs clanging from the thousands of temples; feeble old men crying "Ganga!" with their fast departing breaths; and wailing funeral processions following the dead, fill the ear with an intermixture of sounds never to be forgotten.

Here Buddha first preached his wonderful doctrine. The cries were hushed, the sacrificial altars no longer reeked with the blood of goats and buffaloes, and pilgrims ceased to look to the Holy City and the sacred river for salvation. A code of morality had taken the place of ceremonial observances. Idolatry and worship of every kind was forbidden, and right living enforced. Buddha died and his system degenerated. Having forbidden the worship of idols he put a stop to all devotion, the life of the soul. Following the natural instincts of his nature man must worship. Consequently the dead Buddha was deified. Temples were erected to his memory, and shrines, inclosing hairs from his sacred head, were adored by the devout disciples, and Buddhism became a worse form of idolatry than they had known before.

At length the Brahmins rallied, and expelling the adherents of Gautama from India, destroyed their temples and re-established the old faith. Once more Benares became the life of the nations, the "Mother of their faith." It was made so holy that all dying within a radius of five miles around went to Paradise regardless of their own wishes. Even the hated Moslem and abhorred beef-eating Englishmen were not exempt from this speedy transportation to glory.

O, wondrous city! thy three thousand years of vice and magnificent crime are waning to a close. Thy gorgeous temples must soon be cleared of their hideous images to give place to yet a new worship, and thy surging multitudes will sing a new song, and embrace a new faith never to be supplanted. Even thy dead shall find a sweeter repose than that on the bosom of Ganga!

CHAPTER VIII.

"Where is thy God?"—*Ps. xlii: 3.*

PRINCE MEKARA, with his wife and child, reached Rangoon in good time, and after parting from Ko-Tha, who begged that they would send him the Light if it was ever found, they sailed for Calcutta. A prosperous voyage soon brought them across the Bay of Bengal, and sailing up the Hoogly, one of the mouths of the Ganges, they landed at Calcutta. Mekara was in too great a hurry to reach Benares to spend more time than absolutely necessary in the "City of Palaces." So procuring a boat as soon as possible they set out on their journey up the Ganges, scarcely noticing the palatial residences of the great social city, or the brilliant equipages driving with lordly magnificence along the famous esplanade. They were no longer interested in social pleasures.

Benares, seen from the river, presents an entirely different view from Benares seen from within. The narrow, crowded streets are hid from view, and there can only be seen the ornamental roofs of the houses and the gilded spires of the pagodas, rising in terraces above, and the long ghauts reaching down to the water, covered with people of both sexes and all ages, who are passing continually to and from the river.

The prince had traveled by night in order to avoid, for the sake of Mahdri and the child, the fierce heat of the sun, which was just rising one morning as his peacock-shaped boat glided into view around the bend of the river. A view of the Holy City, thus seen for the first time at sunrise, thrills the soul like the remembrance of a delightful dream, so gorgeous appear the crimson sunbeams bathing the dark-red buildings, and glittering on the burnished spires of gold.

"Surely," thought Mekara, as he saw the heavenly vision and the throngs of seemingly happy bathers, "among so many devout worshipers I shall find the knowledge I seek."

Pushing his way up the crowded steps into the city he found a traveler's bungalow, in which he placed Mahdri and Manohara, and ordering refreshments for them, he hastened back to the river, leaving them to rest while he conversed with the Brahmins.

By this time almost the whole population of the city, numbering nearly two hundred thousand, with many more from a distance, had assembled at the river. Standing in water up to the waist they performed their ablutions, then filling their brass lotas with the sacred water, they brought it upon the bank, and pouring it out as an offering to the rising sun, they fell on their faces and worshiped in silence. Some fashioned images from the Ganges' mud, and gazing fixedly upon them, repeated their prayers, then threw them into the river as of no further use.

Mekara passed here and there through the throng, watching every movement, and endeavoring to draw some conclusion from their actions as to the nature of their religion. Seeing a Brahmin approaching from one side he left the crowd and went forward to meet him. The Brahmin, who had just performed his ablu-

-tions, shaved, and clad in his snowy robe, presented the very picture of contentment which shone on his good-natured face.

"Salaam! noble Brahmin," began the prince, "art thou at leisure now?"

"Peace to thy turban, Sahib. I am always at leisure to give aid to those who need it. Is there anything I can do for thee?"

"There is. I want to know something of the Hindu faith and the nature of the being whom you worship. Something whispers to me of a Personal, All-powerful Being who made the worlds. Knowest thou aught of such an One?"

"Thine instincts are true," replied the Brahmin, "thy question simple and easily answered. The sacred Vedas tell us of one God, even Brahm, whose spirit pervades all space, and by whose power the worlds were created and all that in them is. He is the wind that blows; the light of the sun; the perfume of the flower; the moisture of the clouds; and the vital breath of the body. The stars are his eyes, the earthquakes and thunders his laugh. Without him nothing can exist, for he is the soul of all."

Mokara was overjoyed to hear this plain declaration from the Brahmin, for now he felt that he was in possession of the knowledge he sought. But not yet satisfied he determined to glean all the light possible while with him.

"Tell me more, noble Brahmin," he said, "of that Great Being, and how I may come to a correct knowledge of him."

But the Brahmin shook his head. "Ask no further," he replied, "I have told thee too much already. It is not intended that any but Brahmins should know the teachings of the sacred books. All thou art required to do is to obey our commands."

"But," insisted the prince, "how can I obey thy commands intelligently unless I know of some reason for so doing? Consider, I am a stranger here, and know nothing of thy religion. I have come all the way from Ava seeking the knowledge which thou hast in power to reveal to me. Read to me, I pray thee, from the sacred book that I may learn of God."

The Brahmin gazed for a moment in mute astonishment and pity at the prince for his intrepid boldness.

"Thou dost not know what thou hast desired," he said at length. "Hast thou not heard that a Sudra's head would cleave asunder to listen to the reading of the Vedas?"

"But I am not a Sudra," insisted Mekara.

"Then thou art a Pariah, an outcast, which is worse. Still, if thou wilt follow my directions I will read and thou mayest hear without danger. Dip thy hand three times into the sacred stream, pouring the water over thy head, so shalt thou be purified."

Watching the other until he had performed this holy office, the Brahmin drew from the folds of his robe the sacred parchment and read this invocation:

"God is One! Creator of all that is! God is like a perfect sphere, without beginning and without end! God rules and governs all creation by a general providence, resulting from first determined and fixed principles. Thou shalt not make inquiry into the essence of the ETERNAL ONE, nor by what laws he governs. An inquiry into either is vain and criminal. It is enough, that day by day, and night by night, thou seest in his works, his wisdom, his power and his mercy. Benefit thereby.

"By one Supreme Ruler is this universe pervaded; even every world in the whole circle of nature. Enjoy pure delight, O man! by abandoning all thoughts of this perishable world, and covet not the wealth of any creature existing. .

"To those regions where evil spirits dwell, and which utter darkness involves, all such men surely go after death, as destroy the purity of their souls.

"Let my soul return to the immortal spirit of God! and then let my body, which ends in ashes, return to dust!

"O, Spirit who pervadest fire, lead us in a straight path to the riches of beatitude! remove each foul taint from our soul; who approach thee with the highest praise and the most fervid adoration!

"God, who is perfect in wisdom, and perfect in happiness, is the final refuge of the man who has liberally bestowed his wealth, who has been firm in virtue, and who knows and adores that Great One! Remember me. O, OM, Thou Divine Spirit."

Mekara's heart filled with joy as he listened to this sublime description of his own ideal God; but, looking at the crowds thronging the water, and seeing the strange inconsistency of their worship, he asked:

"Why, O Brahmin, do those people, knowing that there is one God, even a Spirit, worship images of mud on the river-bank, and hideous figures in yonder golden temples?"

"They do not worship the images."

"But do I not see them bow before them, pray to them, and pour libations of sacred water upon them? What is that but worship?"

"It is worship," said the Brahmin, "but offered to God in the image, and not to the image itself."

"I do not understand," replied Mekara. "How is God in such a creation of man's hands?"

"Did I not just read from the Veda that God is every-where, and if everywhere, and in everything, is he not in the idol?"

"Why, then, do they have images? Surely such a God as is there described would delight more in the devotion of the soul than in these outward, and often disgusting, practices."

"Canst thou not yet understand? God is a spirit. Can he be seen? How then shall the vulgar, untaught, un-thinking mob worship him whom they see not? The idea of an unseen, intangible God is too abstract for them; they cannot grasp it. There is nothing actual for the mind to rest upon. · Therefore, we give them idols. On these the mind is concentrated, and the de-votion ascends to God, which otherwise would wander over the wide universe."

The prince was beginning to lose faith in the religion of the Brahmins. "If God is invisible," he asked, "how has any one ever seen him that they may repre-sent him in carvings of stone, mud, or wood? And what idea can any one derive of God by gazing upon your oily-headed Ganesha with his elephant trunk?"

"It is a matter of little importance," replied the Brahmin, "whether they have a right conception of him or not. The uneducated really think that the idol is God and worship it as such. Worship is all that we require of them, and it is as sincerely paid to one object as another. In one sense the image is God, since God is everything. Consequently their devotion is not lost. In that sense I, too, am God."

"Thou God?" cried Mekara, in astonishment. "Canst thou not sin?"

"True, I sin," he replied, "but that is on account of the flesh. God is like fire. A flame is pure Throw dirt upon it and it smokes, giving off a bad odor. That is not from the fire, but from the dirt. So the God in me is pure, but surrounded by impure matter. He hates sin, but it arises from his contact with the flesh."

Confused by this strange logic of idolatry, Mekara knew not what to think.

"How may we become free from sin ?" he inquired.

"By continual mortification of the body," replied his instructor; "by strangling all mortal desires, passions, and affection of every kind. . If life be made continual pain from which death would be a happy release, then sin would be purged and the pure, immaterial soul set free. Some attain that perfection in this life, others pass through many states of existence before their final release. Eternal happiness may be secured by performing the various ceremonies connected with public worship, bathing in the sacred river, or even by silent meditation and fasting. All who die in this holy place are saved. Yet many who, in addition to their own salvation, wish to obtain release for the souls of departed friends, practice additional austerities, and accumulate a surplus of righteousness to be carried with them. Such are the thousands of ascetics who daily go about the streets in rags or almost naked, delighting in bodily torture ; and such are the hundreds of thousands of devotees who shall assemble here this day. Remain here and be content, for no soul from here can be lost. Observe the different rites and ceremonies, and shape thine own life accordingly. Nevertheless, if thou wouldst see farther into our system thou mayest go to the Grove of Sorrow, near a tall mountain shrine which stands near the left bank of the Ganges, two days' journey from the city. It is a place of great reputed sanctity, and here are a thousand ascetics, under a Brahmin, practicing as many different penances. But methinks thou wilt see enough here to satisfy thy soul. May Brahm give thee light, and Vishnu preserve thee. We must part!"

With these words he walked on, leaving Mekara to ponder the things he had heard. The latter stood watching the retreating figure of the Brahmin, and the confused crowd moving to and fro, his mind filled with indecision concerning the strange doctrine he had heard. What spirituality is there in devotion paid to senseless stone? And how can bodily infliction purge the immaterial soul of its pollution? These thoughts racked his brain and afforded him food for reflection for many days to come. He was aroused from his reverie by a sudden commotion in a group of bathers on one of the principal ghauts. The crowd surged backward, leaving an open space on the steps, down which hastily came two men bearing a litter, and followed by a wailing procession of men, women, and children.

The bearers placed the litter by the water's edge and removed the snow white linen cloth that covered it. Mekara came near to look upon the supposed corpse; but, to his surprise, saw the emaciated body of a rich merchant, still alive, and struggling for breath. He stretched his thin, bony hands imploringly towards the river.

"I have sinned!" he gasped, "and the streams of life run low. Place me in the arms of the Sacred Mother quickly. Only on her bosom can my soul find peace!"

Gently lifting him from the litter, they placed him in the water up to his breast, while the weeping relatives crowded on the banks to catch his expiring words. His lean arms clutched at the water before him ; his great dark eyes were already covered with the film of death, and his wan lips scarcely were able to articulate. The bearers held him by the shoulders and supported his feeble head. A spasm passed over his haggard features. His lips moved. "Holy Mother!" he faintly cried, "thou who art my life—receive—my—soul!" His head fell forward on his breast ; his arms dropped to his sides, and they were about to lift him out. Suddenly, as if the departing spirit had forgotten something of infinite importance, he raised his head convulsively and screamed: "Ganga! Ganga!" with all the energy of his last escaping breath, and throwing himself backward lay in the water, a corpse, his spirit caught away in the arms of the Sacred Mother.

The body was placed again on the litter and the cloth drawn over it. A barge now approached and deposited upon the bank a pile of wood and straw. The wood was formed into a pen between two stakes and filled with the straw. On top were placed several layers of dry wood, and the body, closely wrapped in scarlet, was laid upon it and covered with a cloth of gold. When all was ready a priestly Brahmin cried, so as to be heard above the wailing mourners: "What sayeth the widow? Does she choose to eat fire, or no?"

A Hindu widow is accursed if she survives her husband ; cast out from society ; forced to pass her days in solitary confinement and the utmost self-denial ; never sleeping on a bed ; never wearing any jewelry. Without her husband her soul is nothing, but linked with his in the embrace of death, both may go together to Paradise. She makes her own choice.

At the voice of the Brahmin the relatives stopped for a moment their wailing to hear the decision. The poor woman lifted her tearful eyes to the golden domes of the temples where she had so often worshiped ; looked wistfully upon the broad, placid stream of the river and the children clustering around her, then bent a yearning look upon the body beneath the cloth. Only for a moment did she hesitate ; then, "It is decided," she said. "I will go with him!"

Once more the wailing began. Descending into the river, she bathed her body for the last time in its beloved stream, then tying about her waist a cloth, in the corner of which was fastened a quantity of parched rice, she marched, at the head of her children, seven times around the pile in sunwise procession, throwing the rice upon her relatives in passing; then ascending the pile, she lifted the cloth, and, placing the withered arm of the corpse about her neck, embraced it lovingly. The two bodies were now tightly bound together with cords and heavy pieces of wood laid upon them, across which was placed a long bamboo pole, held down at each end by a stout Brahmin to prevent the victim from rising. The priest read aloud from the Shaster, directing how the ceremony was to be performed. The oldest son applied the sacred torch; the smoke ascended to the sky. The wailing grew louder, and the whole immense throng yelled and beat upon their gongs to drown the shrieks of the poor, loving creature, struggling in the burning mass. Two men stood behind those who held down the pole and poured water upon their heads to protect them from the heat. The struggles soon ceased; the dry pile crumbled quickly to ashes; the blue smoke rolled away; the ashes were thrown into the river, and the great crowd thought no more of the every day occurrence, but a family had been destroyed in that one short hour, and two more had been added to the innumerable hosts of the Children of the Ganges.

CHAPTER IX.

> " Tell me, my secret soul,
> O tell me, Hope and Faith,
> Is there no resting place
> From sorrow, sin, and death ?
> Is there no happy spot,
> Where mortals may be blest
> Where grief may find a balm
> And weariness a rest?"
>
> —*Charles Mackay.*

THE PRINCE, who was much shocked at this barbarous deed, congratulated himself that Mahdri was not present to witness it.   Brought up under the Buddhist faith, which forbids the taking of animal life, neither of them had ever witnessed the death, by violence, of even an inseot.   Buddha taught that all souls failing to attain Nirvana in this life were doomed to another round of transmigration from the lower order of animals up to man again.   Consequently even a mischievous flea might be inhabited by the soul of some erratic grandfather who had gone astray from the teachings of the law ; for this reason they were not to be disturbed.   What must have been the shock to the tender-hearted princess, then, had she beheld the cremation of a living human, especially of her own sex, and a devoted wife and mother !

The heat of the sun was now becoming too oppressive to be borne, as it was reflected from the water and the polished steps of the ghauts.   Most of the bathers were dispersing to their homes, and Mekara, fatigued

with his long journey and nights of wakefulness, determined to go to his bungalow and try to rest while he
thought over the events of the morning, or sought repose
in sleep.

Towards evening he wandered with his wife and child
through the streets, watching the endless processions
come and go ; and listening to the learned and bigoted
Brahmins as they discoursed on the corners, explaining
to gaping crowds the way to heaven. Here many, who
had seemed the most devout worshipers at the river,
were earnestly trying to excel in lying, cheating, and
stealing, as if their religion demanded it. Practices
which would make a moral Buddhist shudder to behold.
But what did it matter? Ganga was near and her
waters "cleanse from all sin."

Fakirs in every stage of nudity, some of them coated
from head to foot with dried mud, or hideously striped
with berry juice, ran from street to street, continually
yelling for Shiva. Both Mekara and Mahdri had tried
in vain to conjecture why so many of the sacred bulls
crowded the narrow streets and to what use they could
possibly be put, but that matter soon explained itself.
An old pilgrim came tottering down the street, supporting his feeble frame with a cane. He had the appearance of having come a great distance, his breath came
in short, quick gasps, and his eyes looked eagerly forward as if he feared his strength would fail him before
reaching his destination. Those nearest to him could
hear his dried tongue lisping, through his toothless
gums, the magic name, "Ganga! Ganga!" He was
poor and had no friends to carry him. He paused on a

A Fakir.

corner in sight of the holy stream ; his form reeled, and a look of despair came into his yearning eyes as he clutched the wall for support. Suddenly a sacred bull appeared in front of him ; a new light entered his eyes ; and staggering forward he grasped the animal by the long bushy tail. A generous Brahmin now ran up with a brass lota filled with Ganges water which he poured over the head of the old man, whose sins passing through his hands along the sacred medium, were forever lost, and he fell to the ground, dying in a full assurance of faith that his soul would awake in Paradise ; for, had he not died in the Holy City, in sight of the divine Mother, clinging for refuge to Shiva's favorite steed.

Coolies hastily snatched up the yet quivering body, and bearing it merrily down the steps, dumped it into the river, where it floated peacefully away in company with many others who had enjoyed a like happy fate.

The travelers next visited the temples, where they saw, for the first time, sacrificial blood flow from burning altars. Grave-faced Brahmins, with long white beards, chanted their mantras in response to the bleating of the kids, and lovely nautch girls, clad in light, flowing drapery, with golden bells tinkling about their graceful ankles, danced in circles over the stone-paved floor.

Other temples were inhabited solely by monkeys, who gazed impudently at the curious intruders.

"Why worship monkeys?" The question occurred to Mekara; but there was no one in the temple to answer, except the ridiculous little gods themselves.

Hanumat, the baboon god, is represented in the great Epic, Ramayana, as the son of the God of the Wind,

Temple at Benares.

and as such was often employed by Rama when in need of a swift messenger. For his services to this mighty king in his great campaign against Ceylon, he was rewarded with perpetual life and never-fading youth. He is renowned for no good deeds or noble traits of character, yet is devoutly worshiped by millions.

The prince lost no opportunity of inquiring into the meaning of every ceremony he saw performed. But the more he saw and heard of the religion of the people, the greater was his surprise to see the inconsistency between the teachings of the holy books and the practices of those who professed to follow them. The Vedas proclaimed One God, Immutable, Omniscient, and Omnipresent. Why then should there be such a lack of an object of worship as to authorize the deification of monkeys, bulls, and rivers?

The temples, with their gilded pinnacles and smoking altars, were devoted to worship; the unnumbered hosts of pilgrims came with hearts overflowing with worship; and those who dipped themselves in the Ganges at sunrise did it as a form of worship. But to whom? Out of the millions who annually visited her banks was there one who worshiped God? No; not one. The question now arose in the mind of the prince, "Why is all this?" Then the words of the Brahmin, spoken that morning, recurred to him. "It is not given to any but Brahmins to understand the Vedas." "How different," thought he, "from the religion of Ko Tha-Byu, which had been revealed to the common people, the simplest of the land!"

Reader, dost thou know what has been the greatest curse the world has ever seen? The answer is obvious: Priestcraft.

(69)   AN INDIAN TEMPLE.

Who was responsible for the illiteracy of the masses during the Dark Ages? Who butchered the servants of God, and drove them like sheep to the slaughter? Who, with Satanic cunning, is trying to sap the foundations of our own fair republic? Who holds Mexico in chains? Who opposes the man of God in Cuba? Who is responsible for the gross ignorance, superstition, and vice in every land, civilized or savage? The answer to all is, THE PRIEST! THE PRIEST! God send the happy day, when only the One Great High Priest, who is "touched with the feelings of our infirmity," shall stand between a loving Father and his trusting people!

After wandering till nearly night among the mazy labyrinths of streets, Mahdri, who had no interest in the city beyond a natural feminine curiosity to see the sights, became exhausted from the long tramp; which being observed by her husband, he reproved himself for having led her so far, and proposed to return at once to the bungalow. There they sat till late in the night on the upper balcony; she, amusing herself with the child, and he, looking thoughtfully out over the city. A thin mist had risen from the river through which the full moon glimmered, "shorn of its beams."

Hundreds of spice-lamps set afloat on the silvery tide of the river by amorous maidens, betokening propitious returns from anxious lovers, twinkled like stars, or phantom Will-o'-The-Wisps, as they moved along. Red lanterns flared from the deep dark streets below; and flames of cocoanut-oil lit up the temples on the cliff. The great piles of stone buildings and golden domes, touched by the dim light of the moon, with a back-ground of mist, gave the appearance more of a fading sunset picture painted among the clouds, than of the sad reality it was.

A spirit of worship thrilled Mekara's bosom as he looked on the lovely scene, and he longed to throw himself on his face and pour out his soul in devotion.

"But to whom?" he thought. "Shall I worship yon lovely river? I know, from natural causes, it is a blessing to the whole land; but no more so than my own Irrawaddy. Shall I pray to the sacred bulls or monkeys? They have no instincts common to the human soul, nor could they understand the words of my mouth. Shall I pour oil on the elephant-head of Ganesha, or drape his thick neck with garlands of flowers? The senseless stone would never know it. Shall I give offerings to a God who is Spirit? I fain would worship him; but alas! I know not how to approach unto him, nor with what words to address him. Oh, the light is long in coming! I thought I had received it when the Brahmin read to me of a God, but his actions belie his words. I will patiently labor and wait."

Thus, day after day, and night after night, did he pass in the Holy City; but each day only served to reveal unto him, more and more, the vanity and folly of its gross idolatry. Within a week of daily application he was convinced that the "Mother of the Faithful" could never afford him the rest for which he sought, and he determined, as a further test of their religion and practices, to visit the grove suggested to him by the Brahmin on the morning of his arrival.

Making known his intention to Mahdri, she expressed delight at the prospect of leaving the crowded city, and willingness to accompany him anywhere. So in the cool of the afternoon, just before sunset, they set out in a boat on their journey up the river.

Their destination lay beyond Allahabad, "The City of God," situated at the juncture of the two sacred rivers. Its high-sounding title promised to Mekara the fulfillment of his hopes, and he stopped to make further inquiry; but a few hours sufficed to reveal the fact that the inhabitants were no better informed than those of Benares, but were engaged in the same abominable practices, even to excess.

Weary with journeyings, and searchings to and fro, and almost in despair, he turned his back upon India's two most holy cities, and appealed for comfort to the heart of Nature, landing that night at the banyan temple where first we found them.

Will he find rest?

Ah! troubled prince, thou hast never known sorrow and heart-pangs such as shall soon be thine, when, through Brahmin duplicity, thy beloved wife and child——but we must not anticipate.

BOOK SECOND.

CHAPTER I.

" Moon after moon our lord sat in the wood,
So meditating that he forgot
Oftentimes the hour of food, rising from thoughts
Prolonged beyond the sunrise and the moon,
To see his bowl unfilled and eat perforce
Of wild fruit fallen from the bough o'er head,
Shaken to earth by chattering ape or plucked
By purple paroquet. Therefore, his grace
Faded ; his body, worn by stress of soul,
Lost, day by day, the marks thirty and two
Which testify the Buddha. Scarce that leaf
Fluttering so dry and withered to his feet,
From off the sal-branch, bore less likeness
Of spring's soft greenness than he of him
Who was the princely flower of all his land."

—Arnold.

MEKARA had told his story hurriedly and passed over the minor parts of his history ; but by the time he was through the sun was high in the heavens ; and Mahdri, returning from the village, had prepared a meal of rice and curry, and sitting down with the child, she waited quietly until her husband should be ready.   Asita was invited to partake of the refreshments, but declined, as a Brahmin could not receive food from the hands of a lower caste.   So while they were eating he helped himself from the lota at his side.

Only a few moments sufficed the prince to allay his appetite, for when the soul hungers the body craves but

(73)

little. Asita waited until he had finished and washed his hands from a chattie of water, then began:

"Thy story, O prince, is one of thousands who are troubled with thoughts of the soul, its relation to the Soul of the universe, and its eternal destiny. My brother in the Holy City told thee aright. Brahm is all, and in all. Without him there is nothing; and the highest state of blessedness is to be absorbed finally into the bosom of the great Original from whom all have emanated. The body is nothing but a cage containing the divine spark which alone gives character to its possessor. The soul is holy, and contact with the flesh defiles it. Consequently, if the desires of the body can be quenched, all love and affection uprooted, and carnal sensibilities destroyed, the soul will be freed as water from a compressed sponge.

"Our religion admits of no proselytes. To be a Brahmin is to be born such. But, even in this, thy destiny lies in choice, and not fate, nor even the will of the gods. The fetters of caste bind us fast while in this body, but when freed by death the soul next enters whatever degree it was prepared for in this life. Even a Pariah as thyself can aspire to be a Brahmin in the next life, from which there is only one step to final absorption, the blessed end to all human trouble. The more severe self-torture we practice the greater happiness we shall enjoy.

"As I said, thy future destiny is altogether a matter of choice. Within this forest is a great multitude of ascetics, each practicing a different mode of infliction according to the dictates of his own mind. I will conduct thee, therefore, to the Grove of Sorrow, where thou shalt converse with each and choose for thyself."

Mekara sat in silence, meditating on what course to pursue. Having met with disappointment in both Benares and Allahabad, he was now confronted with the same difficulties met with there. But he was determined to let no opportunity pass unimproved, so he decided to go and converse with the ascetics at least, and hear from their own lips the progress they were making in soul-purifying.

Asita paid no attention to this hesitation, but lifting his crooked trunk from the couch of roots and grass, he stood, with staff and lota in hand, ready to go. Mahdri took up the child and essayed to follow; but Asita objected, saying it was no place for a woman; and bade her to remain with the child and rest, promising to return before sunset. She insisted, and it was only when reassured by her husband that she consented to remain; for with a woman's quick intuition, she had already begun to distrust the wily Brahmin.

The forest which they now entered was one of the most lovely in all India. Cypress, bamboo, plantain, mango, palm and tamarind trees were mingled in the most luxurious confusion. Birds of gorgeous hue flitted from branch to branch, and sang merrily from their shady recesses; monkeys swinging with their long arms, or hanging by their tails from over-hanging limbs, performed the most ridiculous antics; herds of gazelles browsed by the path, and fearlessly lifted their large eyes to the face of their new visitor, as if accustomed to the companionship of mankind.

After winding for some time through the intricate paths of the forest, they at length reached a vast glade where the over-hanging foliage was so dense that the rays of the sun never entered. The ground was as smooth as a floor, having been trodden, for long years past, by innumerable feet; wierd, half-stifled cries ever and anon resounded through the dim vaults, like wails from the region of Despair, strangely unnatural in such a spot. Hundreds of human forms were moving, standing, or reclining, among the trees in every conceivable position. Some walked continually to and fro with strings of beads about their necks which they counted, repeating, over and over, a thousand times a day, the sacred Shasters. Some, who were yet only novices in practice, employed their time in going about with bowls of rice from which they took little balls with their fingers and thrust into the open, dried-up mouths of those who had already become helpless through long abstinence. One poor creature was standing like a statue, his feet close together, and his arms lifted straight above his head. For five years he had been standing thus, not moving a muscle of his limbs. His skin hung wrinkled and hard, like weather-beaten leather about his form. His muscles had dried into stiff, inflexible cords. His arms seemed like dead, sapless branches of a tree, ready to drop off at the least jar. The blood had almost ceased to circulate through his mummy-dried flesh; and through his clinched palms the nails had pierced, growing out through the festered skin on the back, writhing and twisting like serpents' head. His eye-balls, looking straight in front of him, were immovable in their shriveled sockets. His long, matted hair had grown down around his head and neck to his shoulders, and it was only when the breeze lifted the mass hanging over his brows that he could see at all. If the development of the soul is attained by the mortification of the body, surely his spiritual nature must have reached a height almost to perfection.

Here lay a helpless being on the ground woltering in a pool of blood drawn from his own body and limbs with a flint. Here, suspended from a limb in a basket, was a child as beautiful and sweet as Manohara. For two days it had hung there without food, wailing piteously, while the great cannibal ants devoured its tender flesh. The little one was fretful from teething, and Asita, having persuaded its mother that it was possessed of a demon, induced her to let him expose it to the ants. If it lived unharmed for three days he promised to return it as cured; but if devoured by the ants, its mother was congratulated that she was rid of a demon.

Off to one side two slow fires were burning; between which sat a naked fakir "mortifying his body." His flesh was swollen and flushed, and through his cracked skin the watery blood was slowly oozing and dripping to the ground; and yet he seemed happy in anticipation of the reward offered in the pardon of his sins.

Mekara looked with disgust and horror on all this self-imposed torture. Turning to the Brahmin he asked:

"Is there no other hope of gaining eternal happiness?"

"Thou hast already been told that the ways are many," replied Asita. "These all practice their several austerities from choice and not from coercion. The soul may be freed from sin by milder means, as bathing in the Ganges and solemn meditation, but the degree of happiness depends upon the severity of the pain endured.

"It is now almost noon, and I must return to the mountain and bring away the food left there by the pilgrims. These must be fed a little that they may live until the body is conquered; then we will carry them to the Ganges to die in its waters. Stay thou among these till I return. Question them, and learn from each the progress he is making toward the heavenly goal."

Mokara needed no second invitation; he was too anxious to learn for himself the feelings of those who seemed so intent on their own destruction. As far as the eye could see, forms were visible in gloom. Some were rolling like swine in the dust crying, day and night, "Ganga! Ganga!" Some were suspended from the branches, head downward, their long hair growing like moss to the ground; and some hung from swings in different positions. Mokara wandered at pleasure among them, talking freely to those who were still able to articulate. To his surprise, he found each one perfectly satisfied with his condition, and fully confident that his way was right.

At length, weary in body from so much walking, and sick at heart from the sight of so much wretchedness, he sat down by the trunk of a bo-tree to await the coming of Asita who had promised to return in a short while.

The zephyrs fanned the tall cypress tops above, the birds sang, and the soft chime of pagoda bells, scarcely perceptible, fell on his ear. With ears open to the joy of Nature's bright world above him, and eyes beholding human wretchedness around him, he mused.

"Is it indeed the lot of man to always suffer thus amid the loveliness of his surroundings ? Why is the world so filled with beauty if we are not to look upon it ? Why do the birds sing so cheerfully, and the strains of music sound so sweetly, if we are not to listen to them? Why are wives and children given to us if we are not to love them? Could I ever enjoy pleasure that was denied to my loved ones? Strange, strange, teaching this!

"Asita delayeth his coming."

CHAPTER II.

—*Spencer Wallace Cone.*

AFTER the departure of Mekara and the Brahmin, Mahdri washed the rice-bowl and placed it with the little earthen curry-pot in a recess of the tree. She then set about amusing Manohara until her father should return. The two young gazelles that had slept under the tree the night before, came out from the shade of the forest, and walking familiarly about, eagerly picked up the bits of food that had been dropped. Manohara was delighted at the sight of the lovely visitors, and scrambling from her mother's arms, toddled to them; and prattling all the endearing baby talk she had ever learned, she stroked their glossy necks and peeped into their beautiful eyes. They entered fully into the sport, and made her laugh heartily as they rolled her on the ground with their velvet noses, or capered shyly around as if afraid.

Mahdri looked on with all a mother's love; but when the gazelles grew tired of sport and went back into the forest, she saw that the child was sleepy, and placing her in the swinging-basket, she rocked it back and forth singing a lullaby.

> " Sleep, darling, sleep :
> A mother's care
> And a father's prayer
> Shall safely keep
> The baby so fair.
> Sleep, darling, sleep !
>
> Thy father shall bring
> Thee peace and love ;
> The devas sing
> Thy joy to prove ;
> And silver bells ring
> In the pagoda above.
> Sleep, darling, sleep !''

At length the weary brown-eyes closed, and the little one slumbered. Spreading a vail over the basket, Mahdri was preparing to go in search of berries for dinner, when she was alarmed to see Asita returning alone.

"Where is the prince, my husband ?" she asked excitedly.

"I left him with the devotees," replied Asita, "until I should return to the mountain for food, which the pilgrims have left by this time. Thy husband is safe. Is the child asleep ?"

"She is," replied the mother, with a glance at the basket.

"Mahdri, dost thou know her fate if she should live ?"

"I know not, unless it shall be even as my own has been. The future to me is dark. I try not to think about it. My husband is seeking the light, and when he shall have found it he will tell me. Resting in that hope, I give myself no concern, either for myself or the child. We follow him."

6

"Ah, how little thou knowest of human destiny!" replied Asita. "She can never share thy fate, neither canst thou share his. The religious barriers between woman and man are as insuperable as the social barriers of caste between man and man. The child is now at,the age when all Hindu girls must be given in marriage; but thou, a stranger in a strange land, and a Pariah besides, hast no one to whom she may be given. A woman without a husband is a disgrace forever. The only merit possible for her to attain is by the most ser- vile obedience to him who has the rule over her. She may, in that case, be born in the next life as a man of high caste, whence salvation is easily secured; but otherwise her soul is condemned to inhabit the body of a brute, from which there is but little hope of release by means of good deeds. The future happiness of the child, as well as thine own, depends upon thyself. It may be secured by one act quickly done, though the affliction may seem hard for the present. Think of what I have said till my return, when I will further instruct thee. But remember this: The pleasure or grief experienced in this short life is nothing compared to the happiness or misery which shall be the reward of the next."

With these words he turned and proceeded in the direction of the mountain.

Mahdri stood as if dazed. Deep religious emotion, for the first time, stirred her soul. But even then her only concern was for her child. Raising the covering of the basket, she gazed fondly upon the sleeping form The long silken lashes, drawn peacefully over the brown eyes; the cheeks, dimpled and rosy; the chubby limbs encircled by golden bands, the only memento of the Golden Face; and the dark, glossy ringlets tossed loosely about the round little head, formed a picture as lovely as that which adorns the cradle of any American mother, and equally, if not more dear to the poor, yearning heart that had nothing save husband and child to love. Gazing with a soul full of tenderness upon the little one, she said:

"Can it be true, my sweet babe, that life has in store no joy for thee? While the lovely Nautch girls dance like devos in the temple, and while the Hindu children play in the rich zenanas, sipping like humming-birds from all the sweets of life—must my dear one be an outcast, disgraced, and shunned by all? Oh, it cannot, it must not be! I would give my own life to make thee happy!"

Lost in contemplation of her child's destiny, she thought no more of her former distrust of the Brahmin, but looked up eagerly as his deformed shadow once more fell at her feet.

"Holy Brahmin!" she cried, "tell me what I may do to secure the happiness of my child."

The old man's keen, black eyes sparkled with delight to see her anxiety.

"As I said, Mahdri, one act will release her, both from the disgrace resting upon her in this life, and the misery in store for her in the next. This act thou art also in duty bound to perform for another reason. Thy husband, when at Benares, made a vow to the gods which he has never paid. Both demand a human sacrifice."

With quick apprehension, she turned to the basket.

"My child!" she cried, "Oh, do not tell me I must part from her."

"Only think," insisted the Brahmin, "all thy husband's pangs of soul removed, thou shalt secure thine own redemption by that most holy act, which alone can save the child. Eternal sorrow shall be hers if this is not done, for the curse of womanhood, which might thus be removed, will rest forever upon her, and thy conscience will sting thee for neglect.

"Ganga is a more merciful mother than even thyself. The little body, cradled on the waters of the Ganges, shall be joyfully received by the great Mother, and her soul shall pass immediately into a body of nobler order, perhaps even a Brahmin. If thou shall refuse to do this, life ever afterwards will be a burden, and thou shalt continually reprove thyself, saying: 'I have borne a child into the world subject to disgrace among men, and eternal banishment from the presence of the gods. My husband's vow is unpaid. I, myself, must degenerate into a brute, because I refused to obey the holy Brahmin who has power over even the gods.' Can a mother's love allow this?"

Mahdri remained in stupefied horror, looking first at the Brahmin, then at the sleeping child. At length, regaining her power of speech, she said:

"Buddha forbade us to take the life of even an insect, and shall a mother murder her own child?"

"Thy husband has renounced the religion of Buddha," replied Asita, "and even if he had not this act would be right under the circumstances. To kill a beast is murder, because the soul which it contains would be driven into a still lower being; but to sacrifice a child, of one's own flesh and blood is a meritorious deed, combining with it both maternal worship and infant salvation."

Mahdri looked sorrowfully and thoughtfully upon the basket; then folding her arms with a look of determination, she turned and said:

"I am resolved. I will leave the child to her father and throw myself into the Ganges. Will that be sufficient?"

"That would save thyself alone; being thy own act and committed on thine own body, no benefit could arise either to husband or child. In fact she would be left in a worse condition than ever, without even a mother's care. Consent; it is the only way. Thy husband can then return from the forest, and together, you can enter life again, assured of future happiness."

The mother's heart was breaking as she weighed responsibility with love.

"Give me time to decide," she entreated; "at least another day to enjoy the companionship of my darling."

But Asita was too cunning to allow her time for deliberation. Knowing that if he could not induce her to act while thus confused, she would be sure to refuse after reflection; and all hope would be lost if Mekara should learn his designs. So he insisted on immediate action.

A new difficulty arose to Mahdri.

"How could I ever meet her father and show him an empty cradle?" she asked; "and how could I convince him that I had done right?"

"Never fear," replied the artful Brahmin, "thy husband himself desires it, and bade me persuade thee. His religious convictions are so strong that he has consented to part with the dearest idol of this life in order to secure rest and peace for all his family. 'Tis his request, and not mine, that thou should'st perform this sacred duty. For what benefit could it be to me? Consider, and act."

Doubting, fearing, loving, stood Mahdri. Asita had promised, encouraged and harrassed her till she had no thought, feeling, or action of her own. Almost unconsciously she lowered the basket from the tree, and lifting out the still sleeping child, turned in the direction of the river, bearing the precious burden clasped tightly to her beating heart.

Asita stood leaning on his staff watching her eagerly.

Just as she reached the river bank the child struggled, and reaching out her arms called in baby tones for her play-mates, the young gazelles. Then opening her eyes and seeing where she was, she lay passively in her mother's arms looking confidingly up into her face. Mahdri quickly drew the vail over the little face that she might not be deterred in her purpose by the pleading look of the soft eyes. Unclasping one of the little bracelets she thrust it into her bosom, murmuring, "It is thy father's command, sweet child, that I should do this awful deed. Had he not so wished I could never have done it. But he knows best, and we must obey."

Approaching an opening among the rushes, in full view of the broad, placid stream below, she gazed longingly, for a moment, upon the little form in her arms; then turning her face, that she might not witness the deed of her own hands, she, with all her might, threw the little one far into the stream; then ran shrieking from the spot, but not too soon to hear the heart-piercing, half-stifled scream of terror as the child struck the water.

Asita's eyes danced with delight as he beheld the deed, and chuckling to himself, he glided like a phantom into the woods.

"Aha! Aha! my prince," he said. "One more tie severed and I will have thee safe. The mother shall soon follow the child."

Mekara could never become an ascetic while encumbered by domestic ties; and the Brahmin knew full well that he would never consent to part with wife and child; hence, this strategy.

Mahdri never stopped till she sank exhausted under the banyan-tree beside the now empty basket. She then realized, for the first time, what she had done, and burying her face in the long grass she burst into a frenzy of tears.

"O, my child! my child!" she cried, "to think thy downy couch must be exchanged for a crocodile's jaws! Even now I see his shining teeth piercing thy tender flesh. Would I, too, were dead!"

The young gazelles once more came in from the forest and walked about under the tree as if seeking their little play-fellow. They approached the empty basket, side by side, and looked in inquiringly. Then, as if understanding the mother's grief, they stood bleating by her side, and placed their heads down to her face. Clasping each about the slender neck she cried:

"Ah! you, too, miss sweet Manohara. Her little feet shall no more leave their tiny tracks in the dust of the plain; her glad voice no more enliven the gloom of our exile! Happy are you who know not a mother's grief."

CHAPTER III.

—Edwin Arnol .

MEKARA looked up anxiously as Asita approached the tree against which he was leaning.

"Hast thou seen my wife and child?" he asked.

"I saw them under the banyan-tree playing with the young gazelles. They are well and happy," glibly replied the old idolator.

"Hast thou decided to adopt Asceticism in any of its forms?"

Mekara shook his head. "I cannot see," he said, "how the soul is to be purified by any of the means I have seen. Methinks that bodily filth would lead to spiritual pollution, and that too much seclusion would rather dwarf than expand the soul. My faith is yet too weak."

Asita was content to teach him first the practice which was most easy, in the hope of stimulating him to further austerities afterwards, so he began cautiously.

"Wilt thou do a favor for me while I go to another shrine in the forest?"

"Name it."

"Yonder is a group of maimed men—some without feet, some without hands, and all unable to feed themselves. Take this bowl of rice and give to each a morsel. I shall not tarry long."

Mekara promised, and received the bowl from the hands of the Brahmin, who moved off hastily through the forest in an opposite direction from that in which he had come, but changing his course when out of sight.

Mekara took the bowl and began feeding the helpless victims of superstition. He had found one man deprived of both hands and feet, but whose tongue had escaped the burning-iron; with him he entered into conversation.

"Why, O brother," he asked, "do ye all practice such horrid and unnatural tortures; is it not a crime against Nature?"

"It is to cleanse the soul from sin, Sahib; has not Asita told thee as much already? He promised me that with the loss of my limbs I should receive atonement for all the sins of my youth. I think nothing of these bodily pains if thereby I am purified within."

"If I mistake not," said the prince, "thou art a Sudra; what, then, will become of thy sanctified soul after death?"

"It will enter another body of higher caste."

"Will it then be exempt from the sufferings imposed during this life?"

"No; the same agonies must be endured in each successive stage until its final absorption."

"Surely," said Mekara, "there must be some means by which the soul may be permanently released. I see no reason why a being, sanctified in this life, should be subject to suffering in the next. Art thou sure that thou hast not missed the way?"

"We have been taught no other," responded the fakir. "if thou knowest of a better, tell it."

"Alas!" said Mekara. "For that I have long been seeking, but have found it not. We are, all alike, groping in darkness."

.   .   .   .

The calmness of despair had come over Mahdri, and while the gazelles went out on the plains, she sat motionless on the grass, brooding over her irretrievable loss, and thinking what she could do with herself.

A quick, halting, step was heard approaching, and looking around she saw again the bent form of Asita. Suspecting some evil design in his hasty return, the distrust of the morning arose again within her, and she was about to accuse him of the murder of her child ; but something in his strange, excited manner restrained her, and seeing that he had something to tell, she arose and, looking at him with stony eyes, waited.

" Mahdri," he began falteringly, and with seeming hesitation, " it becomes my painful duty to break to thee the tidings that the second greatest curse visited upon woman has this day befallen thee. *Thou art a widow.*"

Her heart gave a great throb and was still ; her muscles twitched convulsively, but she remained motionless. Folding her arms, she said simply:

"Go on. My heart is broken. I can bear anything now."

"While I was gone," he continued, "thy husband having seen all the devotees, grew weary while awaiting my return and went to the Ganges to bathe. It was where the river runs through the woods and is lined on each side with dense jungle. Through this a path has been cut down to the water's edge, where we carry the dying to expire in the water. Underneath the overhanging branches of the thicket is the abode of the sacred crocodile whïch devours the bodies. Thy husband, not knowing the nature of the place, and I not being there to tell him, went into the water, not suspecting any danger and was immediately seized by the huge beast."

"Ah!" she cried, "would that I had listened to the voice of my husband and remained in the palace of the Golden Face! Then would my child, at least, have been saved, and I should have escaped this double calamity. And now the last hope of life is gone!"

"Grieve not for them," replied Asita, "their lot is better than thine. Indeed, nothing better could have happened to them. To die in the Ganges, and, also at the mouth of the sacred crocodile, is worth a whole life of Asceticism, or a voluntary death elsewhere. They shall be born of high caste."

"But," mourned Mahdri, "what shall I do, a poor, despised widow, and far away from mine own country? For my husband and child I lived. I had no other love, no other desire, save to be with them. Compared with this life of horror, death is sweet. I, too, will die in the Ganges."

"That is now the only hope," said Asita. "The law of Menu concerning the Suttee of widows cannot here be carried into effect. Thou has not the corpse of thy husband, nor even his sandals, with which to enter the flames. But, to insure greater merit, I would advise thee to go to the Holy City where there will be a great festival to-morrow. Hundreds rush down the ghauts and are drowned in the river, thereby atoning for all sin and disgrace. Be thou one among the number. Go to the village yonder and a boatman will carry thee gladly. I advise for thy good."

She stood for a moment, doubting, then laying the rice-bowl and curry-pot in the basket, she placed it on her head and walked away towards the village ringing her hands.

Sorrow has its reward, and deep grief only serves to make brighter the succeeding joy. Spring is the more pleasant because it follows the winter. The sun shines brighter after a storm. Gold is purer for passing through the fire. So shall it be with Mahdri. Her light heart had never been made to feel before this day, and the depths of her soul had never been stirred. The Lord hath selected her as a chosen vessel and will speak to her by the wayside.

CHAPTER IV.

MEKARA was still talking with the devotees when Asita returned. Handing back the now empty bowl he expressed his intention of returning to the banyan tree as the gathering gloom showed that the sun would soon be down, and Mahdri would be anxious. Asita sought to detain him.

" Canst thou not remain through the night," he asked, " and continue the work just performed ? Surely good deeds have their reward and thou shalt obtain rest and peace, as, by degrees, thou art absorbed in such a life. Remain, I pray thee."

"Impossible. Leave my family unprotected through the night, and suffering suspense from my absence ! "

"Ah! I fear thou art too much absorbed in such cares to ever attain perfection of soul. Knowest thou not that we must put aside even conjugal and parental love ? "

"Remember, though," said Mekara, "I have a wife and child already. Would it be right to leave them to wander in a strange country unprotected? Surely I could not be required to do such a base deed."

"Thou art relieved of all responsibility regarding them," replied Asita.

"In what manner ?"

"Their souls have made their passage, and their bodies repose on the bosom of Ganga, the divine Mother."

Mekara was thunder-struck, scarcely comprehending what he heard.

"What!" he said, "didst thou not see them safe under the banyan at noon? What knowest thou more than I?"

"There are Thugs in the forest who worship the goddess Kali. Their occupation is to rob and slay human victims in worship to her. Both thy wife and child wore bracelets, ear-rings and anklets. Thugs, in passing, took them captive and were bearing them alive through the forest on their way to Kali's temple where they were to be sacrificed. I saw them but now in the wood, and cried to them to stop. Seeing me they hastily strangled the victims, stripped them of their ornaments and threw the bodies into the river."

"Be not grieved, O prince, it is best. They have thus both escaped the curse resting upon womanhood."

Mekara was overcome with remorse and grief. "Oh, why did I ever leave them," he cried, "even for an hour, alone in the forest! Lead me quickly to the place that I may rescue their bodies to be burned!"

"It is too late now," replied Asita, "the water is full of crocodiles and both have been devoured ere this."

"Show me the way any how," demanded Mekara; "I would behold the place where they died that I may weep over them."

The Brahmin could make no further excuse and moved off reluctantly, closely followed by the impatient father.

At length they reached an opening in full view of the river.

„ Here," said Asita, " is the place I saw them last."

Mekara rushed to the bank and looked down. The long grass had not been trampled, the mud in the edge of the stream was untouched, and there was no sign of a struggle, or even an approach to the bank.

Realizing the deception that had been practiced upon him, he suspected the design of the old Brahmin. Filled with rage and grief as a lioness for her whelps, he seized the old man by the beard, and, shaking him till his loosened teeth chattered in his head, and the dry bones popped in the withered skin, he cried.

"False Brahmin, thou hast lied! No one in all this land except thine own evil, designing self could look upon the fair form of my Mahdri, or into the innocent eyes of little Manohara, and take their lives, either for spoil or sacrifice. Confess to me that thyself art their destroyer; else I will suspend thy wasted body from the branches of a tree for the vultures to pick, that the Ganges may never be desecrated by thy foul carcass!"

"Confess!"

Shivering with terror, and frenzied with rage, the Brahmin screamed:

"Wretch! dost thou dare to lay hands upon a Brahmin? I have lost caste, and the gods will smite thee dead for this act!"

"I fear no gods that will protect such as thou art. Tell me at once, what, with designing hand, or lying tongue, thou hast done with my wife and child!"

Humbled with fear, the old priest replied:

"I confess. It is no harm for a Brahmin to lie, if, by so doing, he can accomplish designs for the gods. I persuaded Mahdri to throw herself and babe into the river, both to save them and make thee free to become an ascetic   I did it all for thy good."

Mekara dropped his hand as if stung; and looking upon the shivering, crouching form with intense loathing, he said:

"Thou hast miserably failed in thy purpose. I regret that I ever came in contact with thy evil presence. But I have learned the true nature of Brahminism, and the bigotry of Brahmins. Deceiving the people and causing them to believe it a high privilege to minister unto you; the fat of the land is brought by deluded thousands, as offerings to the gods, passing through your voracious mouths. Go! and may the hissing flames of the pyre consume thy crackling flesh ere thou shalt be permitted to lead others astray!"

Turning, he left Asita crest-fallen and chaffing; while he returned towards the banyan tree. The gazelles were lying on the grass. But not even a handkerchief remained to remind the widowed father of his loved ones. Going to the river he found where Mahdri had stood with the child; and looked anxiously but in vain for traces of their bodies, not dreaming that one was yet in the village below.

Having seen enough of the Brahmin religion, coming so near the truth in its original theories, but so debasing in practice, he determined to visit the mosques of Mohammed. So loosing a boat from the ghaut, he turned his back upon the banyan grove, the mountain shrine, and the lovely plain, where he had been made to suffer so much. It was now past sunset and the moon soon arose, aiding him to guide his boat up the river.

The god of the Karens was almost a stranger; the god of the Brahmins, a myth. What will the god of Mohammed be?

CHAPTER V.

"Why do the heathen rage, and the people imagine a vain thing?"—Ps. ii-1.

As Maiidri entered the village she beheld the inhabitants in unusual commotion. Some huddled together
in groups as if discussing an affair of great importance,
while the Brahmins chatted wildly in the market-place.
She paid no attention to the confusion, but proceeded
at once to the ghauts, intent upon securing a boat to
depart immediately for the Holy City. But she looked
in vain for those who had the boats in charge. Not
one was to be seen anywhere. So she started for the
market-place, inquiring of every one she met for a boatman. But everybody seemed excited, and could give
no answer, save to rush for the market-place. The
commotion gradually attracted her attention from the
gloomy thoughts of her sorrow, and she began to take
some notice of the surroundings.

A man stood on an elevation and seemed to be making
an effort to address the people, but their continual noise
prevented his being heard. Mahdri spoke to a woman
near by and asked what it all meant.

"Not much," replied she; "a man, who has broken
caste and escaped prison, is trying to teach a new
religion, and the Brahmins will not let him be heard.
A white man was with him this morning, who went on
up the river, but he left these behind."

And she handed Mahdri a slip of printed paper.

curious to a Hindu, accustomed only to the dried leaves written upon with a stylus. It was headed

"THE TRUE GOD,"

and spoke of his character and his relation to man, of Jesus and his atonement for sin, signed by

FELIX CAREY, of the SERAMPORE MISSION.

Mahdri lost sight of her grief for a moment as she contemplated the wonderful tidings. Here, at last, was a knowledge of God, and a release from sin with its accompanying sorrow. Was it not even this for which her husband was seeking? True she had never been interested in religion before, but the memory of their long quest gave her curiosity to learn, for her dead husband's sake, something of the God he sought. "Oh!" she thought, "would that he had lived to see it. What he sought for and found not has come to me without seeking."

The uproar in the street still continued as long as the speaker tried to talk. Suddenly he folded his arms and a hush, as of death, pervaded the whole throng. Every ear was intent on listening, as the words of a song arose in a clear, sweet voice. The attention of a Hindu, no matter how boisterous, can always be attracted by poetry or song. These were the words:

> "O! thou, my soul, forget no more
> The Friend who all thy sorrows bore;
> Let every idol be forgot,
> But, O! my soul, forget Him not.
>
> Eternal truth and mercy shine
> In Him, and he himself is thine;
> And can'st thou, then, with sin beset,
> Such charms, such matchless charms, forget?

> O ! no ; till life itself depart
> His name shall cheer and warm my heart ;
> And, lisping this, from earth I'll rise,
> And join the chorus of the skies."

It was the voice and the words of Krishna Pal, the first Hindu convert to christianity.

Mahdri's tears flowed freely as the spirit of God touched her soul, and echoed in her heart the strange, sweet words, "The Friend who all thy sorrows bore." She wished that he had spoken longer, but when the song was ended the Brahmins again interfered, and, distributing his tracts, he left for the river.

Mahdri had already lost faith in Asita and his innuman prescriptions for sorrow; and she longed to tell this kind-looking man her story and learn more of his religion • At length her desire overcame her timidity, and, following him to the boat, she made known her request.

Krishna was overjoyed to hear her inquiry; for he was leaving in disappointment, thinking that his visit had effected no good. Having disposed of all his tracts he was about to return to the mission for more, as his companion, Felix Carcy, had taken the most of them up the river. But now he gladly seated himself on the bank and related to Mahdri all the wonderful things the Lord had done for him; God's mercy in the great plan of redemption, and the inconceivable joy and peace that come to those who worship him aright. He told her of how he had broken caste, and was banished from home and friends, yet was happy in the consciousness of having done it all for Christ.

Mahdri listened eagerly ; a new interest aroused within her. Hitherto she had worshiped husband and child, but as she heard the story of God's love, her heart went out to him in earnest prayer, and she worshiped God of the bible.

Krishna, seeing how it was with her, proposed to baptize her at once.

"Why is that?" she enquired.

"Not for any merit there is in the water?" said Krishna, "nor that the Ganges is better than any other, but to show, that as Christ died for thee, was buried, and rose again, even so thou hast died to sin and risen to a new life. It is only an emblem—a sign to the world."

By this time many of the villagers had collected around them, curious to see what they were about to do.

Krishna offered a short prayer of praise and thanksgiving to God, then leading Mahdri by the hand into the water, baptized her in the name of the Father, Son, and Holy Ghost.

"Now," said Mahdri, when they had come up out of the water, "I have here no friends, nor any one to care for. Let me go with thee, I pray, to the Mission and learn to work for Jesus. He alone has saved me from suicide this day, and for him I wish to live."

Krishna willingly consented, and getting into the boat, they left behind the spot that had been the scene, in one day, of events long to be remembered.

"The chain of caste is broken, and who shall be able to mend it?"

CHAPTER VI.

AGRA, once the favorite capital of the illustrious
Emperor, Akbar, outshone all the cities of the Orient
in royal splendor, and unrivalled architecture.

Hither Mckara bent his course. The King of kings,
who so adorned Babylon the Great, and made her mistress of the world, never conceived of such magnificence
as glittered in Agra. And the marvelous hanging
gardens, a wonder of the world, built for the pleasure
of his queen, could not compare with the wonderful
Taj Mahal, a mountain of jewels erected above Shah
Jehan's wife, the lovely *Nour Mahal.* No monument
erected by man ever approached it in sublime beauty.

Once a school-boy, on a north-bound train from Nash-
ville, stood at the rear window of the coach to catch
the last view of the landscape of his native country.

Gradually the different parts of the city blended together; the river was lost from sight; the lines of
streets vanished, and the houses mingled together as
one mass; only here and there a tall factory-chimney
could be distinguished, sending forth its tortuous volumes of smoke. But the capitol, at first, unseen on its
lofty base, rose into more prominent view as surrounding objects vanished. Mile after mile, intervened; the
green line of forests were lost in the dim horizon; but

(101)

the marble walls yet stood proudly in sight. The horizon crept over the hills and came between; the blue curtain of the sky dropped down, shutting from view all other objects, even the colossal hill of its base; yet it stood, seemingly without foundation, without color or perspective, a beautiful shadow-graph in the heavens, an airy, unearthly form that impressed the soul with a feeling of awe which was not relieved until a curve was turned and an intervening hill obstructed the sight.

Such gives only a faint impression of a first view of the Taj. A cluster of white bubbles float and dance in the shimmering air like phantoms of luminous cloud. Approaching, they gradually assume shape and settle on their respective towers, the great dome in the midst; all seeming ready to burst into the air, or float away with the breeze. The traveler involuntarily exclaims: "Is it from heaven or earth?"

Nor does a nearer view discredit its celestial design; it seems too pure, too airy, for earth; even after assuming form and settling on its immense base. The river Jumna flows beside a wall of red sandstone, itself a marvel of sculpture, ornamented with a gate most exquisitely carved. Within is a garden with paved walks; blooming groves, and sparkling fountains; a paradise for loveliness.

"Passing under the open demi-vault, whose arch hangs high above you, an avenue of dark Italian cypresses appears before you. Down its center sparkles a long row of fountains, each casting up a single slender jet. On both sides the palm, the banyan, and the feathery bamboo mingle their foliage; the song of birds meets your ear, and the odor of roses and lemon-flowers sweetens the air. Down such a vista, and over such a foreground, rises the Taj." *

Its pure white marble walls, delicately carved, and ablaze with jewels, stand high above surrounding trees and mosques, crowned with a cluster of minarets and domes; and surpassing the descriptions of El Dorado's fabled palaces. Though of stupenduous structure, its size is never fully comprehended; so exact is it in proportion and so delicate in finish. The walls throughout are ornamented with inscriptions from the Koran in inlaid letters of black marble; and the gigantic entrances as intricately wrought as an ivory jewel casket.

It was seventeen years in building, for which twenty thousand men were employed. The various provinces furnished gems and precious stones in abundance; jasper from Punjab; carnelians from Beruch; turquoise from Thibet; and agates from Yemen.

The beholder gazes with admiration and awe upon the glittering pile, almost afraid to approach, lest it should rise and float away; until weary with looking, he goes away only to be drawn back, again and again, to feast his soul on the music of its silent poetry.

Mekara had left the Ganges and crossed, by land, to the Jumna; thence proceeding, as before, in a boat. As he saw the wonderful structure, standing thus away from the noise of the city, his heart gave a thrill of hope.

"Ah! here," he cried, "must be the temple where the Moslem worships God; so pure, so grand, so unlike the gaudy shrines of Brahma, Vishnu and Shiva. Here will I enquire. All is peace and quiet. How suited to worship and devotion!"

____
* Bayard Taylor.

He stood within the magnificent gate-way; and, though the gilded splendor of Benares had not evoked his admiration; though mourning for wife and child; his soul intent only on the search for God; so impressed was he by the scene, that he forgot for a time his grief, in contemplation of what his eyes beheld. He paused for a moment and gazed on his surroundings with bated breath; then reverently approached the entrance to the building.

A sloping passage, whose walls and floors have been polished by the hands and feet of thousands, leads to a chamber below. Down this Mekara walked, holding carefully lest he should fall, and whispering to himself:

"Here is where the worshipers go to offer sacrifice. No sound? I wonder if the Muezzin is here of whom I may enquire."

He reached the chamber. The light was dim, and the air was redolent with the perfumes of the ottar of roses, jasmine, and sandal-wood. No altar for sacrifice, no evidence of worship of any kind, but in the centre was a sarcophagus of white marble, "exquisitely inlaid with blood-stone, agate, carnelian, lapis-lazuli, and other precious stones," and inscribed to the wife of Shah-Jehan, "The Light of the World." A wreath of fresh roses lay upon the top. The whole was surrounded by a screen of marble, six feet high, among the interstices of which were woven designs of lilies, irises, and other flowers, thickly interspersed with precious stones. The scene was sweet, solemn, and impressive; but Mekara was disappointed. Could all this noble building have been designed merely as a monument for the queen of a Mogul lord?

Retracing his steps, he ascended the marble steps to the great hall above. At the entrance he paused. The first sight thrilled him, and he stood speechless, almost unconscious. Stern, strong-minded men, standing thus have burst into tears at the rapturous sight. It was simple, beautiful, grand. The pen cannot describe the effect of it. The floors of polished marble reflect as in a mirror, the jeweled walls and mosaics of the ceiling above. Not a sound is heard, yet music of the sweetest melody seems to breathe from the air and touch the tenderest chords of the soul. No voice, yet the silence is eloquent.

He removed the sandals from his feet in reverence, and stepped cautiously toward the centre. Even his soft foot-fall resounded like the distant tread of thousands, and it seemed that he could hear the pulsations of his own heart. The walls here, as elsewhere, were thickly inlaid with Koran inscriptions in letters of black marble. He found none of these of especial interest, till, casting his eyes upward, he saw, above an arch, the inscription, in blazing letters of gold, ALLAH AKBAR! ("God is great.")

Here, after months of wandering and suffering, he found once more the great Name, the Yuwah of Ko Tha-Byu. His heart was sore with grief; his body worn and fatigued; and his soul, long filled with intense yearning, now burned with fierce desire; and falling on his face, he cried in anguish to the Being whose name he saw, "O, God pity me!"

Like the swell of a great organ, the walls resounded in tones, loud, but soft and tremulous. Round and round, from side to side, echoed the reverberations, growing softer and sweeter as they neared the fretted vaults above; until, entering the great dome, they circled shrill and sweet; gradually dying away in soft undulations, as if the angels, or shining devas of the air, had caught the words and borne them away to the gates of the sky.

Was the prayer answered? In heaven it was heard and from New England the answer comes.

Mekara lay almost stunned with surprise at the sounds, but soothed with the blissful sensations produced. When the last echo died he quietly arose and glided softly from the building. All this had been emotion. As yet he had not received the light he was seeking. On either side of the Taj was an elegant mosque of splendid workmanship. Realizing his mistake in having entered a tomb instead of a place of worship, Mekara went at once to these; but both were closed, no services were held there. They were built to balance the effect of the Taj, and not for worship.

Disappointed again, he turned his face towards the city.

It was now late in the afternoon, and as he passed through the garden of Ram Bagh (garden of Rama), he saw a long row of shrines, facing the river, before little black idols. Lamps were lighted in front of them and a Hindoo stood before each, waving a torch back and forth, and crying, "Ram, Ram! Ram, seeta Ram!" Then having poured Jumna water over the images, and twined wreaths of flowers about their oily necks, departed with a clear conscience of duty performed.

Anointing the Gods.

Mekara recalled a quotation in Tamil, from one of the old clasic poets:

"The lifeless stone a god you call, and flowers in offering bring;
Around and round with muttering sound, fool! many a prayer
    you sing;
But will the lifeless stone speak out?   Will God within it go?
Yes, when the pot in which 'tis cooked the curry's taste shall
    know."

No comfort could be derived from such scenes as this, so he entered the city and retired to a bungalow for the night.

Next morning he roamed through the city of the Moguls seeking to learn all he could of the Moslem religion.   The zenanas were of extravagant beauty, and the rich occupants lounged within, fanned by punkas, or swinging fans, and waited upon by attendants in gorgeous livery.   Wealth and sensual enjoyment seemed to be the end for which they strove; and he knew, from the history of past conquerors, that a thirst for power was one of their ruling passions.

When the bells rang for prayers every man, woman, and child of Mohammedan faith bowed with their faces toward Mecca and prayed.   No idol, nor image of any kind, was to be seen.   This pleased Mekara, to know that he had, at last, found a religion void of idols. But when he learned the reason of all turning their faces as they did, he thought:

"Is it not as much idolatry to worship a place as an image?   What better are they than the Hindus who make pilgrimages to Benares?"

He visited the Pearl Mosque, rightly thus named from its simple beauty.   Essaying to enter, he received a peremptory order to halt, and a Mussulman near by cried.

"No idolators allowed within!"

"I am not an idolator," said Mekara.

"Dost thou worship Allah whose prophet is Mohammed?"

"I know him not. I seek a God whom I may worship. Idols I abhor."

"Dost thou believe the Koran?"

"What is that?" enquired Mekara.

"Our Sacred Book, containing the principles of our religion."

"I never saw it. Read to me from it that I may know its teachings."

"Wilt thou first accept our faith?"

"I cannot until I know what it is."

"Our religion was established by the sword, and its doctrines taught afterwards. It is an abomination for an unbeliever to be allowed to look. into, or hear read, the pages of the sacred Koran. This much will I tell thee, there is one God and Mohammed is his Prophet. Embrace our faith, and thou shalt have for thyself a copy of the Koran."

"But," said Mekara, "how can I acknowledge a creed I know not? I believe there is one God; but of him I know nothing for certain, and what evidence have I of the fact that Mohammed is his Prophet?"

"Thou hast our word for it," replied the Mussulman, "that the Holy Book so declares; but further words are useless; go back into the city, observe our practices, and then judge of our creed. When thou art ready to embrace it, return and I will then instruct thee in all our vital doctrines. Peace go with thee." And he gave a gesture with his hand as a token that the conversation was closed.

"Strange doctrine this," thought Mekara as he turned once more into the busy street. "I had hoped to find my ideal in the God of Islam, but many of their practices are revolting. Oh, that I could find such a God as the Karens once knew! How I would love and serve him the remainder of my days!"

For almost a week he loitered in the streets and houses, watching closely every season of prayer and every religious service, often standing at the door of the mosques and looking upon the worshipers at their devotions, striving to catch every word spoken in reference to the religion in question. The more he saw and heard, the more dissatisfied he was with it. He never returned to the Pearl Mosque for instruction. Not finding an answer to the question of his heart, he proceeded again up the Jumna and stopped at Delhi.

Delhi! A vision of the lovely gardens described in "Lallah Rookh" floats before the eyes at mention of the name; a perfume of tropical flowers is wafted by the breeze, and a sound of poetry greets the ear. The very soul is oppressed by the gorgeous display of Oriental magnificence.

Palaces by the river side, dazzling in the sunlight and reflected from the water below; barges floating on the Jumna with shining banners; bazaars draped in richest tapestry; balconies resounding with music and dancing; golden pinnacles and marble pavilions, characterized the Imperial City of the Moguls.

Like a flower that has been more than once cut down, the romantic city has risen, time and again, from ruins of former glory. For miles over the country, amid luxuriant vegetation, may be seen the picturesque remains of ruined temples, deserted shrines of the expelled religion of Buddha, dilapidated forts, and crumbling palaces.

Every foot of ground has been deluged, again and again, with human blood; yet the rose blooms as if a crime had never stained the Eden bowers. Here Timour, in one day, slew one hundred thousand prisoners. A great multitude; but the restless world took no notice. Like the mist of the morning, they passed away and were forgotten. Shall they ever be remembered more? Aye, and sadly, too. Each had a soul, and that soul knew not God. We shall behold them in the Later Day as they stand with their murderers before the tribunal of God. It is a terrible thing to see a human life wander in gloom and then expire in darkness. May God preserve the poor wretches who yet grope and fall, crying in despair, throughout that lovely land!

Mekara's soul was sick of opulent display combined with spiritual poverty. Religion in Delhi and religion in Agra were the same. He could not endure to remain.

Buddhism had no God; Brahminism worshiped God through images; Mohammedanism had almost conceived of his true nature; but perfect satisfaction came not yet.

"I will cross the Himalayas to China," he said.

Back to the Ganges he again pursued his course. He stopped at the gate of Hurdwar. Here were millions gathered to the annual feast. From every direction and in all garbs, they came; from the far off Deecan, from the Punjab, from Cashmere, and China; old and young, rich and poor. All had sinned and must cleanse themselves in the celebrated fountain where Brahma, the Creator of the world, performed his ablutions.

Thousands of fakirs were here, of every description, even more horrible than those in the Grove of Sorrow.

At the tinkling of a bell four hundred thousand men and women rushed down the steep ghauts to bathe in the stream. Thousands were crushed beneath the feet of the eager multitude behind, and the sacred mother bore their forms rapidly away, struggling and gasping, yet saved (?).

Thus, for thousands of years, has the voracious mother eagerly devoured her children; and Juggernaut smiles to see his wheels of stone crush his dark road of bleeding victims, grinding their crackling bones into the ground made soft with their spurting life-blood.

Truly the being without God has a miserable life, a miserable death, and the hereafter—Who can tell?

Mekara could bear no more. Up the mountain side he struggled. On a lofty peak he stood and surveyed the vast wilderness of crags, ice, and snow, which marked the stormy home of Indra.

There, in view of the "Celestial Empire" far below, his soul thirsting, and his voice calling for God, we leave him.

May He who watcheth the sparrow's fall listen to the heathen's cry.

CAR OF JUGGERNAUT.

BOOK THIRD.

CHAPTER I.

THE June sun was shining brightly, the bees working busily, the birds singing sweetly, the plow-boys whistling cheerfully, and everything combining this soft summer day to gladden the hills and vales of New England. The little village of Bradford, Massachusetts, lay basking in the sunshine, the sparkling Merrimac flowing peacefully by. Scarcely a sound of life was heard in the streets; even the clinking hammer of the blacksmith lay silent near the slumbering embers of the forge. It was the dinner hour.

The girls in Bradford Academy were grouped around the teacher, eating their lunch and discussing merrily, as girls always will, the latest gossip of the day—picnics, balls, dresses, ribbons, boys, and innumerable other matters of equal weight and importance. Lunch

(114)

and the grave questions involved having been at length disposed of to the entire satisfaction of all, the fair participants dispersed to the shade outside.

"Harriet! Harriet!" called a sweet, clear voice from the rear of the building, "come around here in the shade, I want to see you."

In the shade of the house a swing had been constructed, in which was seated Bradford's most charming belle—a plump girlish figure just turning "sweet sixteen." Her face was oval, bright with intelligence, and habitually over-run with the light of the warm, impulsive nature of her soul within; eyes deep and dark; head round, and covered with a profusion of glossy black curls, that streamed behind her as she moved back and forth in the swing, or dangled mischievously over her ears and cheeks when she was still. Her countenance was all animation as she watched eagerly in the direction of girlish voices which she heard at the end of the house.

Presently a light, fragile form appeared at the corner, and she who had been addressed as Harriet came gently toward the girl in the swing.

"What is it, Ann?" she asked as she seated herself by her friend. Her manner was less ardent than that of her companion; her voice not so clear, but more mild and expressive.

"Oh!" replied Ann, "haven't you heard? Why Mrs. Roy is going to give a grand ball next week, and both of us are to be invited. I heard Emma talking about it this morning, and I want us to decide what dresses we shall wear and how the flowers are to be arranged in our hair. Oh, I can hardly wait till the time comes!   Next week is so far off; but it will give us time to arrange our dresses.   Say, what do you think?"

A faint shadow stole across Harriet's face, and her voice assumed a more serious tone, when, after a moment's reflection, she said: "I shall not attend the ball."

"Not attend the ball!" exclaimed Ann, almost gasping with surprise.   "Why, Harriet, what has come over you?   How can you think of missing this, the grandest affair that has been in Bradford for a year?   Surely, dear, you are jesting.   Now say you were, and that you will go."

"I am sorry to disappoint you, Ann," she replied gently but firmly, "but I do not think I shall ever attend another ball, especially when in school.   Such things consume a great deal of our time from study, and then there is really no profit in them."

Though much addicted to pleasure, Ann, owing to her naturally quick mind, had never been once accused of negligence in the preparation of her lessons.   So she could not take this for an excuse.

"Fie!   Harriet, there is nothing in that.   You know I go to such things as much as any girl in school, and yet I am not troubled about my studies.   There must be something else behind that you should suddenly take such a stand as this.   We have always been the best of friends; now tell me what is the real cause of your refusal to go with me?"

"To tell you the truth," replied Harriet thoughtfully, "my conscience disapproves of such.   I can't honestly think it is right."

"Conscience, indeed!" said Ann. "I can't believe a word of it. It all comes from your associating with that young preacher, Mr. Newell. I do wish you would give him up, Harriet. Just think of how much enjoyment you will be deprived, if married to such a man. I wouldn't have a preacher if he was the only man living. Not that I don't like them, but because I should be expected to be so good, and give up so much of what is life to me. I am truly sorry for you, Harriet, and I do wish you would reconsider your decision, and go in spite of your clerical beau."

Harriet had a very sensitive nature, and she was cut to the heart by the light remarks of her bosom friend. She made no reply, but her eyes filled with tears as she looked at her fair tempter reproachfully. Seeing which, Ann leaped to the ground and impulsively clasping the slender form in her arms, kissed away the tear-drops and begged her to think no more of what had been said.

The school bell put an end to further conversation, and winding their arms about each other's waist they walked together into the house.

We thus introduce to our readers her whose name shall ever be sacred to every Christian heart, Ann Hasseltine, and her bosom friend and school-mate, Harriet Atwood. Being the youngest daughter, Ann had been made much of by all, and, perhaps, too freely indulged by those who loved her best, and who wished to be first in the ardent affections of her heart. Hitherto, thoughts of a serious nature had never entered her mind. Naturally impulsive, she threw her whole soul into whatever she did, whether it was to fashion playhouses for dolls when a child, solve intricate problems in algebra when a school girl, or whirl in the giddy maze of the dance when a society belle.

Mrs. Hasseltine had never felt the power of the Christian religion in her own heart, and, as a consequence, was incapable of impressing upon her children a feeling of its true importance. Nevertheless, from a consciousness of maternal responsibility, she had sought to inculcate into their minds the moral code of the bible and the principles of morality. All of which had been readily received by the vivacious child, but laid as readily aside when her short dresses were hung in the closet, and the calls of worldly pleasure admonished her to lay aside all such "childish things"

Such was the natural course of her disposition   What will it be when touched by the spirit of God?

We shall see.

CHAPTER II.

It was a dark, stormy night. Among the pine-clad hills of New England the wind sobbed and moaned, and dark, phantom-like clouds scudded across the sky like ships at sea without a rudder. How different from the calm, peaceful nights in India, when the wandering prince lay under the open sky listening to the soft tinkle of distant bells, or watching the luminous path of the fire-fly, while his restless soul dwelt in the dark, distant future.

At the little country tavern, on the road from Sheffield, they were making preparations to retire, when a voice was heard without; and, opening the door, the landlord saw a benighted traveler alighting from his horse at the gate. Having delivered his horse to a boy, who now appeared, the stranger entered the house, and taking off his wraps which were hung away by the landlord, he seated himself by the fire that roared cheerfully in the great log fire-place.

As revealed by the fire-light, he was young, almost a boy in appearance, his form of slender structure, and his face, though delicate, prepossessing in appearance, combining a look of bright intelligence with strength of character, showing that his spirit, if not his body, was capable of strong endurance. His dress could neither be characterized as costly nor foppish; yet it was so fastidiously tidy and arranged with such a studied neatness and sense of propriety, as to display his agile form to the best advantage.

The old landlord had a Yankee curiosity to know who it was so far from home as to be caught on the road in such a night. So prefacing his remarks with the hope that he might not be considered at all inquisitive, he proceeded to besiege the young man with such a continual storm of questions as could only be thought of by an interlocutor in a minstrel show, or a lawyer in a criminal suit.

The stranger seemed lost in abstraction, and only answered the old man's questions at random as he dried his boots on the hearth, and gazed thoughtfully into the glowing embers underneath the logs. After dispensing with a hearty supper, however, he became more talkative, and by bed-time had communicated to his host the fact that his name was Adoniram Judson, a graduate of Brown University, and, at that time, connected with a theatrical company in New York.

The old landlord was a genuine Puritan of the Plymouth Rock type, and this information gave him occasion to vent his indignation against such organizations as tended to corrupt the morals, and destroy the better nature of the people; all of which had no seeming effect upon his guest. Young Judson was an infidel. At length, feigning sleep, but in reality, wishing to be rid of his unplesant company, the young man requested to be shown to his room; and following the light of a flame from a pine-knot, he was led into a dingy apartment at the rear of the building. The host apologized for giving him no better quarters, saying that a sick man occupied the guest chamber which was next door. Arranging everything as comfortable as possible, and stopping a draught of cold wind which came through the broken pane of a window, with the impromptu covering of a pillow, he bade his guest good-night and closed the door behind him, saying that he must watch all night with the sick man.

On the morning before, which was Sunday, the young actor had stopped at Sheffield, and out of respect to his uncle, who was pastor of a church there, he attended services. But instead of his uncle, a very pious young man had preached a most impressive sermon by which he was deeply affected.

To-night he could not sleep, but lay tossing on his pillow from side to side, trying to clear his mind of the doubts and skepticism long implanted there. The blasts of wind howled mournfully without, the shingles rattled on the roof, and ever and anon a groan would come from the sick room. The two apartments were separated by a single partition of rough boards, and the flickering light from within struggled through the cobwebs of the cracks and made long, straw-like streaks across his own bed, as if bringing him in sympathy with a fellow-sufferer.

Towards midnight it seemed that the sick man was becoming worse, for the groans became more frequent, and occasionally a loud curse or blood-curdling yell would be mingled with the sobbing of the wind and rain without. The restless listener in the dark was tormented beyond measure by these sounds which seemed to come as mournful echoes to his own heart-cries within.   As the sick man grew worse the cracked voice of the old landlord could be heard reciting passages of Scripture or offering the comforts of religion, which seemed rather to enrage than console the poor sufferer.   At length, after a more severe outburst than usual, the groans and curses ceased, and after a few short stifled gasps all was still and the shadows ceased to flit along the wall.

The worn traveler now turned his face and tried again to sleep, but it was not until nearly dawn that he fell into a restless slumber.

Next morning at breakfast he enquired after the condition of the sick man.

"Dead," replied the old man.   "And such another death I pray God I may never see.   Without faith in God, and without hope in Christ, he has gone to meet his doom."

Judson did not relish such serious reflections, and sought to change the subject by asking,

"Who was the young man and where did he come from?"

"Where he came from when he came here, I can't tell," said the landlord.   "He staggered in here one day, already delirious, and could give no rational answer to my questions.   I put him to bed and when he grew worse, I looked in his pockets and found a letter addressed to Mr. George Sanders, of Brown University."

The young man's knife and fork fell rattling on his plate, and his hands dropped to his sides as if paralyzed.

"What!" he cried, "George Sanders, my old schoolmate who graduated with me last year?"

"I suppose he must be the same," replied the old man, "for the letter was dated more than a year ago, and I judged it to be from his mother. I wrote to her at once and expect her here to-day."

Mr. Judson arose from the table in much agitation.

"Show me the room immediately," he said, "I wish to see for myself, if it is indeed my old friend."

The landlord led the way to the chamber, and drawing back the sheet that shrouded the corpse, disclosed the stark, distorted features of what had been a youth just budding into manhood.

"Poor, poor George!" said Mr. Judson, looking sadly upon the emaciated wreck of former days. "Who would have thought a year ago when you graduated, the pride of your class, that you would now be lying thus, far from home, with not even a school-mate to soothe your dying hour though under the same roof. 'Tis sad to think that such a star of promise should be thus shrouded in darkness. Nothing accomplished in this life. And the next—Alas! we both denied a future existence. Your Past was an opening rose-bud, your Present a withered flower, and your Future, for all we know, dust and ashes. Shall I ever lie thus?"

Then turning, he asked, "Have you made arrangements for his burial?"

"Not definitely," replied the old man. "I wished his relations to come first and suggest what to do."

"Then, here is money," said Mr. Judson, handing him a roll of bills. "Bury him decently and take the remainder for your care of him. With his memory I also bury my former life. From this day forth I will strive for something nobler than either of us sought before."

Turning from the room, he ordered his horse, and extending his hand to the old landlord, who grasped it warmly, while tears of gratitude streamed down his furrowed checks, he who had entered the tavern an infidel, rode away, a penitent, seeking light.

Who, but an all-wise God, could have seen the elements of a great missionary in the follower of a theatrical troupe? Who but Jesus of Nazareth would have called Saul of Tarsus to bear the gospel to the Gentiles?

"How unsearchable are his judgments, and his ways past finding out!"

CHAPTER III.

IT was Sabbath morning after the ball.   Ann Hasseltine was standing in the parlor waiting for her father to come and go with her to church.   She had risen early that morning in order to spend an unusual amount of time in the preparation of her toilet; for she realized that her well-clad figure had attracted special attention at the ball; and, was not she the belle of Bradford?   She surveyed herself in the large mirror with evident satisfaction, and indeed, there was no one who would not have been proud of the image reflected there.   Her new spring costume was beautifully made, and fitted her handsome form with becoming grace. The fair, round face, and twinkling dark eyes were perfect; and the short, curly locks artistically arranged to show her face to the best advantage.

The sound of a bell was heard through the open window.   Drawing the curtains aside, she exclaimed impatiently as she saw the people passing, " I do wish papa would come on; there is the second bell now, and the people are all going in.   I wanted so much to see Harriet before church ! "

Then, walking to the center-table, she began carelessly turning over the leaves of a book lying there.

It was Hannah Moore's "Strictures on Female Education." Suddenly a line italicized from the bible struck her attention, "*She that liveth in pleasure is dead while she liveth.*" She read no further, but stood with her eyes riveted on the words, while she made the application of the passage to herself. She was so much engrossed that she scarcely heard her father's voice as he called at the door, "Come on, Ann, I am ready."

Seeing she was too much interested to hear, he spoke again more sharply, "Daughter!"

"Yes, papa," she said quickly, and closing the book as if just remembering it was church time.

"Come on, we are late and must hurry." And with cane in hand he stepped briskly into the street, she walking beside him in silence. It was something unusual for her not to be chatting vivaciously about everything she saw, but her father thought perhaps she was pouting, and, in his hurry to be in time, gave her no more attention.

The girls were all arrayed in their best that day, but Ann, for the first time in life, cared not if others excelled her in dress. The sermon was eloquent and full of spiritual teaching, but she heard it not. Even Harriet was scarcely noticed as they passed at the door. One single thought filled her mind and distressed her soul: "She that liveth in pleasure is dead while she liveth."

During the months that followed she lost all relish for amusements, and became so awakened as to her spiritual condition that she even longed for annihilation. As formerly, she had given all her attention to pleasure-seeking, she now turned all the faculties of her ardent soul in the quest of salvation, and ere long she found the peace for which she had so earnestly sought. The change in her life was radical, from extreme worldliness to earnest piety. At school she was inspired with a new zeal in her studies; not as formerly with a desire for human applause, but because she felt the responsibility of preparing her soul for greater usefulness in life. The bible was now her daily companion, and as she pondered over its pages she was struck with the thought of its applicability to all classes and conditions of mankind.

"Why," thought she, "may not the scriptures be taught to the poor African slave and to the wild red men of the West? Why are these precious truths kept so close by our people while others are dying for the want of them? I wish I had the power to diffuse the Gospel. I would go anywhere if only I might be permitted to lead others to the light."

Little did she dream of the field soon to be opened to her, or the use to which God would put the knowledge she was now so eagerly acquiring. She continued her bible study with aid of the best commentators, preparing herself for something, she knew not what.

After the completion of her course in the Academy, at the earnest solicitation of friends, she consented to teach a school. There she first had an opportunity to make application of the plans she had formed of evangelizing others. Much to the astonishment of her pupils, she opened every morning with prayer, and lost no opportunity to lead their minds to a higher life, as well as to instruct them in their regular branches.

How different her life now from the time when we first knew her! The refining fires of conviction have purged her soul from all its vanity and delight in worldly pleasures, and now, wholly absorbed in making others happy, she is lost to self, and yet enjoys continual peace.

The Lord hath chosen her for his own use, and is shaping her character and developing her faculties in such a way that she may be best able to perform the great life-work whereunto he hath called her.

CHAPTER IV.

AFTER the scene at the tavern Mr. Judson, true to his promise, retired from the life on which he had entered, and returned home deeply convicted. At the earnest solicitation of two of the professors in Andover Seminary, he placed himself under the instruction of that institution. The laws of the Seminary demanded evidence of strict evangelical piety as a conditi n of matriculation; but as he could, as yet, claim no satisfactory hope in Christ, he was enrolled as a special student His new religious surroundings gradually wrought a wonderful change in his nature, and soon light from the Cross dawned upon his spiritual vision, and he was enabled to accept the sacrifice of Christ for the atonement of his sins.

Once more the finger of God is seen moving mysteriously among the pages of our history.

The Rev. Claudius Buchanan, an ambitious churchman, had visited Calcutta from England, and seeing the efforts of the "poor mechanics" Carey, Marshman, and Ward, as they were struggling to diffuse the light of the gospel, he wrote to a friend in England expressing himself slightingly in regard to the infant enterprise. But when further developments were made, difficulties removed, and the standard of truth permanently planted on Indian soil, he conceived a more favorable opinion of their labors, which led him, on his return to England, to preach in Bristol a sermon, entitled "The Star in the East." The sermon was printed in book form, and a copy found its way across the waters, and by some mysterious way into the hands of the young student at Andover Seminary.

Though coming from a strange and distant source, it was the message of God to him, borne on the wings of poor Mekara's prayer from the Himalayan crags. Quicker and more forcible than the electric current that bears man's thought through the caverns of the ocean, is that unseen, powerful medium, the Spirit of God. Though its poles be separated as far as India from Massachusetts, yet its pulsations thrill the brain and throb in the heart so perceptibly that there can be no doubt as to their reality; though, for the time, we may not know whence they come nor whither they go.

The little book fulfilled its mission, and Mr. Judson determined to go to the rescue of the heathen who were wandering in darkness waiting for the dawn to appear.

At that time there was not a single missionary organization in America, and he was left without any one to consult, and with no hope of financial aid. At length Samuel Nott, a member of his own class, was found to be interested in the same subject, and together they decided to adopt Asia as the field of their life-work.

Several other young men soon entered the Seminary who were also interested in missions, but whose attention had been mostly directed to the North American Indians. One by one they were finally convinced by the earnest speeches of Judson and Nott that Asia was the field most demanding their labors.

The General Assembly of the Congregational Church, of which they all were members, was to convene at Bradford in June. They drew up a petition to be laid before this body, begging to be sent under its auspices as missionaries to Burmah.

CHAPTER V.

ALL Bradford was alive with bustle and excitement, preparing for the meeting of the Assembly. Mr. Hasseltine and family, being among the most prominent members of the Congregational church, were expecting to entertain many of the visitors who should attend. No pains were spared to have homes and church in order, for such an occasion was rare at a small place like Bradford.

During his winter vacation, before the Association convened, Mr. Judson returned home on a short visit to his parents. As yet he had not had the heart to tell them of his intentions in regard to his future field of labor. His father, justly proud of his son for his mental attainments, was overjoyed at the prospect of his becoming a great minister. One evening while the family was seated around the fireside engaged in a pleasant conversation, the old man, who had just received his mail, looked up from a letter he was reading, and with a look of paternal pride beaming from his eyes, said: "Listen here, Adoniram; here is a letter from the Rev. Dr. Griffin, who proposes to make you his colleague in the largest church in Boston! A splendid beginning, I must say, for a young man just through the Seminary."

"And think, how near home you will be, too," added his mother.

The young man's heart was breaking as he listened to the plans they were dotingly arranging for him, and he could not bear to break to them the great dream of his life. His sister, sitting near him, also made a remark as to the pleasant arrangement it would be to have work so near home. Turning to her he ventured to reply.

"No, sister, I shall never live in Boston. I have much farther than that to go."

"Why, brother, what do you mean?" she cried.

"I am going as a missionary."

"What's that, Adoniram?" hastily asked his father, who had overheard the last word of the conversation.

"I have decided to begin my life work in Burmah," replied Adoniram. He then proceeded to lay before them the workings of the Spirit with him, how his life had been saved from ruin by the hand of Providence, how the little book had fallen into his hands, and the lasting impressions made upon him to bear the light to those who sat in darkness, and in the shadow of death. His father saw the wisdom of his choice, and though deeply grieved and disappointed, offered no opposition. His mother and sister remonstrated with him earnestly, and besought him, for their sake, to revoke his decision. But finding he was not to be deterred from his purpose, they burst into tears. He thus witnessed the first hardship that a missionary is called upon to endure.

The eventful day of the Assembly at length arrived. The great men and women of the land and dignitaries of the church were seated together in Council. Before this august body the petition of the Andover students was read. Being entirely different from anything that had ever appeared before, and advocating a measure which, till now, had never occurred to the religious mind of America, it created quite a sensation, and met with considerable opposition. But the young applicants were not to be lightly put aside, and they followed in earnest speeches in answer to the oppositions that were brought up; especially did the eloquent, soul-stirring appeal of Mr. Judson carry with it weight and conviction. After a warm discussion, however, the request was granted, and the young men appointed missionaries to Burmah, and a board appointed to arrange for their support.

Through the personal instrumentality of Mr. Judson they had been appointed by the London Missionary Society in the event they should fail in America. They now withdrew themselves from its patronage, and made preparations to go entirely under the direction of the Board appointed.

After the meeting adjourned—was it an accident or Providential?—the young ministers were assigned to Mr. Hasseltine's for dinner. They were received with genuine, old-fashioned hospitality, and made to feel perfectly at home; which is the height of bliss to a student, whether he be a preacher or not.

Mrs. Hasseltine, with matronly grace, presided at the head of the table, her older children near; and Mr. Hasseltine sat with the young ministers at the other end.   Ann, who was the youngest daughter, waited on the table.   Her heart had been wonderfully stirred that day as she listened eagerly to the speeches of the young men in regard to the great question which they had advanced.   Especially was she impressed by the address of Mr. Judson as he painted, in living colors, the condition of the heathen.   All the impulses of her nature were aroused, and she felt that she would be willing to make any sacrifice if only she might be permitted to go to their rescue.   As she moved gracefully about the table, she gave silent and strict attention to every word that was said on the important subject, her eyes often resting with interest on Mr. Judson, by whose neat person she was attracted, not less than by his becoming address, and earnest, consecrated zeal. Little did she dream that he, fully conscious of her bewitching charms, was composing, in the bottom of his plate, his first love verses in her praise.

That evening, when assembled in the parlor, they were thrown together, and after an hour of delightful conversation they were impressed with their mutual fitness for each other.

He escorted her to church that night, and, ere the meetings of the Assembly had closed, he was convinced that she was the one whom the Lord had provided as an helpmeet to him.   During the two years that intervened before his departure to Asia, he won her hand, as he had her heart at their first meeting.

Love at first sight is not often deep, or of the purest type; but where two kindred natures have thus been prepared for each other, mutual recognition comes soon and strong.   They loved solely from principle.   She did not love him for the dangers through which he should pass; neither did he love her because she did pity them.

In this, as in everything else, Ann took into her confidence her bosom friend Harriet, and endeavored to persuade her to go with them, no longer objecting to her "clerical beau," Mr. Newell, but urging her to consent to marry him as he, too, was contemplating the step and only hesitated on her account. "Only think, Harriet," she said, "I shall be all alone, not another white female in the whole country. We have always loved each other and been together; it will be hard for us to part. There we can both assist our husbands and do some little good in holding up their hands, besides being a mutual solace to each other.'

Harriet's gentle nature soon yielded to the entreaties of her more adventurous friend, and together they made preparations for the sad departure.

Girls of this day, even those who accompany their husbands to foreign fields, cannot appreciate the sorrows of these two at leaving home. The facilities of travel were so few, and a long voyage accompanied by so many dangers and delays, that the departing missionary could scarcely hope to see home again. The enterprise was new, and met with disfavor with the majority; and the country to which they were going was unexplored, not even the sword of the white man having found its way thither. Old people considered it a mad freak, and their girl friends thought it a ridiculous wedding tour.

The grief of the families is too sacred to be revealed, even at this late day. No rash promises had been made to win their daughters from them. When called upon to consent to his daughter's marriage, Mr. Hasseltine received a letter from Mr. Judson containing the following:

"I have now to ask whether you can consent to part with your daughter early next Spring, to see her no more in this world; whether you can consent to her departure to a heathen land, and her subjection to the hardships and sufferings of a missionary life; whether you can consent to her exposure to the dangers of the ocean; to the fatal influence of the southern climate of India; to every kind of want and distress; to degradation, insult, persecution, and perhaps, a violent death? Can you consent to all this for the sake of Him who left his heavenly home and died for her and for you; for the sake of perishing immortal souls; for the sake of Zion and the glory of God? Can you consent to all this in hope of soon meeting your daughter in the world of glory, with a crown of righteousness, brightened by the acclamations of praise which shall redound to her Saviour from heathens saved, through her means, from eternal woe and despair?"

Both Harriet and Ann were warned of their hardships, and anticipated a life of danger and suffering, yet of joy, because accounted worthy to suffer for the Master's name. They spent the last days of their maidenhood in visiting the scenes made dear to them by the associations of the Past. They went again to the old church, and knelt in prayer at the sacred altar where the peace of God had come to them; then to the school-house, over whose familiar desks they had bent their youthful heads in study, and on whose playground they had so often skipped the rope in childish glee; to the river where they had often wandered at evening, and on whose grassy border we leave them, Harriet and Ann, dreaming of the Past so sweet, and talking of the Future so dark.

CHAPTER VI.

AFTER having been led through strange events in distant lands, the reader's attention is directed again to Burmah, the land of The Golden Face. No country is fairer; yet, till the present century, the great world was unconscious of its existence. Here fled the adherents of Gautama, when expelled from their native land, and established the religion of Buddha. Every sunny slope is crowned by an image of Gautama; every flowery glade and every gloomy cavern conceals a representative of the pensive god. Scarcely, throughout its whole extent, is there a spot where the pagoda is not seen.

Prince Gautama sought to reform Brahminism. For this cause he left his beautiful palace and the embrace of his lovely wife, to live an ascetic on the mountains. When light came to him under the bo-tree, revealing the causes of human sorrow and the remedy, he proclaimed to the world a religion whose pure creed has never been equaled by human philosophy; approaching so near the truth, yet a temple founded upon the sands of human deeds, ignoring the "Rock of Ages" standing so near.

"There are no gods who hear prayers," says Gautama, who now became Buddha, "consequently your salvation depends, not upon worship, but upon the obtaining of merit by doing good deeds. These commands obey and sin shall be removed:

'Do not kill:

'Do not steal:

'Do not lie:

'Do not commit adultery:

'Do not drink intoxicating liquors.'

"By a strict adherence to these, the soul, instead of transmigrating, will be permanently freed from the shackles of the flesh and enter Nirvana, the abode of sweet forgetfulness, of ' ceaseless, stirless rest.' Ceremonies and prayers effect nothing. Only live true to these principles of Morality."

The Buddha passed into Nirvana. His followers were left without a leader. Then the former cravings of the soul for something Supernatural became too strong for the simple moral principles; and making unto themselves idols in his image, they worshiped them with prostrate bodies and offerings of fruit and flowers. The most costly and most sacred pagodas are believed to contain some relic of Buddha, such as a tooth, a hair, or even a nail from his body. All devotions are mechanical; all prayers without faith. No human cry of wretchedness or misery can arouse the senseless repose of Buddha. He sleeps, silently sleeps forever; and all they can hope is annihilation at the end, when the restless soul ceases to wander from being to being, man or beast.

Such is the religion of Burmah; and the despised Karens dare not to speak the name of YUWAH outside their solitary homes in the mountain glens. All hope of future reward being based on meritorious performances, the Burmese excel in hospitality; but kindness is always shown, not for the good of the recipient, but for the personal advantage of the dispenser. Consequently gratitude is unknown; for he who receives a favor recognizes that his benefactor is only acting through selfish motives. This renders them the most haughty and arrogant of any nation living. He who would imbibe a new religion would be subject to the ridicule and disdain of the people, besides the implacable displeasure of the king.

Rangoon, the chief sea-port of the country, is a low, marshy place, composed of dingy bamboo huts; and brick or mud residences for the higher classes. The traveler, entering the mouth of the famous Irrawaddy, and confronted with this wretched landing-place, can scarcely believe the stories he has heard of the lovely fields beyond, to which it is the door.

Under the direction of the Serampore Mission, Felix Carey had once come here to establish a mission. A spacious house was built as headquarters and the work begun. But again the restless desire for wandering, to which he had long been addicted, took possession of him. He married a native, and, moving to Ava, accepted the office of embassador for the English, leaving the great mission house deserted as if the emissaries of the cross had besieged the citadel of the country and then left their weapons and armor in despair. The building was situated just without the walls of the city, and there, in unbroken solitude, a native Christian, a female, took up her abode, fearing to be seen in the city after having renounced the national religion. Hers was a soul that had been born again through the teachings of young Carey, and then left as a helpless babe, famishing and dying for the bread of life.

One July morning she heard a great uproar in the city, and on looking out, saw almost the whole population of the town on their way to the beach where a foreign ship had just landed. On board appeared, what was to them, a novel spectacle. A white couple, man and woman, of youthful appearance, stood on deck. It was Adoniram Judson with Ann, his trusting bride. Looking around we see no traces of Harriet, Mr. Newell, and the others who were appointed to come with them. These two are alone, and both their faces are sad, though full of hope and trust. A large chair was brought out, in which Ann was seated; then two bamboo poles were thrust between the rounds, and four natives marched away with it on their shoulders, Mr. Judson walking beside them, and the eager crowd following behind. Reaching a tamarind tree by the wayside the bearers placed the chair on the ground that she might rest a moment under the shade. This gave the multitude an opportunity to obtain a nearer view of the object of their curiosity. Crowding up, they stood in a circle around the chair, gazing with awe upon its pale occupant. She was tired from her long voyage, and sat with her head resting wearily on her hand, her face hidden by a large sun-bonnet. Some, desirous of seeing her countenance, crept timidly near, and, stooping, peered under her bonnet. Seeing their curiosity her former mischievous spirit returned, and forgetting for a moment her recent sorrows, she smiled at their inquisitiveness, at which they all fell back with the crowd, laughing loudly. The bearers again took up their burden and moved on amidst the shouts of the multitude. They went first to the custom-house. The native officers were seated on mats on the floor of the veranda. Rising, they proceeded to search Mr. Judson, but asked permission that a female should perform the same office for his wife. This done, they repaired immediately to the mission-house without the city, and dispatched the bearers again for their baggage. The solitary inmate at the mission received them joyfully, and, though unable to communicate with them, did all in her power to make them comfortable.

The baggage having come, they set about furnishing their new quarters. Hammocks were suspended from hooks in the wall; a table constructed near a window for Mr. Judson's books, and their various souvenirs, gifts from friends at home, arranged around the room, in the center of which stood the comfortable rocking-chair presented by Mrs. Hasseltine on the day of their marriage. Ann showed herself an able and tasty, as well as cheerful, housekeeper, and by nightfall she had the satisfaction of seeing her home furnished as elaborately as any in the city.

Till now their work had restrained their thoughts from wandering back to the scenes of the past. But when night came on they sat out on the veranda overlooking the river, and feasted their eyes on the scenery of a night in a strange country. A youthful pair just beginning their wedded life, neither could hope to be

again received under the parental roof. The happy
evenings spent in the family circle, around the fireside
of their New England homes, could only be remembered as of the past. They have no firesides here; no
winter; no family circle; even their companions in the
mission were absent, and Harriet—Oh, where was Harriet? Silently they sit, hand in hand, thinking. The
great ship in the harbor moves, and like a spectre,
glides from the wharf down the stream, bearing away
with itself every sign of civilization. They were left
alone, these two, to struggle in the darkness, against
the mighty tide of ignorance and superstition surrounding them. Sorrow, such as the reader cannot as yet
comprehend, overwhelmed them. Tears fell on their
clasped hands as they sat together. Yet was there no
regret for the choice they had made. They had all
faith and confidence in God, but no matter how strong
the believer's hope, there are times when the natural
tears unbidden flow. They knelt in prayer, then she
went into the room, and sitting down at her desk, wrote
a long, trustful letter to her sister at home. Mr. Judson
sat without in the darkness, pondering the great field
of his life work, and praying for guidance as to the
best means of accomplishing it.

Only two against millions, yet we have the promise,
"One shall chase a thousand, and two shall put ten
thousand to flight."

CHAPTER VII.

—Whittier.

MANY and varied had been the events of that eighteen month's voyage, which separated the missionaries from their homes. Ann and Harriet had embarked with their hnsbands, shortly after their marriage, for Calcutta, the remainder of the party having preceded them in another vessel. Deeply consecrated, indeed, must be the youthful heart that can bravely turn from the ties of home and all congenial associations; from a brilliant prospect of future usefulness and popularity in his native country; and penetrate the thick darkness of an unknown heathen land. Now launched on the treacherous deep, as the last faint ontline of their familiar landscape faded from view, they each realized that they had renounced *all* for the sake of the Kingdom of Christ. But the long months that were to intervene before their arrival in India were not to be spent in pensive dreaming, nor idle repining. The time was embraced as an excellent opportunity for preparation for the great work which they were soon to begin. Separated from the world and its conflicts, with only the ocean about them, and its Maker and Ruler above them, they had sweet intercourse with God. They also held services in which they preached to the passengers and crew. But the greater portion of the time was spent in study. But they acquainted themselves with the country to which they were going, its peoples, languages and customs, as much as they were able. They also studied works on Theology; and Mr. Judson engaged in the translation of the New Testament out of the Greek into English.

They safely crossed the Equator, though they were almost suffocated by the intense heat. On rounding the Cape of Good Hope they encountered rough weather for twenty days, after which they were anxious to see land of any description, anything to relieve the feeling of the unstable, rolling, waves. After nearly four months they heard the thrilling cry: "Land ahead!" To the eager, storm-worn, passengers the distant blue-summits of Golconda awoke emotions equaled only by a view from the heights of "The Delectable Mountains." They sailed for several days in sight of the land, sometimes near enough to distinguish the delightful groves of orange and palm trees. They now make their way among the spicy islands that cluster about the mouth of the Ganges, and enter the Hoogly. The air is fragrant beyond description with the perfume of flowers. Either shore was covered with clumps of the wonderful mango, and other trees, which sheltered the innumerable cottages that clustered like hay-stacks beneath them.

Mr. Judson and Mr. Newell were detained for some time in Calcutta in an unsuccessful effort to obtain permission from the English officials to settle in India, the

East India Company being violently opposed to the evangelization of the natives. They then accepted an invitation from Mr. Carey at Serampore, to which place Harriet and Ann were borne at a rapid gait in a palanquin. No ladies were to be seen in the streets, and the natives thronged them in annoying crowds.

The venerable Dr. Carey met them with great joy, and conducted them at once to his home. In this delightful retreat they found opportunity to regain their strength, and to acquire a better understanding of the work of the missionaries. The latter never alluded to the denominational differences between themselves and the new comers, but treated them with the greatest respect and hospitality.

The native Christians were much interested in the new missionaries, and as soon as it was known where they were going, a female, differing in some respects from the natives, found her way to the presence of the ladies, and in broken English made known her name.

It was Mahdri.

She told the story of her past life in the court, their wanderings in search of God, and the loss of husband and child, reproving herself often, and bitterly, as an infanticide. She besought them to use every means to enlighten her benighted countrymen, and to soften the king's heart; saying that she herself hoped to return, when better qualified, as a teacher.

This pleasant sojourn at the mission was not to last long. The East India Company looked with distrust upon all such enterprises as would tend to draw from themselves the favor of the down-trodden people. After ten days Mr. Judson and Mr. Newell were summoned to Calcutta, where an order was read to them to depart at once from their territories. Sending for their wives they prepared to embark on a vessel bound for the Isle of France; but when ready to start, it was found that the ship could accomodate only two. Harriet's health was so delicate that it was necessary for her to be removed from the hurry of the city, and the perplexities of delays. Consequently it was arranged for her and Mr. Newell to go first, the others to follow at the first opportunity.

While waiting for another ship to sail for the Isle of France, the Judsons accepted the hospitality of some resident Christians, in whose house they remained for three months, closely watched by the English officials. Mr. Judson found some theological works in his chamber, and began their study during his delay. Ann, now left without a female companion, also took up the reading for pastime. The works contained a treatise on baptism, which subject had of late greatly disturbed Mr. Judson's mind. Ann was at first alarmed at his unsettled state, and warned him of the unpleasant consequences of a change of church relations at that time. But he could not rest till he had decided the matter. So she united with him in the investigation of the subject which led to their adopting the Baptist faith. Although realizing that they were forever separating themselves from the auspices and sympathies of the Board which was organized for their support, and calling down upon themselves the censure of their dearest friends, they recived baptism. Humanly speaking, they had nothing to gain, and all to lose. The Baptists of America were a weak body, and inactive as to missions. It may have been the hand of Providence in thus arousing them to a sense of duty.

In a few days the ship containing the other missionaries, after many delays, arrived, and it was found that Mr. Rice had also undergone a change of views.

This fresh arrival exasperated the officials who now issued a peremptory order for the whole party to go at once on board a ship bound for England.

Mahdri had accompanied them as far as Calcutta, and she could not bear the thought that they should be hindered from going to Burmah, though Mr. Carey had made them believe it inaccessible. She learned from a native servant that a ship was about to sail for the Isle of France, which intelligence she immediately communicated to Mr. Judson. He applied at once for a pass to go on board, but was denied. Relating the circumstances to the captain, he consented to take them without a pass; and Mr. Rice, with Mr. Judson and his wife, took passage for their destination after so much delay. But they had not proceeded far down the Hoogley before they were overtaken by a government dispatch commanding the pilot to proceed no further, as passengers were on board who had been ordered to England. They were rudely put ashore at a mean tavern, where they remained for three days almost in despair, and seeking vainly some means of escape.

Mahdri, learning of their detention, went boldly before the magistrate, and after much pleading, procured from him a pass for the missionaries on the "Creole" which they had left.

They were sitting disconsolately at their dinner one day, and discussing their misfortunes when a coolie hastily entered and thrust the pass in Mr. Judson's hands and departed without a word.   Their hearts overflowed with joy at this unexpected deliverance, though they had no idea whence it came.   Procuring a boat they set out immediately to reach the "Creole" which they found just setting out to sea.

At length, after a weary perilous voyage, the shore of the green isle appeared.   They recognized Mr. Newell among the crowd, and Ann rushed on deck to greet her old schoolmate, thinking, of course, she would also be there to meet them.

"Harriet! Harriet!" she cried, "Mr. Newell, where is Harriet?"

The poor man could speak not a word, but with trembling finger, pointed upward, and falling on Mr. Judson's shoulder, burst into tears.   Ann stood by in great distress.   Divining the cause of his grief, she begged him to tell them all.

Calming himself at length, he told them of their arrival at the Isle, with its unfriendly climate; of Harriet's sickness with no nurse but himself; of her death, like the fading of a fragile summer flower, and of how he buried her with her new-born babe, in a nameless grave.

Ann was almost distracted at this heart-rending news.

Poor, poor Harriet! Is this the end to the noble life which you two loving hearts planned?   Must you be thus cut off before reaching even the field of your life-work?   Having gone forth weeping and bearing precious seeds, shall you not return rejoicing, bearing your sheaves with you?   Aye, the hallowed green mound shall be visited by many pilgrim feet from afar, and its verdant grass shall be watered by the tears of other noble saints who shall be moved by your tragic death to emulate your noble heroism. Rest in peace. The angels of love shall ever stand guard over the lonely grave.

Ann herself had a very severe attack of illness while on the island. Mr. Newell, unable to reconcile himself to his unutterable loss, departed soon; and Mr. Rice, with Mr. Judson's consent, returned to America to inform the Baptists there of their action, and to arouse them to lend their assistance in the prosecution of their great work. It was soon found that the island was unfavorable to the establishing of a mission; and, as they had given up all idea cf going to Burmah, Mr. Judson and his wife decided to establish a mission on an island near Malacca, to reach which they must sail by way of Madras. But on reaching the latter place no vessel was found ready for sailing except one bound for Rangoon, Burmah. Fear of the East India Company forced them to embark on this; and thus, led by the hand of God, they were driven to the country to which he had at first directed their minds.

The sorrowing but hopeful company that left Salem, Mass., eighteen months before, had been diminished, one by one, till now only two were left; and they could no longer claim recognition from the great body before which the young Andover students had made their fiery speeches. Trusting in God that he would arouse his people to their support, and bless their labors in the unfriendly country to which he had led them, they landed at Rangoon as was related in the former chapter.

The reader now understands the sorrow of that first night spent in the deserted mission house.

BOOK FOURTH.

CHAPTER I.

"Nay, though the heart
Be consecrated to the holiest work
Vouchsafed to mortal effort, there will be
Ties of the earth around it, and, through all
Its perilous devotion, it must keep
Its own humanity."

—Whittier.

THOUGH surrounded by millions of fellow-creatures, the condition of the missionaries was, for several years, inexpressibly lonely. When an untutored rustic finds himself for the first time in the streets of a large city, he wanders aimlessly to and fro, looking wistfully into the heedless faces of the thousands who pass him by, and feels more alone in the crowded throng than Crusoe on his solitary isle. So with Mr. Judson and Ann Unacquainted with the Burmese language, there was no one with whom they could communicate. Trusting in the goodness of God and relying on his unfailing mercy, they were content to find mutual solace in each other. They wrote to their friends as often as conveyance could be found for their mail. The following extract from a letter written by Ann to the bereaved husband of her beloved Harriet reveals the feelings of her heart, and the obstacles to be overcome:

"Rangoon, April 23, 1814.

"*My Dear Brother Newell :*

"A few days since we received yours of December 18th, the only one we have ever received since you left us at Port Louis. It brought fresh to my mind a recollection of scenes formerly enjoyed in our dear native country. Well do I remember our first interesting conversations on missions and on the probable events which awaited us in India. Well do I remember the dear parental habitation where you were pleased to favor me with your confidence relative to a companion for life. And well do I remember the time when I first carried your message to the mother of our dear Harriet, when the excellent woman exclaimed with tears in her eyes, 'I dare not, I cannot speak against it.' Those were happy days. Newell and Judson, Harriet and Nancy, then were united in the strictest friendship, then anticipating spending their lives together in sharing the trials and toils, the pleasures and enjoyments of a missionary life. But alas! behold us now! In the Isle of France, solitary and alone, lies all that was once visible of the lovely Harriet. A melancholy wanderer on the Isle of Ceylon is our brother Newell, and the savage, heathen empire of Burmah is destined to be the future residence of Judson and Nancy. But is this separation to be forever? Shall we four never again enjoy social, happy intercourse! No, my dear brother, our separation is of short duration. There is a rest—a peaceful, happy rest, where Jesus reigns, where we four soon shall meet to part no more. Forgive my gloomy feelings, or rather forgive my communicating them to you, whose memory, no doubt, is ever ready to furnish more than enough for your peace.

"As Mr. Judson will not have time to write you by this opportunity, I will endeavor to give you some idea of our situation here, and of our plans and prospects. We have found the country, as we expected, in a most deplorable state, full of darkness, idolatry, and cruelty —full of commotion and uncertainty. We daily feel that the existence and perpetuity of this mission, still in an infant state, depends in a peculiar manner on the interposing hand of Providence; and from this impression alone we are encouraged still to remain. As it respects our temporal privations, use has made them familiar, and easy to be borne; they are of short duration, and when brought in competition with the worth of immortal souls, sink into nothing. We have no society, no dear Christian friends, and with the exception of two or three sea captains, who now and then call on us, we never see a European face. But then we are still happy in each other; still find that our own home is our best, our dearest friend. When we feel a disposition to sigh for the enjoyments of our native country, we turn our eyes on the miserable objects around. We behold some of them laboring hard for a scanty subsistence, oppressed by an avaricious government, which is ever ready to seize what industry had hardly earned; we behold others sick and diseased, daily begging the few grains of rice which, when obtained, are scarcely sufficient to protract their wretched existence, and with no other habitation to screen them from the burning sun, or chilly rains, than what a small piece of cloth raised on four bamboos under a tree can afford.   While we behold these scenes, we feel that we have all the comforts, and, in comparison, even the luxuries of life.   We feel that our temporal cup of blessing is full, and runneth over.   But is our temporal lot so much superior to theirs?   Oh, how infinitely superior our spiritual blessings!   While they vainly imagine to purchase promotion in another state of existence by strictly worshiping their idols and building pagodas, our hopes of future happiness are fixed on the lamb of God, who taketh away the sin of the world.   When we have a realizing sense of these things, my dear brother, we forget our native country and former enjoyments, feel contented and happy with our lot, with but one wish remaining—that of being instrumental in leading these Burmans to partake of the same source of happiness with ourselves."

    .   .   .   .

Mr. Judson, having procured a Burman teacher of rare attainments, gave himself diligently to the acquisition of the language which is peculiarly difficult, both in structure and manner of expression, besides having no adequate grammar or dictionary to aid in translating.   Ann, on account of her domestic affairs, found less time to devote to study, yet, from her frequent intercourse with the natives, she learned to speak the language more readily than her husband, though with less knowledge of its grammatical structure.

Realizing the advantage to be gained by obtaining the favor of the civil authorities, Ann determined to make the acquaintance of the wife of Mya-day-men, the Viceroy of Rangoon.   She accordingly visited the government house, but her highness not being up at the time, she was received by the inferior wives of the Viceroy. These, though extremely polite and respectful, could not restrain a demonstration of their innate feminine curiosity relative to such a rare novelty as a white female dressed in her foreign costume. They subjected her to a close scrutiny, and, after minutely examining each article of her apparel, successively trying on her gloves and bonnet, they were firmly convinced that she was no less an object of interest and wonder than his royal holiness, the great white elephant. At length the door opened and the Vicerine appeared, richly dressed, and smoking a long silver pipe. At her appearance the other wives timidly shrank away and sat in a crouching position around the walls of the apartment. Her highness was very gracious, and taking her guest by the hand, seated her on a mat by her side, sincerely apologizing for her delay, as she was unwell. Receiving a bunch of flowers from one of the women, she selected several, and proceeded to ornament her cap, at the same time asking many questions in regard to her visitor. Among other things she inquired if she was Mr. Judson's highest wife, thinking that he, like the Burmans, practiced polygamy.

"I am the only one he has," replied Ann, "for it is the custom of Americans to have but one wife at a time."

"Have you any children?"

"I have not. Our first child was buried in the ocean before we ever reached the land of the Golden Face."

"How sad! Will you tarry long with us?"

"We expect to remain here as long as we live, or until his Majesty shall forbid."

"I am so glad. Then I can see you often."

Further conversation was prevented by the entrance of the Viceroy. His long robe and enormous spear, accompanied by his own savage looks, caused Ann to tremble, but she was reassured by the gruff kindness of his greeting, and found courage to decline his offer of rum and wine. At length, thinking that her visit had been sufficiently prolonged, she arose to go, whereupon her highness again took her hand and led her to the door. "You must come to see me every day," she said, "for you are like a sister to me and I shall always be happy to see you." Thanking her for her kindness, Ann made a low salaam and departed. Great reason did she afterwards have to be thankful for the friendship of the wife of Mya-day-men.

CHAPTER II.

—Rev. J. Lawson.

Two years have passed since we found the little
family first in Rangoon; years of vicissitudes and
varied changes. Let us intrude, for a moment, on the
sanctity of their home circle at this time. Mr. Judson
seated as usual at his study table, is diligently engaged
in solving the long unbroken lines of Burman enigmas
through which he must learn to communicate the Gospel
to the people. His eyes wander often from the page
before him, and rest with loving tenderness on something at his feet. On a mat by his chair, and in full
view of his face, lies a laughing blue-eyed boy of seven
months whom they call Roger Williams. The little
one tosses his baby hands and kicks with delight as he
meets his father's gaze; lying thus for hours, perfectly
contented if he can only see his father's face. Ann is
heard in an adjoining room moving busily about like
the diligent house-keeper she is; when, in want of
something in her press, she enters the room. The eyes
of little Roger follow her from the time she enters till,

(157)

finding what she wants, she moves towards the door, smiling and speaking caressingly to the little form on the floor. The blue eyes fill with tears as the young mother passes by without taking him; seeing which she turns and stooping, takes him in her arms, imprinting a kiss on his rosy lips. He coos with delight at this maternal demonstration, and when replaced on his mat, allows her to return to her work.

During the long period of preparation and lonely seclusion, God has sent this little beam to brighten the gloom that else might have settled over them, and to keep warm the hearts that might have otherwise forgotten the strong ties of nature and become indifferent to those softer feelings that only a parent can experience.

For a year and a half they had toiled ceaselessly, when, on account of failing health, caused by overwork in a strange climate, Ann was compelled to take a sea voyage and a change of air. After due consideration of the matter, and to some extent overcoming the pangs incident on such a separation, she consented to leave Mr. Judson alone and visit Bengal. Mya-daymen was very kind and sent with her a female attendant; which was peculiarly accommodating, as no Burman woman was allowed to leave the country, and her expenses were paid by the Viceroy himself. The captain of the vessel on which she sailed, refused pay for her passage and yet provided everything necessary for the comfort of one in ill health. The physician at Madras who treated her, also returned the proffered fee, saying that he was glad to have been of service to her. Much recuperated in strength, she returned, after three months, to Rangoon, and together they continued their labors. Soon after this an added light entered their lonely chamber, and with hearts overflowing with joy, love and praise, they lived happily in the daily performance of their duties.

"The little white child" was an unheard-of curiosity in Burmah, and the eager natives vied with each other in paying their homage to the little visitor.

Although Mr. Judson was, as yet, unable to preach to the people in their native tongue, the conduct of himself and wife had won even the confidence of the natives who were unaccustomed to honesty, veracity and deeds of uncompensated kindness, such as the missionaries daily exemplified; and by the addition of the child they drew around them a circle of admiring and sympathizing friends, though from the teachings of their religion they were, in a measure, destitute of the finer affections of the human heart. Not, as yet, fully comprehending the intents of the "teacher," they were being gradually prepared for the unfolding of the wonderful truths which he was preparing to give them.

. . . .

It is morning in the month of May. The air is yet cool and balmy, and sweet with the fragrance of opening, dew-laden flowers. The smiling red sun is just appearing in the soft Indian sky, and "feathered songsters" hail the opening day. The first cheering beams straggle through the cracks of the bamboo shutters and reveal the silent objects within. The "teacher" sits with bowed head at his study table. The night lamp is burning low. A faint, half-suppressed moan is heard from the opposite side of the room. There in the shadow sits Ann, gazing wistfully upon a shrouded cradle, weeping silently, and anon praying to God for strength. Little Roger has been taken from them. Like a flower that opens its bosom to the light, and, for a few days, emits a sweet fragrance blessing its stay and then fades; or like a sweet-voiced bird that lights in the open window, startling the echoes with its cheerful song and then flies away, never to return, the angel spirit has flown, leaving darker than ever the gloom of their exile.

God knows best. The time had come when their labors must begin. The magnitude of their undertaking admitted of no division of labor. The care and affection bestowed on the child amounted to almost idolatry, and God hath said, "Thou shalt have none other Gods before me." The tender flower was exotic to the unfriendly climate of its birth, and the Great Gardener hath transplanted it to his own Paradise where the chilling frosts never bite, and the fierce monsoons never blow.

> "Hushed be the murmuring thought! Thy will be done,
> O Arbiter of life and death. I bow
> To thy command—I yield the precious gift
> So late bestowed; and to the silent grave
> Move sorrowing, yet submissive. O sweet babe!
> I lay thee down to rest—the cold, cold earth
> A pillow for thy little head. Sleep on,
> Serene in death. No care shall trouble thee.
> All undisturbed thou slumberest; far more still
> Than when I lulled thee in my lap, and sooth'd
> Thy little sorrows till they ceased   .   .   .   .   .
> Then felt thy mother peace; her heart was light
> As the sweet sigh that 'scaped thy placid lips,
> And joyous as the dimpled smile that played

Across thy countenance. O I must weep
To think of thee, dear infant, on my knees
Untroubled sleeping. Bending o'er thy form,
I watch'd with eager hope to catch the laugh
First waking from thy sparkling eye, a beam
Lovely to me as the blue light of heaven.
Dimm'd in death's agony, it beams no more!"

Their Burman acquaintances came in during the day, and looking sadly on the little waxen figure, tried to console the weeping young mother; but their words of sympathy only added pangs of pity for them. They could only say, "He has gone to Nirvana." There all is Lethe, forgetfulness, annihilation. Not even could they give the more cheerful consolation of the beautiful Hindu faith, that his soul was absorbed into the Great Soul like a bottle of water broken in the ocean, or a " dew-drop slipping in the shining sea."

In the evening, followed by forty or fifty Burmans and Portuguese, they bore the little casket to a clump of mangoe trees in the yard where a grave had been dug. When the bereaved parents had lifted their hearts to God in a song of praise and resignation, and the father with trembling lips had offered a fervent prayer, resigning the departed spirit to Him who gave it, the beloved features were hid away, and arm in arm they returned, sorrowfully but trustfully, to their home, no longer a home.

On the morrow the wife of the Viceroy came in great state, attended by two hundred lords and royal officers, to condole with the distressed mother. She reproved her for not informing her sooner so that she could attend the funeral. She showed every kindness in her power and again invited Ann to visit her.

11

Ofttimes mothers in this Christian land, surrounded by loved ones and all the luxuries of life, when deprived of one of their nestlings, repine at the Providence of God, and refuse to be comforted. What must have been the sufferings of this poor mother, in a land where no congenial friend was ever seen, and but few comforts of life to be had. Yet we hear her say, "Though I say with the prophet, 'Behold and see if there be any sorrow like unto my sorrow.' Yet I would also say with him, 'It is of the Lord's mercies that we are not consumed, because his compassion fail not.'"

Noble, heroic trust!

CHAPTER III.

—*Moore.*

Two years have passed since the death of little Roger. On May 20, 1817, Mr. Judson finished the translation of the Gospel of Matthew, which was the beginning of that monumental task he had undertaken of translating the whole Bible into Burmese. At the opening of this chapter we find him ready to begin public preaching, to which he has long looked forward with great eagerness. But during this time, from 1816 to 1818, occurred one event which served as a foretaste to the experiences which are to be described in succeeding chapters.

Mr. Rice, returning to America from the Isle of France, had succeeded in arousing a missionary spirit among the Baptists, who now organized for the support of the laborers in the field, and also appointed Mr. and Mrs. Hough to go to Rangoon as co-laborers with the Judson's. The patient toilers were much encouraged and strengthened by this addition to their force, especially as Mr. Hough was a printer and brought with him a printing press and fout of type in the Burmese character, a present from the Serampore Mission. This was the first printing press ever brought to Burmah, and the incident of its introduction is interesting to notice. The first printing ever done in the world was a copy of the Bible, so it seems that the Lord reserved the introduction of this great art for his own cause, as the first use to which it was put in this great empire was to print tracts and Bibles. Mr. Hough being unacquainted with the language, confined himself exclusively to the mechanical part of the work, while Mr. Judson did the writing and composing. The tracts were soon circulated, and as sowers of seed, they could only pray that some might fall on good ground.

One day Mr. Judson was sitting as usual with his teacher when a Burman of respectable appearance, and followed by a servant, came into the zayat and took a seat. To Mr. Judson's questions of greeting he scarcely replied, and seemed to be ill at ease. Suddenly he surprised them by asking:

"How long time will it take me to learn the religion of Jesus?"

"Such a question," replied Mr. Judson, "cannot be answered. If God gives light, the religion of Jesus is soon learned; but without that a man might study all his life and then never know it. But how came you to know anything of Jesus? Have you ever been here before?"

"No."

"Have you seen any writing concerning Jesus?"

"I have seen two little books."

"Who is Jesus?" asked Mr. Judson.

"He is the Son of God," replied the man, "who, pitying creatures, came into this world and suffered death in their stead."

"Who is God?"

"He is a being without beginning or end, who is not subject to old age and death, but always is."

The effect of this frank confession on Mr. Judson cannot be conceived. For years he had lived in this land of atheists, and never before had he heard a Burman acknowledge an Eternal God. Producing a tract and catechism, he handed them to the man who recognized them at once, and immediately began reading from place to place as if perfectly familiar with them Mr. Judson now tried to explain to him more of God and Jesus, but he would not listen intently, and seemed anxious only for another book.

"I have finished no other book," said Mr. Judson, "but in two or three months I will give you a larger one which I am now translating."

"But have you not a little of that book done now —hich you will graciously give me?"

Mr. Judson considered for a moment, then thinking it best to grant this voluntary request, folded and gave to him the first two half-sheets containing the first five chapters of Matthew, whereupon he arose and departed immediately as if satisfied. May the Grace of God be with him in reading.

Mr. Judson now determined to begin public preaching, but though fully acquainted with the structure of the language, he did not feel competent to preach in the tongue without the aid of a native assistant. The English Baptists had once established a mission in Chittagong, the natives of which speak Burman Several of these had been converted and baptized, and then the mission was abandoned for some cause. Mr.

Judson decided to go there, gather together the scattered converts, encourage them to be firm in the faith, and, if possible, to bring back one or two of them to assist him in beginning public worship. He intended a voyage of only three months, as the vessel on which he sailed was to return in that time. But he trusted himself on a treacherous ocean, as will afterwards appear.

Mr. Hough was left in charge of the mission premises, and the society of his wife somewhat compensated Ann for the separation from her husband, especially as she so rarely saw any one with whom she could converse in her own tongue, except Mr. Judson.

Nothing transpired to blight their prospects till the three months were past, at the end of which time Mr. Judson was expected back. Then, to the great dismay of the missionaries, a ship arriving from Chittagong reported that neither Mr. Judson nor the ship in which he sailed had been heard of in Arracan. The same news also came from Bengal. These tidings were distressing beyond measure to the devoted wife at home, who pictured to herself her beloved husband driven far away on the dark waters, or his bones bleaching in the coral groves below.

It is said that misfortunes never come singly, and it was true of the missionaries. Mya-day-men, the friendly Viceroy, was recalled to Ava and another sent in his place. Like Pharaoh that knew not Joseph, the new Viceroy had never heard of the white teachers, and looked upon them with suspicion. War was rumored between Burmah and England. The proud King believing that all the world, like his own servile subjects, must quake at the name of the Golden Face, essayed to drive the English from Arracan. Mr. Hough, suspected of being an English spy, was rudely seized and dragged to the court-house where he was told if he did not tell the truth in regard to his presence in the country they would write with his heart's blood. It was falsely reported that a royal order had come for the banishment of all foreign teachers, and Mr. Hough, unable to speak in Burman, was detained from day to day on the most flimsy excuses, until Ann, suspecting that he was detained for the purpose of extorting money from them, and that without orders, determined to make an effort for his release. The family of the Viceroy was absent and it was not etiquette for a woman to appear alone in the presence of his highness. Yet, with that intrepid daring that never was known to shrink even under the most hazardous enterprises, she, like Esther, taking her life in her hand, ventured into the palace uncalled for and found favor. Having plainly stated the facts to the Viceroy, he ordered the immediate release of Mr. Hough, and commanded that the missionaries should not be further molested.

So far from being an end, this was but the beginning of disasters. That fearful epidemic, the cholera, so much dreaded in southern climates, began to rage with alarming violence. The mission house was just without the walls of the city, near the place for the burning of the dead. Day and night the horrible noise of the death-drum was heard continually, announcing, in rapid succession, the departure of poor unguided spirits into Nirvana. Litters bearing the bodies of the dead were continually depositing their ghastly burdens without the walls to be burned, and returning for more.

All day long the dense smoke from the funeral pyres
rolled in clouds above the mission house; and at night
the pestilential marshes were lit up by the lurid glare
of burning flesh.

The mission was now in a distressing condition. The
natives, conscious of the intolerance of the government
for foreign religions, were frightened away by the arrest
of Mr. Hough, and most of the learners were prevented
by the plague. Mr. Judson had not been heard of for
six months and it was believed that the vessel on which
he sailed was lost. Neither Mr. Hough nor his wife
could speak the language, and disheartened by the
state of affairs, they contemplated a removal to Bengal,
at least until the war was over. Already all English
ships were fleeing from the harbor and now only one
remained, the last chance of escape, and that ready to
sail. They daily importuned Ann to forsake her post
and go with them, assuring her that if Mr. Judson
should come the ship would not be allowed to land, and
if yet living, they would be certain to meet him in
Bengal. Harassed beyond measure, she was urged on
board against her will. Even then the thought of Mr.
Judson's returning and finding his home deserted and
his wife gone, he knew not where, induced her to steadfastly refuse at the last moment and return to the
mission house, there to abide alone till he should come,
trusting God to protect her from harm. There, her eyes
beholding the still burning dead, and listening to the
hoarse mutterings of war, she stood at her post and
waited.

Nor was her confidence in vain. Within a week she
had the inexpressible joy of greeting her returning

husband, though but a skeleton of his former self. His brow was marked with the traces of recent pain, and his whole person exhibited signs of the deepest suffering and privation. The vessel on which he sailed had encountered adverse winds, and was driven into the open sea, anchoring after many weeks in a distant part of India, hundreds of miles from their destination. During that long protracted voyage the provisions had given almost entirely out, only a few grains of rice being allotted as the daily portion of each. Mr. Judson had a violent attack of sickness on board, and his frame, racked with pain, and his body burning with fever, with no water to quench his raging thirst, he only prayed to reach land where he might die and be buried. When at length the vessel came to anchor in the mud of Masulipatam, and he saw English faces approaching he fell on his knees and wept for joy, for never had a white face appeared to him so beautiful before. He was kindly received and cared for till able to travel again, when he was sent by palanquin to Madras, thence sailing for Rangoon.

Though disappointed in obtaining one of the Arracanese converts to assist him, he nevertheless determined to pursue his original plan of beginning public preaching. This was more than ever necessary since Mr. Hough had taken with him the printing press, and he had no other means of communicating to as many people as formerly. He began at once the erection of a zayat in which to hold his daily services, and in one room of which Ann could instruct her class of Burman women whom she had gathered around her.

CHAPTER IV.

" Whence comest thou ? "

—Job i: 7.

HALF way between Rangoon and Ava is Prome on the
Irrawaddy, one of the chief cities of the country,
scarcely less important than Rangoon as a commercial
center. Several vessels were anchored in the harbor,
among which was a small fishing smack owned by a
swarthy, weather-beaten Burman. The master was
scolding loudly, and berating the innocent helmsman
because one of the crew had forsaken them just as they
were ready to embark and another could not be procured. About this time a man appeared on the wharf
approaching in the direction of the vessel. He was a
person of splendid physique, though having the appearance of being much worn, and, on account of trouble
or grief, prematurely old, yet he could not have been
more than forty years of age. His dignified bearing
was strangely out of keeping with his dress, which was
that of the simplest menial. At a first glance his face
seems familiar, but his down-cast look and simple
appearance belie our first impressions. Crossing the
plank, he stood on deck, seeing which the master turned
and accosted him.

"Who are you?" he said.

"My name is Moung Ing," replied the stranger.

"What do you want on here?"

"Having heard that you had lost a man, I came to apply for his place."

"Have you any experience in managing a vessel or in catching fish?"

"None whatever, but I thought I might learn."

"Strange application that. I have no use for beginners. First learn your trade and then apply for a position."

Here the helmsman interposed.

"Master, the man seems in earnest and will doubtless do his best. We have no other, why not at least give him the trial of one trip?"

The master only scowled as if admonishing him to hold his peace.

"Certainly," said Moung Ing, "I would try to do all in my power, and I hope my close application will compensate for my want of skill."

At length, after some debate, and finding that there was no other alternative, he was received on trial, and they proceeded down the river. They expected to stop for a day or two at Rangoon, and then go as usual to the sea coast. Moung Ing applied himself so assiduously to his duties that in a few days the captain, naturally of a hilarious temperament, began to be much pleased with him, and praised him extravagantly, calling him a "good fellow" and the "best of the crew." It was not on account of his outward surroundings, and his being among strangers, but seemingly, from some inward sentiment, that Moung Ing was unusually reticent, especially for a boatman. So much absorbed did he often seem with his own thoughts, that he scarcely noticed the jocular remarks of the garrulous

captain, or the uncouth jests of the kindly old helmsman.

On the third day they came in sight of the glittering pinnacle of the Great Golden Pagoda of Rangoon.
The river was now full of boats, moving in every direction, and the air confused with a jargon of sounds.
Moung Ing was not in the least interested in the Babel
around him, but remained as taciturn as ever. They
stopped at an upper landing, and a man who seemed to
be acquainted with the captain came on board, full of
news, and bearing a folded paper tightly clasped in his
hand. He said there was much commotion in the city
on account of a man who was teaching a new religion,
and sending " little books " all over the land. At the
first mention of a new religion, Moung Ing's face lighted
up with a strange animation.

" Whence came the man? " he eagerly asked.

"From over the sea toward the West," replied his
informant.

" Of what race is he? "

" Of the pale-faced."

" What does he teach? "

" He says there is One Eternal God to whom we must
all give account. This is a part of his book."

Moung Ing grasped eagerly the folded sheets and
scanned their contents. It was the five chapters of
Matthew which Mr. Judson had given away, not knowing the result, yet sending them forth as bread cast on
the waters.

Moung Ing returned the manuscript and inquiring
minutely as to the location of the mission house,
returned to his work as silent as ever; but there was

an elasticity in his tread, and a brightness in his eyes, such as his companions had never observed in him before.

"Can it be true," he thought, "that the time has come at last, and God will reveal himself to me? But I have so often hoped and been so sadly disappointed I can scarcely believe as yet. We land to-night, and to-morrow I will go myself to see the white teacher from the West."

Thus the morning star sheds its beams on Mekara in disguise. Be patient and hopeful, O prince, the sun will rise in the morning!

CHAPTER V.

Two miles out from Rangoon, on a beautiful hill,
stands the great Shway Dagong Pagoda, a wonder of
the empire. The gently sloping hill is graded with
terraces, thickly dotted with smaller pagodas, and
embowered with shade-trees. The top is perfectly flat,
containing an area of about two acres. On this, and
entirely covering it, rises the gilded pile, as if it were
an extension of the hill, though its sides are gold. The
enclosure surrounding the hill is densely thronged with
miniature temples, little pagodas, images of Gautama,
great stone vases, standing in rows for the reception of
offerings, lofty pillars draped with banners of gold,
embroidered muslin, lights burning steadily before the
faces of images, garlands of flowers loading the air
with fragrance, tombs, zayats, and carved figures of
every description. It is held the most sacred of all
pagodas, because it is believed to enshrine four real
hairs of Gautama. There is said to be a shaft of solid
gold extending from bottom to top, and the summit is
covered with a great golden umbrella visible for many

miles. The road connecting the pagoda with the city is literally a street whose entire length is lined with continuous rows of pagodas, many of them almost as splendid as the Shway Dagong itself.

Every morning the vast population of the city goes out in mass to worship. The road is filled its entire length with an innumerable throng. They proceed with waving, crimson banners, streaming paper flyers, garlands of flowers, and accompanied by the deafening sound of drums and pealing metal gongs. In the enclosure of the temple some are decorating the images with wreaths of flowers, while others deposit their offerings of fruit and flowers in the great stone vases to be soon carried away by the multitudes of crows that blacken the air, and add their hideous cries to the din of the temple-drums which each votary sounds in order to let the god know of his sacrifice.

This was the great rushing tide of humanity that Mr. Judson wished to stop and turn into another channel. Planting his engines on the bank he began, by imperceptible degrees, to undermine the ancient and seemingly impregnable flood-gates. He had purposely erected his zayat on the side of the great thoroughfare leading to the pagoda, and sitting on the veranda, he daily cried to the passing throng, "Ho! every one that thirsteth, come!" Does it not seem a weak and vain effort, the crying of that one voice against the great clamor of the crowd? Their eyes were filled with visions of the gorgeous ritual, and their ears tuned to the sound of loud music. What had he to attract attention? Only the sweet old story of the Cross. In all ages it thrills the heart and warms the soul. Even here the Spirit of God will show its power, and His word shall not return to Him void. Some, from mere curiosity, stopped to "see what this babbler hath to say," others having seen the tracts, came to inquire the way of life.

The next morning after the events recorded in the former chapter, a man passed by in the crowd, yet he seemed to be no part of it. His eyes rested closely on every surrounding object as if looking for something. When opposite the zayat he heard the usual cry of the man of God. Halting for a moment, he closely scrutinized the face of the speaker, and seemed listening for more, debating in his mind as to whether he should stop. But the surging crowd pushed him on and he moved away like a bubble with the current, pondering with himself, "That was a white man, and the words he utters are sweet to the soul, for who is it thirsts more than I for a knowledge of the truth? I will return another time and seek him."

He had often been disappointed; now he was cautious, though more than ever assured that the truth was near at hand—Moung Ing approached the light.

Several had been visiting the zayat, among whom was Moung Nau who was the first to embrace the new religion. The hearts of the missionaries were joyful as they were at last able to report a convert. Messrs. Colman and Wheelock had shortly before arrived with their wives, and the six missionaries, uniting as a church, heard the experience of Moung Nau and voted to receive him as a candidate for baptism. Two others, Moung Byaa and Moung Thahla, were soon added and the work seemed more hopeful than was even anticipated when the zayat was built.

A learned teacher, Moung Shwa gnong, often came to dispute with Mr. Judson. He displayed great ingenuity in discussion, yet never took any definite grounds.

It is now Sabbath morning and Mr. Judson has preached to a large audience, showing them how to observe the Lord's Day and administering the supper to the disciples. Moung Ing was present at the services and seemed much affected. He had been a daily visitor to the zayat for several days, but finding Mr. Judson thronged with inquirers, had directed most of his conversation to Moung Nau, desiring to hear from others the object of the white teacher, and what the knowledge of God had done for one of his own race. He and Moung Nau read together from the precious five chapters of Matthew, Moung Nau himself calling attention to the sixth, containing a part of the Sermon on the Mount.

"See here," he said, "how superior is the teaching of Jesus to that of Buddha! Here we are told not to do our alms before men to be seen of them, nor to make long prayers, and useless repetition on the streets, but to go in our closets and pray. Oh, it fills me full to think of it! When I worshiped at Shway Dagong I marched in a great crowd with gorgeous display, and when I deposited my offerings I sounded a gong, then I went to my home weary and dusty, my eyes dazzled with gawdy scenes, and my ears ringing with horrid sounds, conscious that no one had seen or heard me but the people. Now I go alone, and in the solitude of my chamber, offer to God the sacrifices of a broken heart and a contrite spirit. No human eye sees me, no ear of man hears me, but God in heaven listens and His

Holy Spirit warms my heart.   Oh, it is a great thing to know God, my brother!"

"Indeed, it must be," said Moung Ing.   "I have sought him these seven years and found him not.   Deprived of my beloved family, through many and distant lands have I wandered, praying and longing, until almost in despair of ever finding him, I have engaged to go to sea that its tempests may help to drown the ragings of my own soul.   Pray to your God that he may reveal himself to me!"

After services Mr. Judson held a long conversation with him and explained the word of the Lord more perfectly.   Ere long he had the satisfaction of seeing the light dawning on his soul.

What a grand thing it is to see the mists of superstition and error roll away before the dark—dispelling beams of the sun of righteousness!   Like over-flowing rivers sweeping across India's burning plains, producing from scorching sands a spontaneous outburst of green fields and waving forests, the Spirit of God bears the Gospel into the soul, washing away its pestilential sins, and from its softening, generating influence spring up fruits unto life eternal.

The fishing vessel was to sail on the morrow, and Moung Ing felt duty bound to fill his engagement, though he desired to remain and receive further instructions.   Mr. Judson regretted very much that he was compelled to take the voyage, fearing that so long an absence, among different people, would, in a measure, destroy the effect produced by his first hearing the Gospel, not knowing the depth of the impression made upon him.   But an object so long sought for is not so easily relinquished. Taking with him some tracts to read, and promising to pray and ponder over the things he had heard, Moung Ing departed next morning on his voyage.

Moung Shwa gnong now became an importunate inquirer, often remaining till night with Mr. Judson that he might have a private conversation with him. But one morning he failed to make his appearance, as did also many of the other inquirers. On investigation it was found that Moung Shwa gnong had been accused to the Viceroy, and that august personage had replied in words of ominous import, "Inquire further about him." This had frightened the inquirers to such an extent that they no longer dared to approach the zayat for fear of offending the Lord of Life and Death.

There had been a great change in civil authority. Not only had their old friend Mya-day-men been succeeded by the present Viceroy, but even the royal household had undergone a revolution. Minder-a-ge-praw, the king, had not discouraged the new religion since he himself had formed a violent hatred for Buddhism, perhaps on account of the memory of his beloved son, Mekara, who had been lost to him through its influence. But a whisper wakes the air. Some say the king is sick. Now a universal hush and death-like stillness pervades the great empire. No one dares to guess the reason; it would be an unpardonable crime, for the "lord of land and water" is called immortal. The attendants wait before -the palace, and the Queen comes out smiting on her breast and wailing, "Ama! Ama!" They look at each other breathlessly and depart. Nirvana has engulfed another soul.

Now great commotion ensues. Mekara, the heir to the throne, has long since been as dead to the royal family. The king's next oldest son is dead, but has left a son, who has been declared heir to the crown. The new king, Nyoung-dan-ghee, has found two powerful opponents in the persons of his father's younger brothers. But he was now Lord of Life and Death, and all must bow to him. The two princes must acknowledge his power or die. The people look on in dread of a great civil war, and long for the rightful king, Mekara. Happy Mekara, sailing away a fisherman on the sea! But all is soon settled. The great Prince of Toung Oo is slain with his family and followers, and the mighty Prince of Pyee buried alive in the mysterious ce.lar of the palace.

The waiting crowd now hears the royal proclamation;

"Listen ye: The immortal king, wearied, it would seem, with the fatigues of royalty, has gone up to amuse himself in the celestial regions. His grandson, the heir-apparent, is seated on the throne. The young monarch enjoins on all to remain quiet, and wait his imperial order."

The new king, so far from favoring his grandfather's course in regard to religion, restored to their former places the banished priests of Buddha and renewed the persecution against all innovations. Like a whirlwind in a flock of pigeons, the imperial disturbances had scattered the audience at the mission house. Only a few of the most zealous remained with the professed disciples. Something must be done, or the mission will perish. Mr. Judson conceived the idea of going to Ava and venturing in person into the presence of the Golden Face and laying a petition at the Golden Feet. Mr. Wheelock, on account of failing health, had departed with his wife for Bengal, and only Mr. Colman remained to accompany Mr. Judson on this daring expedition.

A petition was prepared making known their request, and a tract carefully arranged especially for the perusal of the Golden Face. As it was not customary to appear before him without a present, they carried with them a handsome copy of the Bible in seven volumes, bound in gold-leaf, and each volume enclosed in a rich wrapper. Leaving their faithful wives under the protection of Jehovah, they procured a boat and proceeded with trembling hearts toward the Golden City.

CHAPTER VI.

"The kings of the earth set themselves, and the rulers take counsel together, against the Lord, and against his anointed, saying, 'Let us break their bands asunder and cast away their cords from us.'"

—*Psalms ii,* 2—3.

MYA-DAY-MEN, on his removal from Rangoon to Ava, had become one of the chief officers of the state under the new monarch, and was made a woon-gyee of high authority.

One morning, about a month after the setting out of the teachers from Rangoon, he was sitting in his audience chamber surrounded by various dignitaries of state, his favorite officer, Moung Yo, by his side. It was announced that two foreigners in black were without desirous of speaking with his highness. At a signal from the woon-gyee, Moung Yo retired and presently returned, followed by Mr. Judson and Mr. Colman. Seeing Mr. Judson and recognizing him as an old acquaintance, Mya-day-men arose with evident pleasure in his manner and addressed him cordially.

"Ah, Tsa-Yah, I am happy to see you again, and that in the Golden City of the great King. Whom else from the foreign land have we here?" looking at Mr. Colman, who respectfully bowed in silence.

"Thank, your highness, for the welcome," said Mr. Judson, "and may we always be worthy of your gracious favor. This is Mr. Colman, who only arrived at Rangoon, since your departure. He has not yet learned to speak Burman which accounts for his silence."

With an assuring look at Mr. Colman, he continued:
"And how is the white lady whom my wife loved so much, and who lost the little white child?"

"Mrs. Judson is well, and sends this token of her regards to your excellent wife. Be pleased also to receive this unworthy present for yourself that we may come with favor in the presence of your highness while in the city." Saying which he laid two valuable presents in the hands of Moung Yo who deposited them at his master's feet.

The minister recognized the offerings with a smile of satisfaction, and then inquired how long they intended to remain in the city, and if he could do anything for them.

"Our stay cannot be long," said Mr. Judson, "but its length depends upon the success with which we meet in our undertaking. We wish to come to the Golden Feet and look up to the Golden Face. Can your highness obtain for us entrance into his royal presence?"

"That I shall be glad to do. Moung Yo will conduct you thither at the king's leisure. For the present you must be dismissed as the unsettled affairs of the new monarchy call my attention. I hope to grant you another audience before your departure. Moung Yo, conduct the teachers back to their lodging and see that their request is granted. Let them be introduced first to Moung Zah in the morning, which will save them the inconvenience of applying to all the various officers. Peace go with you."

On their way back to the boat where they made their headquarters, they passed the palace and other public works. As they looked upon the immense structure with its imposing trimmings of gold glittering in the sunlight, and saw the pompous splendor of the court, they thought of the haughty monarch within, now flushed with the bold success of placing himself on the throne as absolute monarch of the land, and exulting over a recent victory in Kathay, which was to be celebrated by a grand parade on the morrow. The country is now his own. The people are his slaves, and their earnings go to him. Without his permission they dare not do anything. Will he grant them the privilege of receiving a new religion? The task seems hopeless, yet the missionaries pray God to incline his heart.

That evening Moung Yo, who lived near the boat, called again and said he would conduct them to the golden palace the next morning. They retired that night with the feeling that to-morrow would be the most eventful day of their lives; a day when success should be assured, or all hope destroyed.

True to his promise, Moung Yo appeared at the boat next morning to conduct them into the presence of his Majesty. They proceeded first to the residence of Mya-day-men, who informed them that the king had been notified of their arrival, and had given orders for their reception at court. Proceeding then to the outer gate they were delayed for a long time as each petty officer must inspect them and be assured that they had authority for entering. Having entered the palace yard they deposited a present for Moung Zah and were next shown to his pavilion near the gate. Several governors and petty kings were present to participate in the great parade of the day. In his royal chamber the Great White Elephant stood gorgeously arrayed in his trappings of silk and gold, ready to step forth and receive the homage of his votaries, as well as to honor the king by thus condescending to appear in public where all eyes could look upon his sacred form. War-horses were pawing in their stalls as if impatient to begin the great pageant. Soldiers in dazzling livery thronged the streets, and gilded barges swarmed the river. The king would shortly appear and all must be ready.

Moung Zah received them very kindly and seated them before the distinguished visitors at his levee. As soon as preliminaries were over Mr. Judson began at once to unfold the object of their visit.

"Your excellency," he began, "in the great country of America we sustain the character of teachers and explainers of the contents of the Sacred Scriptures of our own religion. Since it is taught therein that if we pass to other countries and preach and propagate our religion, great good will result, and both those who teach and those who receive the religion will be freed from future punishment, and enjoy without decay or death, the eternal felicity of Heaven—that royal permission be given, that we, taking refuge in the royal power, may preach our religion in these dominions, and that those who are pleased with our preaching, and wish to listen to and be guided by it, whether foreigners or Burmans, may be exempt from government molestation, they present themselves to receive the favor of the excellent king, the sovereign of land and sea. May it please your highness to present to his majesty our petition, this tract setting forth the principles of our teaching, and also beg him to receive from his humble servants this book containing the Word of our God to his people?"

It would be impossible to describe the feelings of Moung Zah as he listened to this speech. He thought of the past when he had stood by the king, now dead, and heard him denounce his own son. The present king was even more opposed to heresies against the established faith, and what could he hope for these?

He was also joyous to know that there was, in reality, a God, and longed more than ever for Prince Mekara. Then the rightful king would sit on the throne dispensing justice to all, and he could also learn of the true God, the object of his search; then these teachers could be tolerated and the minister himself could learn of them. He was truly desirous of knowing the truth, but feared the consequences, as was evinced by his chicken-hearted manner at the trial of Mekara. Reaching forth his hand he received the petition and read it about half through; but his mind was on a more important subject to him. He dared not show, in the presence of his officers, any interest more than his official duties demanded. Assuming a careless manner, he asked, as if by way of conversation:

"Who is your God? We in Burmah know of no such being."

"God," replied Mr. Judson, "is an Allwise, Eternal Being, without beginning or end, by whom we live, and by whom all things were created."

"Well, what is it you would teach our people to do, once having learned of God?"

"I would teach them their duty as revealed in His Holy Word, the necessity of giving up all to worship Him, and teach them to pray to Him for a new heart, and a true conception of Himself."

Doubtless the minister would have gladly inquired further, but at this point a royal fore-runner appeared, crying:

"The Golden Foot is about to advance. Make ready to meet him!"

Hastily rising, Moung Zah drew on his robes of state saying: "I must seize this opportunity as the king passes, to present you to him. But how can you hope to propagate your religion in this empire? All foreigners are allowed the free exercise of their own religion, but a native can never depart from the belief of the king."

He now hastily conducted them from his own pavilion to the audience chamber of the palace, closely followed by Moung Yo, who bore the precious books to be presented to his majesty. Such imposing splendor, such sickening magnificence, they had never before seen. Passing through the long avenue of gold-covered pillars, they stood in the vast rotunda beneath the lofty dome, on the very spot where the disobedient prince had received his doom. The majesty of the place itself was sufficient to awe one to silence. Only a few great officers of state were present, seated in their respective places. Moung Zah directed them where to sit, then took his seat on one side, Moung Yo sitting behind the gilded present on the other. A few minutes of silence then Moung Yo whispered, "His majesty has entered." Instantly every one except the two missionaries dropped with their faces to the floor; they waited on their knees. Presently a distant ring of golden sandals was heard on the marble pavement; nearer, steady, measured, each approaching footstep caused their hearts to tremble. His magnificent form was richly dressed, and he carried in his hand the jewel-hilted sword. How like his grand father as he appeared on a former occasion! Will his decision be as harsh? His high aspect and noble, commanding eye riveted the attention of all who dared to look upon his countenance. He strided on, careless of surrounding objects, till he saw the missionaries at his feet. Looking down with some surprise and curiosity, he turned toward Moung Zah and asked:

"Who are these?"

"The teachers, great king," replied Mr. Judson.

His majesty was astonished.

"What, you speak Burman—the priests I heard of last night from Mya-day-men?"

"We are the same, O king. The noble Mya-day-men knew me in Rangoon."

"When did you arrive?"

"On the evening before the last we first saw the imperial city and the towers of the golden palace."

"Are you teachers of religion?"

"That is our occupation, and for that we came into the country of the great king."

"Are you like the Portuguese priests?"

"We are not. Our religion knows no priests, for it has no ritual."

"Are you married?"

"We have companions each, who await us at Rangoon."

"Why do you dress so?"

"It is merely the custom of our country."

"What do you desire at the hands of the Golden Face?"

"The petition we bring will answer that question of the King."

Moung Zah now lifted his head from the floor and read, while the king took his seat on the divan, his hand resting on the hilt of his sword, and his eyes fixed on the strangers, though not with displeasure. Having heard the petition he reached forth his hand. Moung Zah crawled forward and presented it. The king read it through deliberately from beginning to end, then returned it in silence. While he was reading Moung Zah received the tract from Mr. Judson and presented it next. With beating hearts they awaited the issue. "O God, display now thy grace! Have mercy on Burmah. Have mercy on her king." Slowly opening the handsome cover, the king read the first few lines:

"There is one Being who exists eternally; who is exempt from sickness, old age and death; who was, and is, and will be, without beginning and without end. Besides this the true God, there is no other God."

He read no further, but with contempt in his manner dashed it to his feet. Moung Zah picked it up and returned it to the teachers. Moung Yo now unfolded one of the volumes by his side and displayed its beauty. The Golden Face never even glanced at it. Though he spoke not a word, they realized that their fate was sealed. After a few moments Moung Zah interpreted the royal master's silence.

"Why do you ask for such permission? Have not the Portuguese, the English, the Mussulmans, and people of other religions, full liberty to practice and worship according to their own customs? In regard to the objects of your petition, his majesty gives no order. In regard to your sacred books, his majesty has no use for them—take them away."

Moung Yo ventured to remark something about Mr. Colman's skill in medicine. The royal countenance turned indifferently toward the silent teacher; the Golden Mouth opening, said:

"Let them proceed to the residence of my physician, the Portuguese priest, let him examine whether they can be useful to me in that line and report accordingly."

The martial music was now heard without, and the shouts of the victors proclaimed the approach of the procession. Rising, his majesty moved proudly and coldly away toward the end of the hall. Throwing himself down on a cushion by a window overlooking the palace-court, he lay listening to the music and watching the glittering pageant below. He had heard for the first time of a God who made him, and who would judge him. The knowledge had been displeasing to him and he had trampled it under foot.

The attendants were frightened. These strangers had come here and evoked the frown of the Golden Face. What might be the consequence? Hastily gathering together the books and tracts, they quickly conducted them to the gates, lest the smoking fire of the king's displeasure should burst into a flame. They were carried first, according to the royal commandment, to the Portuguese priest, who, of course, not relishing the idea of a rival for royal favor, as a consequence, found no good in Mr. Colman's skill. Wearied with the dust and heat of the two miles which they had traveled coming to his house, and disheartened by their repulse at the palace, they retreated to their boat to remain for the day.

Unwilling yet to relinquish all hope, and thinking that they had detected some show of favor in the conduct of Moung Zah, who was second in power only to the king himself, they determined to visit him again the next morning. The minister fearing to receive with favor those who had incurred royal displeasure, assumed an unusual coldness and reserve. He assured them that it was utterly out of the question as to whether Burmans should be allowed to embrace a new religion; punishment was inevitable. He afterwards received, a tract and read it through; then, instead of throwing it down as the king had done, he handed it to one of his attendants to keep. Perhaps the poor soul may read the God-sent message alone, and yet find the knowledge of the true God. He then turned and replied:

"The doctrines and commands are very good, but it will be a long time before Burmans can be convinced that there is a God and a Saviour."

An English officer who had shown them great kindness was, in the meantime, summoned to the palace to tell what he knew in regard to the teachers. The Englishman replied at length, dwelling on the country, the character, and object of the missionaries, trying to vindicate them as much as possible.

"I have been told quite differently," said his majesty. "The Portuguese priest informed me that they were a sect of Zandees, a race that have been of so much trouble to our empire."

"I beseech your majesty to believe nothing of the kind," replied the other warmly. "They are true teachers and only desire to labor in peace."

"Enough of them," said the king. Then laughing scornfully, he said: "What, they have come over here presuming to convert us to their religion! Let them leave our capital. We have no desire to receive their instructions. Perhaps they may find some of their countrymen in Rangoon who may be willing to listen to them."

With heavy hearts the missionaries turned their backs on the Golden City. The last remaining hope was blasted, and the little mission must be abandoned just as they were beginning to succeed. So thought they in the gloom of their disappointment.

CHAPTER VII.

Cowper.

THE city of Pyee, once the seat of a former dynasty, is an important place some two hundred and thirty miles below Ava. On the evening of the sixth day after their departure from the imperial city, the missionaries landed here where they spent the night, having, of course, traveled much more rapidly down the river than during their ascent. Just at night a man appeared at the boat and asked to see the teachers. Mr. Judson sent word for him to be conducted on board to his little room. When the visitor appeared at the door, where the dim rays of the cocoa-nut lamp fell on him, they were astonished to see it was Moung Shwa gnong.

"Why, teacher," exclaimed Mr. Judson, in surprise and alarm, "what are you doing here? Has the mission been scattered?"

"No, Tsa-yah, the mission is as you left it. I was summoned here to see a friend who is very sick, and will return soon. I would be glad to accompany you back if you can wait a day or two."

"We cannot wait," replied Mr. Judson, "as we must hasten to bear the report of our expedition to the disciples at Rangoon."

13   (193)

"May I ask what success you met with at the Golden City?"

"Ah," Mr. Judson replied sadly, "it was worse than no success. The king gave no answer to our petition, refused our present of the Holy Scriptures, and dashed our tract to the ground. We were told that it would be impossible for any who embraced our religion to escape punishment and perhaps death. We also heard an incident of a man who renounced the religion of Buddha, and whose fate was a sign to us of what might follow others from the effect of our teachings. The man embraced the Catholic faith, and the Emperor hearing of it, ordered that he should be compelled to recant. He was thrown into prison and inflicted with continual torture. At length, finding him unsubdued, they had recourse to the iron mall. He was laid upon his back, and with heavy blows, beginning with his feet, they gradually beat his body almost to a pulp, inch by inch, up to his breast. He still pronounced the name of Jesus, and when at the point of death, some who pitied him reported to the Emperor that he was merely a poor madman who knew not what he was doing, and procured orders for his release, but he afterwards died of his injuries. Such must be expected now and more, for that took place under the rule of the former king, who himself had become a violent hater of Buddhism, and the present ruler will use more rigid means to uphold the religion he loves."

"I think, teacher, we should not be intimidated by these things," replied he, "for if God is for us He will yet open a way."

Mr. Judson was surprised to see his confident air and seeming fearlessness, but he yet doubted his sincerity, since it was reported that he had recanted to the Mangen teacher at Rangoon and still worshiped at pagodas. He had never declared himself a disciple, because his high position would cause attention to be attracted to him immediately. Mr. Judson replied:

"It is not for you that we are concerned, but for those who have already become disciples. They could not worship at pagodas, or recant before the Mangen teacher."

He saw the hint and tried to explain his conduct.

"Say nothing," said Mr. Judson. "One thing you know to be true—that when formerly accused, if you had not in some way or other satisfied the Mangen teacher, your life would not now be remaining in your body."

"Then if I die, I die in a good cause," said he, "for I know it to be the cause of truth. My faith has been growing. I now believe in the eternal God, in His Son, Jesus Christ, in the atonement which Christ has made, and in the writings of the apostles, as the true and only word of God. In one of my last visits you told me I was trusting in my own understanding rather than the divine word. From that time I have seen my error and endeavored to renounce it. You also explained to me the evil of worshiping at pagodas, though I told you my heart did not partake in the worship. Since you left Rangoon I have not lifted up folded hands before a pagoda. It is true, I sometimes follow the crowd on days of worship in order to avoid persecution; but I walk up one side of the pagoda and down the other. Now, you say I am not a disciple. What lack I yet?"

"Teacher," replied Mr. Judson somewhat relieved, "you may be a disciple of Christ in heart, but you are not a full disciple. You have not faith and resolution enough to keep all the commandments of Christ, particularly that which requires you to be baptized, though in the face of persecution and death. Consider the words of Jesus, just before he returned to Heaven, 'He that believeth and is baptized shall be saved.'"

This thought impressed him seriously, and he remained for some moments in silence.

"I am sorry for those poor disciples that shall be left," said Mr. Judson, "for it is well that we leave the country since no others will dare to embrace our religion, having heard the king's decision."

Moung Shwa gnong was deeply aroused at this intimation, and, for the first time, showed the real interest he felt.

"Say not so," he said, "there are some who will investigate, notwithstanding; and rather than have you quit Rangoon, I will go myself to the Mangen teacher, and have a public dispute. I know I can silence him. I know the truth is on my side."

"Ah," said Mr. Judson, "you may have a tongue to silence him, but he has a pair of fetters and an iron mall to tame you. Remember that."

Towards midnight Moung Shwa gnong departed, and they retired to rest for to-morrow's journey; yet the thought of how their failure could effect the mission kept them awake most of the night. Six days afterward they arrived in Rangoon.

They had already formed the determination of removing the mission to Chittagong, where, under the protection of the British, they could still preach to a Burmese-speaking people. Gathering the converts together, the details of the whole of the expedition were gone over. Mr. Judson related their failure fully, pictured the persecutions that would be brought on the people by a further propagation of the gospel in Burmah, and announced his reluctant determination to leave them. It was a cruel test for those so recently born again, but the true Christian principle manifested itself in every one of them. Surrounding him they cried, to a man, that they were ready to suffer persecution and even death, rather than renounce their religion.

"Stay," they pleaded, "until a little church of ten is collected and a native teacher is set over it; and, then, if you must go, we will not say nay. This religion will spread of itself. The Emperor can not stop it."

The teacher's heart was too full for utterance as he heard this demonstration of heroism and devotion on the part of the disciples. Recovering himself, he told them of his gratitude to God for their trust, and promised not to leave as long as one held out faithful.

They decided, however, that Mr. Colman and his wife should proceed to Chittagong, and gathering together the scattered converts, reorganize them, and prepare there an asylum for the teachers and disciples in Burmah when persecution should break out.

Mr. Judson and his wife were now left once more alone, in this the darkest hour of their experience, yet the Lord worked mightily in the hearts of the Burmans, and the little church grew rapidly, though in the very face of persecution. Mrs. Judson had a daily class of women whom she taught among whom was Mah-Men-la, a very talented woman, who seemed to be making great progress towards the knowledge of the true God. At length, worn out with excessive labor and anxiety, Mrs. Judson's health gave way, and Mr. Judson was compelled to accompany her to Bengal.

After having arranged for the voyage, several inquirers who had not yet professed Christ, came and demanded baptism before they should leave, for fear that Mr. Judson might never return. He examined them, and finding them firm in the faith, promised to baptize them in the evening. In the mean time Moung Shwa gnong came in. He stayed all day, and by a relation of his mental trials, and strivings with sin, he convinced Mr. Judson that he was truly a disciple. Others came during the day, and as evening approached Moung Shwa gnong became much interested and addressed himself to the teacher.

"My lord, teacher, there are now several of us present who have long considered this religion. I hope that we are all believers in Jesus Christ."

"I am afraid to say that," said Mr. Judson. "However, it is easily ascertained; and let me begin with you, teacher. I have heretofore thought that you fully believed in an eternal God; but I have some doubt whether you fully believe in the Son of God, and the atonement He has made."

"I assure you," he replied, "I am as fully persuaded of the latter as of the former."

"Do you believe, then, that none but disciples of Christ will be saved from sin and hell?"

"None but His disciples."

" How, then, can you remain without taking the oath of allegiance to Jesus Christ, and becoming his full disciple in body and soul?"

"It is my earnest desire to do so by receiving baptism; and for the very purpose of expressing that desire I have come here to-day."

"You say you are desirous of receiving baptism. May I ask when you desire to receive it?"

"At any time you will please to give it. Now—this moment, if you please."

"Do you wish to receive baptism in public or in private?"

"I will receive it at any time, and in any circumstances, that you may direct.'

"Teacher," now replied Mr. Judson, "I am satisfied, from your conversation this forenoon, that you are a true disciple, and I reply, therefore, I am as desirous of giving you baptism as you are of receiving it."

The disciples rejoiced, and the others were astonished, at this candid confession of the hitherto proud teacher; for, though they believed him a Christian they did not think such a man would ever confess it, or consent to baptism by a foreigner.

It was a happy, though solemn scene as Mr. Judson led his little band at twilight to the accustomed pool, and in the silence of evening, baptized them into the name of the Father, Son, and Holy Ghost. Mah-Men-la was in the room with Mrs. Judson when she saw the teacher going to be baptized.

" Ah," she cried, "he has gone to obey the command of Jesus Christ, while I remain without obeying. I shall not be able to sleep this night. I must go home and consult my husband and return."

That night she returned, related her experience and demanded baptism. They received her gladly, and it being very late, she was baptized in a pond near the house, by moonlight. Thus the first female was added to the church, which now numbered ten.

On the morrow Mr. and Mrs. Judson departed for Bengal.

.   .   .   .

After a happy visit of six months at Calcutta, Mr. and Mrs. Judson returned to Rangoon, Mrs. Judson having fully recovered her health. As the ship drew near the city they strained their eyes to see if any of their friends were at the whari. The first they saw was Moung Shwa gnong who stood with his hands shading his eyes, watching the deck. Mah-Men-la and others met them when they landed, and several gathered around them that night at the mission house. Their evening prayer was full of gratitude and praise, for not one had disgraced his calling, though many had suffered extortions from petty officers till forced to flee to the woods.

Things were now more hopeful. Mya-day-men was once more made Viceroy of Rangoon. Those who had accused Moung Shwa gnong to the former Viceroy, formed a conspiracy to destroy him. They met in daily consultation and assuming a triumphant manner, made it appear to poor Moung Shwa gnong that his fate was decided, and he was almost on the point of fleeing for his life. One of the conspirators going to the Viceroy accused the teacher, Moung Shwa gnong, of endeavoring to "turn the priests' rice-pot bottom upwards." Mya-day-men only replied, "What consequence? Let the priests turn it back again." That sentence destroyed the conspiracy, and gave the disciples hope so long as Mya-day-men should hold his administration.

During the succeeding period of peaceful prosperity, Moung Ing returned from his long voyage, much worse physically from wear and exposure, but retaining in his heart the precious truth that he had imbibed before departing, being the second Burman to whom God revealed Himself in saving grace. Stopping at a riverside town on their way in, he had showed his precious copy of Matthew to a Catholic priest, who immediately consigned it to the flames, giving, instead, one of his own heretical pamphlets. Yet, through all difficulties, he had remained steadfast to his principles, and now only desired to be one of the disciples and be with the teachers always. His request for baptism was gladly granted, and he was added to the fold. A happy day was that for Burmah; though, seemingly, but a poor fisherman, his light shall burn the longest of any, and his services shall be more for the general good than all who were converted before.

CHAPTER VIII.

—P. P. Bliss.

MORE than three years have passed since Moung Zah
returned to the disappointed missionaries the golden-
covered Bible. Now again the gilded doors are ajar
and two strangers kneel at the Golden Feet.

Mrs. Judson's health having failed again, she was
compelled to take a voyage to America, leaving Mr.
Judson alone. During this time Dr. Price had arrived,
and being very successful in his profession, a knowledge
of his skill had reached the Golden Ears and he was
summoned to the king's palace. As he was unacquainted
with the language, Mr. Judson accompanied him as
interpreter, leaving the mission in charge of Mr. Hough
who had returned to Rangoon.

The Golden Face was pleased with Dr. Price; received
him graciously and inquired many things of him in
regard to his profession, but took no notice of his companion except as interpreter. Moung Zah recognized
the teacher, however, and asked him kindly about his
welfare in the presence of the king. After the interview was over, and his majesty had retired, the minister drew Mr. Judson into conversation on religious
topics, and gave him some confidential encouragement
to remain at Ava.

Several days after, during an interview, the king noticed Mr. Judson for the first time, though he had been present nearly every day with Dr. Price. Turning he asked:

"And you in black, what are you? A medical man, too?"

"Not a medical man, but a teacher of religion, your majesty."

"What is the nature of your religion? What does it teach?"

"It is a religion of the heart, treating of God and His relations to mankind, and their duties toward him."

"Whence did you come bringing your teachings here?"

"From America, your majesty."

"Have any embraced your religion yet?"

"Not here."

"Are there any in Rangoon?"

"There are a few."

"Are they foreigners?"

The teacher hesitated for a moment, fearing to give an answer that would involve his friends in ruin, but the truth must be told. Further evasion was impossible. So he replied.

"There are some foreigners and some Burmans."

His majesty remained in silence for a few moments, but the expected look of displeasure did not visit his countenance. Presently he asked a great many questions in regard to religion, geography, astronomy, &c., all of which were answered in such a satisfactory manner as to elicit the admiration of all. His majesty presently retired as usual, after which a royal secretary asked some questions and drew the teacher into one of his accustomed dissertations on religion, as if he was in his own little zayat and not in the palace of the most haughty monarch of the world.

Great was the encouragement of that day, the king had heard of his subjects renouncing Buddhism and was not displeased!

Mr. Judson now found himself in great favor at court. The king gave to him and Dr. Price a spot of ground, and had them a temporary house erected, into which they moved from the boat. The restraint from fear of the king's anger being now removed, Mr. Judson was often sent for by the high ministers of state to converse on science and religion. The a-twen-woon, Moung Zah, now became openly interested and improved every opportunity of informing himself in regard to the new religion.

Joining the house which the king had erected for the missionaries, and near the palace, was the handsome residence of Prince M., eldest half brother to the king. The prince is a fine young man of more than usual intelligence, but disabled in his arms and legs from the effects of a paralytic stroke. Being deprived of the common sources of enjoyment, he had devoted much time to literature, and his associations with Portuguese teachers had developed in him a strong taste for the sciences. Having once seen Mr. Judson in company with Dr. Price, whom he had called for medical assistance, he afterwards sent for him, and entered into an interesting conversation. He was much pleased with Mr. Judson's communications, and admired his understanding of the sciences, but he sought more for entertainment in his inquiries concerning the Christian religion than for any personal good. He received a tract very thankfully, and when asked if Burman converts would be subjected to persecutions under government, replied:

"Not under the reign of my brother. He has a good heart, and wishes all to believe and worship as they please."

Soon after, while Mr. Judson was conversing with Moung Zah in the palace, his majesty came forward and again honored him with a personal recognition, inquired many things concerning his country, and authorized him to invite American ships to his territories with the assurance of protection and facilities for trade.

Prince M., who had formed such an attachment for Mr. Judson that he could not bear to be long out of his presence, sent for him often, and, in company with his wife, derived much pleasure from their intercourse. One day Mr. Judson made a full disclosure of his purpose in coming to Burmah, his former repulse at the court, and the persecution of Moung Shwa gnong, and many of their trials in establishing the truth in Rangoon. They both listened with great feeling, and manifested their interest in such a way as to insure him of their sympathy.

Mr. Judson now thought it a good time to press upon the prince the necessity of his own change of heart, and a view of his personal danger in living without Christ. He urged him to make the Christian religion an object of immediate concern.

Like many others before him, the prince hesitated for a moment, weighing the convictions of his heart with his worldly ambitions. After a monent of silence he replied:

"I am yet young—only twenty-eight. I am desirous of studying all the foreign arts and sciences. My mind will then be enlarged, and I shall be capable of judging whether the Christian religion be true or not."

"But suppose your highness changes worlds in the meantime?" urged Mr. Judson.

His countenance fell as he glanced at his emaciated limbs.

"It is true," he said sadly. "I know not when I shall die."

"My lord, it would be so much better to pray to God for enlightenment, when his divine Spirit will enable you to distinguish between truth and falsehood in this great realm of investigation where the arts and sciences of man never reach. I beseech you, think of this more seriously." And he departed.

One day he was in the palace in company with two Englishmen, when the king attracted by the unusual number of three foreigners at once, approached the company but directed his attention chiefly to Mr. Judson.

"Teacher," he said, "I wish to know about those Burmans who have embraced your religion in Rangoon. Are they real Burmans?"

"The same as all other Burmans I have seen, your majesty," replied Mr. Judson, now without fear, for the king's inquiry had expressed more of surprise than displeasure, that a Burman should be induced to give up his religion.

"Do they dress like other Burmans?"

"There is no difference that I can distinguish."

"Are they of the high or low classes?"

"Both, your majesty. I have baptized recently a poor fisherman, and a learned teacher of much note." Little idea had he of the real difference between the two new disciples.

"Do they adhere strictly to their new religion?"

"So far, all have been faithful. We hold daily worship, and I preach to them publicly every Sunday."

"What, in Burman?"

"In Burman."

"Let us hear you preach."

Here Mr. Judson hesitated, should he dare to preach in the king's palace? But the king himself had demanded it, though for curiosity, and an a-twen-woon repeated the order Hoping that good might come of it, he began with an invocation, and an ascription of praise and glory to God, followed by a declaration of the laws of the Gospel; when he stopped.

"Go on," said another a-twen-woon.

Amid the profound silence of the court, he proceeded to declare the perfection of God, when his majesty's curiosity being satisfied, he signed to him to stop. Being asked what he thought of Gautama, he replied that he was the son of a great king, and was a wise and good teacher, but not God This explanation seemed to please some of the ministers who now entered into a spirited conversation in regard to God and Christ, his majesty listening in silence. Moung Zah encouraged by all this, made a remark, which at the time of Mekara's banishment would have cost him his life.

"Nearly all the world, your majesty, believe in an eternal God, all except Burmah and Siam, these little spots!"

His majesty sat for a few moments, in silence, then making a few remarks on other topics, arose and retired.

It was now near the time when Mrs. Judson was expected to return from America, and Mr. Judson prepared to go to Rangoon to meet her, expecting to return with her to Ava and establish a mission there. On communicating his intention to the king in regard to leaving for Rangoon, he inquired:

"Will you proceed thence to your own country?"

"Only to Rangoon."

The king nodded in acquiescence.

Moung Zah inquired:

"Will you both go, or will the doctor remain?"

"It is very hot here," said Dr. Price "and our situation is inconvenient, besides Mr. Judson expects his wife at Rangoon and must go to meet her."

"Then you will return here after the hot season," said Moung Zah.

Mr. Judson looked at the king inquiringly, and replied:

"If it is convenient."

The king again nodded and smiled, and turning to Dr. Price, said:

"Let a place be given him."

Before making final preparations to depart, Mr. Judson held another conversation with Moung Zah, but with little success. The belief that there was an eternal God had long possessed him, as we know from former events, but he could not receive Christ, ranking Him as a great teacher, such as Gautama and Mahomet, but with nothing of the divine about Him. He seemed immovably settled in his convictions, yet, on parting, he said:

"This is a deep and difficult subject. Do you, teacher, consider further and I, also, will consider."

On taking leave of Prince M., the prince desired him to return to Ava and bring all the Christian Scriptures and translate them into Burman that he might read them all. His wife also expressed a great desire to see Mrs. Judson, and enjoined upon him to bring her without fail.

The king invited him to return to the capital to live, and the queen expressed a great desire to see the white lady in her foreign dress.

Such a happy heart Mr. Judson had never had before as he departed this time from the Golden City. The king and all the royal family were pleased with him and interested in his religion. Now he could establish a mission in the capital whence its influence would be felt over the whole empire. And, then, was he not going to meet Ann from whom he had been parted so long? Happy teacher! But sorrow will come.

.   .   .   .

Reaching Rangoon he received a letter from Mrs. Judson stating that she had just left England for America, and it would be several months yet before she could return. This time of waiting gave him an opportunity of finishing his translation of. the New Testament which he had reluctantly abandoned to accompany Dr. Price. He also prepared a synopsis of the Old Testament to be used in the study of the New.

After ten months Mrs. Judson returned, accompanied by Mr. and Mrs. Wade, who now were left with the Houghs in charge of the mission. Eight days after their arrival Mr. Judson set out on his third journey to the Golden City, accompanied by his wife, a Bengalee cook, and Moung Ing, who declared he would never leave them. After an absence of almost a year, Mr. Judson again clasped hands with Dr. Price.

14

BOOK FIFTH.

CHAPTER I.

—*Ella Wheeler Wilcox.*

LOOKING forward to the events soon to transpire, it is hard to realize the truth of the above. The finite mind cannot appreciate the designs of the infinite. As a traveler, stumbling through the mists of the valley, cannot realize that the sun still shines brightly on the mountain-tops; that the sky is blue, and the great world gay; so when we are compassed about with great afflictions, the whole world too often seems dark, and we imagine the Lord has withdrawn His face from us, when, in reality, it is His excessive love drawing a vapor from our surrounding circumstances to refreshen less favored spots elsewhere. Only those who have passed through great tribulations can begin to estimate the fullness of God's mercy, and see how His Providence has ever surrounded them. It was after emerging from the "Valley ot The Shadow of Death" that Bunyan's pilgrims stood on the delectable mountains and viewed, in perspective, the "Celestial City."

The missionaries were met, a few days below the Golden City, by Dr. Price, who informed them of new difficulties in their way at the capital. The war that had long been threatening between Burmah and the English in Bengal seemed now inevitable. A few victims of Burman cruelty had escaped to the dominions of the British in Arracan. The monarch demanded of the English authorities that they be arrested and delivered to him. On their refusal to interfere, he determined to punish them by wresting Arracan from their possession. Flushed with recent victories over the Kathays and other aboriginal tribes, he imagined that the very name of the Golden Face would cause all enemies to tremble, and that the glitter of the golden war-boats would strike terror into their hearts, insomuch that they would flee without offering to resist. The council of a-twen-woons who had been so favorable to the teachers, was dismissed and strangers appointed. Dr. Price himself was out of favor at court.

The changed state of affairs was a severe disappointment to the missionaries after the sanguine hopes in which they had previously indulged.

Dr. Price had erected a house in which they were received, but the brick walls were yet damp, and so affected the health of Mrs. Judson that they were compelled to return to the boat and remain till a house of bamboo could be built on a spot of ground which the king had given to Mr. Judson when there before. Within the incredibly short time of two weeks the house was ready and they moved in; but the thin walls were but poor protection against the heat, which often exceeded one hundred and eight degrees in the shade; and they would be forced to build a smaller house of brick to be used during the hot season then just coming on.

On his first visit to the palace, Mr. Judson met with a cold reception. The king recognized him and accepted from him a small present, but never noticed him again. The queen did not even mention the "white lady in the foreign dress," whom she had formerly expressed such a desire to meet, and as a consequence Ann never ventured within the palace enclosure. Prince M. and his wife alone received them cordially, yet they were averse to speaking on religious subjects, and confined their conversations to the arts and sciences.

Notwithstanding these difficulties, they lost no opportunity of teaching. Mr. Judson held public worship every Lord's day at Dr. Price's. Ann also began her female school as in Rangoon. The first pupils she had were three little girls whom she taught to read. The circumstances connected with two of these sisters are somewhat singular. Their mother had become insane, and their father, being unable to provide for them properly, brought them to Mrs. Judson to rear and educate. Though said to be sisters, and each calling him father, there was a striking dissimilarity in their features and manners. The eldest was a bright, acute little creature; and, judging from her expression, one would think her at least sixteen, but in form she did not seem more than twelve. Mrs. Judson observed the peculiarity and inquired of her father how old she was.

"That I do not know " he replied.

"What, not know the age of your own child?"

"She is not really my child. My wife took her to rear when but a babe, and we have considered her as our own, even as the sister of this one."

"Is her own mother dead, that there is no one to tell her age?"

"It is a strange story, teacher, and I know it not all. Years ago, before my wife lost her reason, one day while I was away from home, the white teacher who was here before you came, brought the little child to my house, seemingly then about a year old. He told my wife her story and requested her to keep the little one, as he had at that time no wife, though he afterwards married a native woman at Rangoon. The child is evidently a Burman, though the teacher brought her over from Bengal. When I returned home from the service of the king she was at my house as my own child. I inquired of my wife her history but the madness had come on her and she could give me no answer. From her ravings, at times, I have gleaned this much. All else seems to have been a secret entailed upon her, and this little box was left to be opened when the child should be fully grown."

From the folds of his vest he drew a little ivory jewelry casket and delivered it to Mrs. Judson.

"It is indeed a strange story," she replied, "and I have a great curiosity to know the mystery of her origin, but will keep the little box for her till she is grown. Is it locked?"

"It is. The key will be found on a cord about her neck, which was there when we first knew her, and has never been removed."

He then took an affectionate leave of the little ones, and Mrs. Judson led them into the house, henceforth to be as her own children. They called her their "white mamma," and she has ever since been known by that title among the Burmans. She gave them her maiden name—one Mary, the other Abbe Hasseltine. Mary, the eldest, was called by the Burmans, Mah-ree—the Burmese for Mary.

Mrs. Judson had had a happy visit to the home of her childhood, which, when leaving at first, she never expected to see again. The old friends of her school days crowded around her, rejoiced at her success in the mission field, and wept with her over the pathetic death of Harriet, whom they all loved. Her relations of missionary trials and sufferings, with their consequent joys, aroused a zeal among her friends at home, and the girls of Bradford Academy organized themselves into an association to raise money for missions. Their first instalment reached her just at this point, and she set it apart for the support of Mah-ree. With her little school of three, she now began teaching, expecting to increase the number as she and her object became better known.

Mr. Judson devoted himself to the translation of the Bible, and each hoped that, in the event of war, they, being Americans, would not be molested.

News was soon brought to the capital that an English fleet had anchored in the mouth of the river at Rangoon, and one morning, just after their worship in Dr. Price's house, a messenger entered and announced that the city of Rangoon had been taken. The intelligence produced a two-fold effect upon the foreigners—one of joy, that they should be under christian rule; the other of fear, lest the consequences should be fatal to them before greater conquests should be made.

Mr. Gouger, an English merchant at Ava, was worshiping with them, and he, of course, had more cause to fear than any of them. We went at once to Prince Thirrawady, the king's most influential brother, who replied that he need not be uneasy, as his majesty had said the few foreigners residing at Ava had nothing to do with the war, and should not be molested.

The whole city was now in the wildest commotion. An army of ten thousand troops was raised and dispatched down the river in their golden war-boats. Not the least doubt was entertained of their success in recapturing Rangoon. The king was only apprehensive lest the name of the Golden Face should so frighten the enemy that they would all escape to their boats before they could be captured as slaves. The king himself sent a pair of golden fetters to bind the prime minister, whom he expected to make his own royal servant. A wild young buck of the palace put in his application for six white strangers to row his boat, and the wife of a woon-gyee ordered four white strangers to manage her household. The eager soldiers gladly promised to supply all these demands, and as they passed down the river by Mr. Judson's house in the war-boats they were dancing and shouting in the highest glee.

"Poor fellows!" said the missionaries; "you will probably never dance again."

The prediction was only too true. They were never to see the Golden City again.

Immediately after the departure of the army the government began to inquire into the cause of the sudden arrival of the white strangers at Rangoon. Some suggested that spies had invited them over. Three Englishmen were then in Ava, and were at once seized and placed in confinement. Mr. Judson and Dr. Price were also examined; but, being Americans and having no communication with the British, they were released. But when they came to examine the English prisoners, it was found from Mr. Gouger's accounts that the missionaries had drawn on him for money, as they received their salary from America, through exchange, by orders on Bengal. The Burmese authorities, ignorant of these customs, thought they were in the pay of the British, and, very likely, spies. On hearing this, the king angrily exclaimed:

"Arrest the two teachers immediately!"

At the mission house all were engaged in their usual occupation, not suspecting any danger. The brick-masons without were busily humming at their work on the new house, Mr. Judson was in his study writing, the little Burman girls were sitting on the floor studying their lessons, and Ann was in an inner room preparing dinner. Moung Ing was washing the rice outside the door, when there rushed up a magistrate holding a black book, accompanied by a dozen ruffians and a hideous spotted-face, whom Moung Ing knew to be an executioner.

"Where is the teacher?" demanded the magistrate.

Mr. Judson, hearing the commotion, appeared at his study door, pen in hand.

"You are called by the king," said the officer, and meant he was now under arrest. The spotted-face, at this signal, leaped upon him, threw him on the floor, and proceeded to bind upon his arms a small cord. This is a favorite instrument of torture, as the arms, pinioned from behind, are drawn together, sometimes stopping respiration, and even producing death, causing the blood to spurt from mouth and nostrils. Ann came rushing in, and seeing what the executioner intended, caught him by the arm.

"Stay!" she said. "I will give you money."

"Take her, too," demanded the officer. "She also is a foreigner."

Mr. Judson here interposed, though till now he had been silent. He pleaded that they had no orders to arrest her, and begged them imploringly to let her remain—which they reluctantly consented to do The scene was heart-rending. Abbe and Mah-ree stood screaming and crying; the brick-layers forsook their work and fled; the Bengalee servants looked on with horror to see their master thus rolled on the floor and trampled upon; the neighbors crowded in, and Moung Ing stood with flashing eyes, as if he would have been glad to resent the terrible indignities. The cruel spotted-face, grinning with hellish delight, drew tighter the cords and dragged the tortured man from the house. Ann begged and entreated him to accept the money and loosen the cords, but he only grinned and gave them another twist as he departed. She now gave the money to Moung Ing, and told him to follow and see if he could not persuade them to relieve Mr. Judson from his suffering. But when the faithful servant again offered the money as they passed into the street, instead of receiving it, the executioner threw his victim to the ground, planting his knees on his back, drew harder on the ropes with diabolic joy, until the poor man shrieked with anguish. Seeing that such attempts only increased instead of alleviating the torture, Moung Ing followed on in silence to see what they would do. First to the court-house. There a crowd had collected, and an officer read the sentence of the king—"to the death-prison!" All who enter there are condemned to die at some time. Moung Ing saw him hurled within and the door closed, then returned and reported to the distressed wife. He told her to be of good cheer, as he did not think they would kill her husband, and he would go himself to the prison enclosure and remain through the night, in order to render any service in his power.

. . . . , ... o

The old governor of the North Gate, Moung Shaw-loo, into whose charge all prisoners are consigned, was sitting in his apartment early next morning, dozing like a lazy Burman will, and entirely alone. The governor was a fat, jolly old fellow, kind-hearted and generous—a rare qualification in a Burmese official.

A bamboo door slowly opened and a man passed gently into the room unobserved. It was Moung Ing, his servant's livery contrasting strongly with his luxuriant surroundings. He advanced up the carpeted hall until he stood in front of its occupant, his face downcast and his eyes on the floor.

The old man started up in surprise and alarm, and exclaimed, "Who art thou, menial, to venture thus into my presence unannounced?"

For a moment there was no answer. Moung Ing was thinking of the cruel indignities inflicted on the teacher, whom he believed to have come all the way from America, God-sent, in answer to his prayers. The royal blood leaped in his veins. The sleeping lion within him awoke. Lifting his head proudly, while there danced in his eyes the fires of Alompra, he spoke in a stern voice, which, had it been pronounced in the great audience chamber, would have caused each hearer to tremble at its power.

"Moung Shwa-loo!" he cried; "dost thou not know me?"

The old man was thunderstruck to hear his name thus familiarly called by a menial; but astonishment gave place to fear and trembling as he gazed on the transfiguration of the man before him. His servant's robe was no longer seen, only the flashing eyes, proudly-lifted head and handsome form. The Golden Face himself could not have inspired such awe in the governor's heart. He saw before him the banished and beloved prince; and realized that he had spoken roughly to him. With pallor on his cheeks and trembling in his knees, he fell to the floor, clasping the prince by the feet and crying:

"My Lord Mekara, forgive me. I did not recognize you. Indeed I did not!"

Stooping, Mekara lifted the old man back to his seat. The royal passion had spent itself, and he was once more simple Moung Ing, the humble fisherman, servant of the teacher and devoted follower of the meek and lowly Nazarene.

"Your Excellency," he said in assuring tones, "be not afraid of me. I would never have revealed myself had it not been for circumstances that have just transpired demanding action on my part, even at the hazard of my life ; for it would be accounted nothing should my nephew, the Golden Face, hear of my presence here, in sight of the palace, which is in reality my own. Can I depend on you to keep my secret?"

"Command me anything, my Lord, and I will do it, to the extent of my life," replied the old man fervently.

"You know the circumstances connected with my banishment. I believed there was a God, and, as a consequence, could no longer worship at pagodas. For that was I disinherited. Since then I have wandered much, seeking God and praying him for light. I have found Him. The white teacher was impressed by His Spirit to bring the glad tidings of salvation, through a crucified Redeemer, to us who sit in darkness. I have consecrated my life to God's service. When I heard of my father's death, instead of coming and claiming my crown, which all would have gladly given me, I chose rather to be a private soldier of the Cross. By learning to preach I can do my people more good than by ruling over them. For this cause I study under the teacher and serve him. But the king has ordered him to the death-prison, whence few come out alive. This prison is in your keeping. The king's commands are executed through you. My request is that you will make the situation of the prisoners as comfortable as possible, and that you will spare the teacher's life, even contrary to the king's decree. You can hide him away, and his majesty will never know it Will you pledge me this?"

The old man reflected seriously for a moment. "It is a hard and dangerous thing, my Lord," he replied, "to disobey the king, and my life would pay the penalty should he know it; but I promised to do anything for you to the extent of my life, and I will do it. He shall not die while in my keeping."

"Good," replied Moung Ing; "and I shall trust you to keep your word. Treat kindly the white lady who shall visit you. Give her every privilege in your power, but say nothing of me. It is not safe that I should remain longer or return any more. God's mercy be with you."

He then passed out as unobserved as when he entered, leaving the old governor amazed at the apparition, as it were, of one whom he thought dead, and at the rash promises which he himself had made.

.   .   .   .

After Moung Ing had returned to the prison the evening before, the magistrate of the city came to examine Mrs. Judson. She had kept a carefully prepared journal of every event since coming to the city, but this, together with her other papers, she destroyed, lest they should be found to have correspondents in England. She then went out and submitted to the search, as well as answer a great many minute questions. The magistrate then departed after placing a guard of ten ruffians about the house with instructions to keep her safe and allow no one to go in or out on pain of death.

As it was now dark she retired to her inner room with Abbe and Mah-ree and barred the doors. There was immediately an uproar outside. The guard ordered her to unbar the doors and come out or they would tear the house down. This she obstinately refused to do, and finding her not to be intimidated by their threats, they resorted to another expedient. Capturing her two Bengalee servants, they carried them around opposite her window and confined them in the stocks; first laying them on their faces till their feet were fastened, then bending them backward till their shoulders lay on the ground behind, a most painful position. Ann could not endure to see the poor creatures thus suffering, and calling the headman to her window, she told him if he would release the servants she would give them all a present in the morning. This was very pleasing to their avaricious hearts, but they did not want her to think it an easy matter to influence them, and only consented after much debating, and many threats. But their diabolic carousing through the remainder of the night allowed her no rest. Climbing up on the walls of the unfinished brick house in front of the window, they yelled and screamed like demons, and made the night hideous by their satanic jests and malicious threats. Thus unprotected, even Moung Ing being away, she passed that first miserable night, equalled only by the sufferer in the death-prison.

The next day Moung Ing returned, at intervals, for food for the prisoners, and reported their condition. Ann was in deep distress because she could do nothing for her husband, being herself a prisoner. She begged the guard to let her go into the city and lay their case before some member of government, but they replied that they dared not, lest she escape. Penning a note, she sent it to the king's sister, begging her to lay the matter before the king. But she was afraid of the queen and refused to interfere.

Burmese Infantry

On the following night the guard, having been softened by gifts of tea and cigars, were not so boisterous,
yet the thought of her husband in chains prevented the
poor tired wife from resting again.

Next morning she sent a note to the governor requesting permission to visit him with a present. He kindly
consented and sent orders to the guards to let her come
into the city. The old man received her very pleasantly,
and seemed ready to grant any request in his power.
She stated to him the true situation of the foreigners,
and convinced him that the teachers, being Americans,
had nothing to do with the war and should not be confined. He replied:

"It is not in my power to release any of the prisoners,
but their situation can be made more comfortable.
There is my head officer who has charge of the prisoners, state fully to him what you desire in that respect."

The officer, to whom he referred her, was one of the
city writers, in whose face there seemed to be a concen-
tration of every evil passion common to the most de-
praved heart of man. Taking her to one side he said:

"Now, lady, not only are the prisoners in my power,
but you also are entirely at my disposal, and your comfort, as well as theirs, will depend altogether on your
liberality in regard to presents, and these must be made
to me privately, that no officer of government may
know it."

This much she had anticipated, knowing from former
experiences that only through a present could she gain
access to an ordinary Burman's heart.

"What must I do," she said, 'to obtain a mitigation
of the present sufferings of the two teachers?"

"Pay to me two hundred ticals, two pieces of fine cloth, and two pieces of handkerchiefs."

She had with her the amount of money demanded, but her house being two miles away, she could not conveniently return, and begged him to receive the money, and not insist on the other articles. He hesitated for a moment, looking with gloating eyes on the money, which amounted to about one hundred dollars; then, fearing to lose sight of so much, he accepted it and promised to relieve the prisoners as much as possible. The governor now gave her an order to the jailer for admittance into the prison, and she sped gladly away, hoping, at last, to meet her husband after those two days and nights of anxious separation and suffering.

CHAPTER II.

—Mrs. Sigourney.

THE death-prison stands on a bare, burning plain.
just without the city, with not even a palm to protect
its inmates from the fierce rays of the tropical sun
that dance and shimmer on its slatted sides, or scorch
its thinly thatched roof. The prison enclosure is a
spacious square, surrounded by a high wall of boards
held together by slats pinned on the outside. Within
this enclosure, and extending the whole length of one
side, is an open shed with the yard wall for its back.
Beneath this, in wretched, squalid filth, live the under
jailers, or children of the prison, with their leprous
wives and vermin-laden offspring. Without the wall
is a structure resembling a square haystack with steep
peaked roof, in which dwells the father of the establishment. All the sons of the prison are condemned
criminals, and may be recognized anywhere on account
of their spotted faces, the sign of outlawry being
branded with a red-hot iron ring on their cheeks; and
the name of their crime labeled in like manner on their
breasts. Their lives are only spared on condition of

(226)

their faithfulness and adaptness to execute all the cruel methods of torture resorted to by the tyrannical government. They have no possible means of escape, as their ineffaceable sign of guilt is ever visible and known. Their only daily occupation is to torture prisoners. The only music that ever greets their ears is composed of the shriek and groans of suffering victims. But as sameness in any occupation in life grows monotonous, they studiously display an ingenious variety in the tortures applied, and only those who make it a life-study could invent, with so few artificial or mechanical appliances, such different modes as they use. From continual and hereditary association with such a life, they acquire a passionate fondness for their occupation and nothing is to them such a source of amusement as to inflict their excruciating pains for the first time on a fresh victim, to see his writhings and listen with fiendish exultation to his ear-piercing cries. They never associate with any but prisoners; never see the great world outside, nor the pagan splendor of the palace. Within the prison walls they propagate their race, intermarrying only with each other and such unfortunate prisoners as they choose to spare for their base purposes. The wretched children, fruits of incest and adultery, grow up with the vice of their parents entailed upon them, born like them, and by association and practice, if possible, even worse—demons and fiends incarnate.

The head jailer bore on his breast the significant title, "loo-that," man-killer. He is described by Mrs. Emily C. Judson as "a tall bony man, with sinews of iron; wearing, when speaking, a malicious smirk, and given, at times, to a most revolting kind of jocoseness. When silent and quiet, he had a jaded, care-worn look; but it was at the torture that he was in his proper element. Then his face lighted up—became glad, furious, demoniac. IIis small black eyes glittered like those of a serpent; his thin lips rolled back, displaying his toothless gums in front, with a long, protruding tusk on either side, stained black as ebony; his hollow, ringed cheeks seemed to contract more and more, and his breast heaved with convulsive delight beneath the fearful word, MAN-KILLER. The prisoners called him father when he was present to enforce this expression of affectionate familiarity; but among themselves he was irreverently christened the Tiger-cat.

"One of the most active of the children of the prison was a short, broad-faced man, labelled thief, who, as well as the Tiger, had a peculiar talent in the way of torturing; and so fond was he of the use of the whip, that he often missed his count, and zealously exceeded the number of lashes ordered by the city governor. The wife of this man was a most odious creature; filthy, bold, impudent, cruel, and, like her husband, delighting in torture. Her face was not only deeply pitted with small-pox, but so deformed with leprosy, that the white cartilage of the nose was laid entirely bare; from her large mouth shone rows of irregular teeth, black as ink; her hair, which was left entirely to the care of nature, was matted in large, black masses about her head; and her manner, under all this hideous ugliness, was insolent and vicious. They had two children—little vipers, well loaded with venom; and by their vexatious mode of annoyance trying the temper of the prisoners more than was in the power of the mature torturers."

Such was the family under whose hospitable care the teachers were gladly welcomed; but the guest chamber —who can describe the grand apartment with its luxurious furnishings?

The prison was a building forty by thirty feet square. The sides were six feet high with a sloping roof fifteen feet high in the center. Around the walls were ranged long rows of stocks, composed of two logs with holes bored between, and fastened together with long, wooden pins; each holding a pair of helpless victims by the feet. There was no light by day except the faint rays that struggled through the chinks between the boards. By night a faint glimmer, only sufficient to "make the darkness visible," shone from a flame of impure earth-oil in an earthern cup, suspended from a tripod in the center. The only ventilation came with the light, and, of course, was equally, if not more, scanty. The prison had not been swept since it was built, yet it had been kept continually filled with the vilest of the land. There were no private accommodations and the consequent stench is indescribable. Here were huddled together more than a hundred people of all ages and ranks, and of both sexes. There sat cursing, a bandit thief and murderer; by his side, in sullen silence, was the a-twen-woon of yesterday, who had offended the Golden Face. Here, at the feet of the judge who delivered his sentence, lies the traitor. There was no distinction of race or caste in the death-prison. The laboring breath of so many filled the room with poisonous gas, added to which were the miasmatic vapors rising like steam from the heated grounds, covered with impurities. Every Burman chews the betel, and the pulp and juice of this abominable article, so like the filthy weed of our own country, covered the floor. The walls and rafters were moldy with the collections of vapors and dust. On the floor were ministers of torture not less terrible than the keepers. The dust seemed alive with hopping fleas of immense size and voracious jaws, and creeping vermin of every kind, so common to tropical countries.

The keepers never fed their prisoners. If one should enter there so unfortunate as to have no friend without who dared or was able to bring him food and drink, he must starve. Even then food was not admitted without a fee to the jailer. Many had no acquaintances in the city, and the consequent sufferings endured are horrible beyond description. Rolling in the heavy dust, vermin gnawing their writhing bodies, mosquitoes in hordes, stinging their fettered feet, gaunt hands and emaciated cheeks; their dry, dusty tongues crying pitifully for water, and their empty stomachs gnawing with hunger, seemed enough to melt any heart; yet the Tiger laughed at their miseries, and derived unspeakable delight from their sufferings. Often they would lie till the last stage of hunger was reached, perhaps on a gala-day. Then the women of the city would be allowed to enter with boiled rice, as a religious duty. The poor famished creatures would madly seize the bowls, gorge themselves on the contents; then the weak stomach, over-laden, would rebel, the muscles relapse, and the wretched creatures fall back, dead!

Such the chamber, accommodations, and room-mates of the teachers, and other foreigners.

A plank slided back at one end, causing the blinded eyes of the prisoners to blink at the sudden entrance of daylight from the outside world. But the entrance was darkened and the form of a man thrust in. It was Mr. Gouger, the English merchant. He was goaded on, over the prostrate bodies of those around him, to the center where the Tiger stood. The old parent received him joyfully, placed his long, filthy arms around him affectionately, and bidding him welcome to his home, at the same time clasping the flesh of his victim's back in his talon-like fingers and giving such a pinch that the poor man squirmed with pain.

"Now, my dear son," said he, "since you have become an inmate of my palatial residence"—and he gave a mischievous chuckle as he glanced at the surroundings —"I must proceed to invest you with the insignia of our royal household. You have on more clothing than is customary in this establishment, so you may dispense with these, which I will appropriate to my private use."

He then stripped him of coat, vest, hat and shoes.

"Now," he continued, "please be so kind as to repose on your back while I attach to your beautiful ankles these handsome rings."

Mr. Gouger glanced at the loathsome floor, in terror at the thought of polluting his body by contact with it, but there was no choice. The giant arms closed about him and laid him down as if he was an infant. His feet were laid upon an iron block and the three pairs of "ornaments' quickly adjusted, the rivets fastened, and the job was done Each blow of the hammer was accompanied by a jest and if, by a skillful miscalculation, the manipulator missed his mark and battered the rusty iron into the flesh, he laughed immoderately, as if it was a rich joke. The courteous host next seized his unwilling guest by the arm, and politely escorted him to the further end of the prison, and stretching him upon his back, left him in charge of the Thief, who was ordered to see that he lacked for nothing (in the way of torture.) The Tiger then returned to his block and awaited other patrons. Two other Englishmen soon made their appearance and were received with equal cordiality. Again the little door opened and the "wan teacher" was crowded in, stumbling over prostrate forms, and looking with horror on the miserable surroundings. To Mr. Judson, especially, was this being rolled in the dust and filth, revolting beyond measure. So fastidiously neat and clean was he in person that he bathed his body in pure cold water every day and his linen never showed the least spot. To him cleanliness was next to godliness, and he shrank more from this contamination with filth than from any other manner of torture. The father, with quick apprehension, saw what was most displeasing to his guest, and arranged matters, as he said, "congenial to his taste," by placing him in the worst place to be found. Another American soon followed, then a Greek, and at last, Dr. Price was led in and placed in the row with the others, filling out the rank.

"Now you have come," said one of the row, "our number is complete, and I suppose they will proceed to murder us. We hoped that you had escaped, you were so long in coming."

But they were abruptly forbidden to communicate again, except in Burman, and remained silent.

It was now growing dark. The flaring earth-oil light began to reveal dimly the silent forms lying in every conceivable attitude on the floor. The Tiger and the Thief now approached the line of white bodies upon the floor, bearing a long bamboo pole. This they passed between the ankles of each, just above the three pairs of fetters. Then placing the ends in the loops from ropes hanging from the rafters, they drew them up by means of pulleys, till the prisoners rested only on the backs of their necks, almost their whole weight supported by the fetters, which, coming together, pinched and cut the flesh in a fearful manner.

Thus shackled, poor Judson lay helpless as a babe. Added to his physical sufferings was the still more severe mental torture of anxiety for his family. Ann who had dared so much with him, and had been such a devoted help-meet to him, what would become of her in the hands of those hard-hearted officers? Yet he never lost faith in God. Sleep was impossible. Some-one suggested, "Let us pray," which each one did, after which they felt stronger to bear their sufferings, and like Paul and Silas, even sang hymns through the night. Thus they wore away the first long night.

Next morning the kind-hearted jailer returned, and graciously lowered the bamboo pole to within a foot of the ground, which allowed the blood once more to circulate through their benumbed limbs.

The door opened and Moung Ing appeared with food, not only for Mr. Judson, but for his companions.

"Give me a present," demanded the Thief at the door.

Moung Ing put a piece of silver in his hand and proceeded to the place where the teacher was lying with his comrades in misery. But the unwholesome odors pervading the place, and the idea of eating with unwashed hands, destroyed their appetites, and they only derived comfort from inquiring of Moung Ing the condition of their families.

That day passed. The sun beat against the thin sides of the building. The air was close and sweltering. The temperature stood above 100°, and the perspiration almost streamed from their bodies, and saturating their scanty clothes which, coming, in that state, in contact with the dust of the floor, soon acquired a color better imagined than described.

Another night; hoisted bamboo; and groans and prayers.

On the morrow a voice was heard without the door. The prisoners started. What music to their ears! Surely this loathsome place had never before heard anything so sweet. The guards grumbled but the voice overcame. The little door opened and a face appeared, a beautiful white face, with head of curly locks. Was it an angel? Aye, more. An angel would not have been so welcome, at least to Mr. Judson. He was now allowed to slip his feet from the pole and drag himself to the door. But the meeting that was anticipated with so much pleasure was painful to both. Revealed by the light of day, he stood with begrimed and impure exterior, a death-like pallor over his features, his face unshaven, and hair disheveled. The poor wife, having last seen him so neat, had not anticipated this, and at sight of him she covered her face with her hands in horror. Only a few words were they allowed to speak with each other, when the guard ordered her to come out.

"I have an order from the governor to come here," she pleaded.

"Come out," he demanded sternly, "or I will pull you out," and he seized her by the arm. She drew back from the door. The shutter was closed, leaving all once more in darkness and gloom. Yet, "ALL THINGS WORK TOGETHER FOR GOOD TO THEM THAT LOVE GOD." Is it true? It is, but how hard to believe!

CHAPTER III.

> " And were not there high words to flow
>   From woman's breaking heart?
> Through all that night of bitterest woe
>   She bore her lofty part;
> But oh! with such a freezing eye,
>   With such a curdling cheek!
> Love, love! of mortal agony,
>   Thou, only *thou* shouldst speak!"
>
> *—Gertrude, from Mrs. Hemans.*

THE death-prison has a remarkable, yet well-selected and appropriate motto—Let-ma-yoon, "hand, shrink not." Says Mr. Gouger in describing their tortures:

"It contemplates the extreme of human suffering, and when this has reached a point at which our nature recoils—when it is supposed that any one bearing the human form might well refuse to be the instrument to add to it, the hand of the executioner is apostrophized and encouraged not to follow the dictates of the heart: 'Thine eye shall not pity and thine hand not spare.'"

New prisoners arrived daily, and almost every day, at a certain hour, an executioner came in, and laying his hand on his victim's shoulder, led him forth as a sheep to the slaughter. Such scenes kept the prisoners in continual terror, for no one knew but that he would be the next one called, and the missionaries, as they saw so many hurried away without a moment's preparation, felt more and more the force of the Saviour's admonition, "BE YE ALSO READY." One event, however, aroused them more than all else. But my pen

refuses to paint the scene, and I surrender it to another.
Mrs. Emily C. Judson will finish the chapter.

.   .   .   .

"The arrival of a new prisoner was an incident calculated
to excite but little interest in the hat-wearers, provided he came
in turban and waist cloth. But one morning there was brought
in a young man speaking the Burmese brokenly, and with the
soft accent of the North, who at once attracted universal attention. He was tall and erect, with a mild, handsome face, bearing the impress of inexpressible suffering; a complexion
slightly tinted with the rich brown of the East; a fine, manly
carriage, and a manner which, even there, was both graceful
and dignified.

"'Who is he?' was the interpretation of the inquiring
glances exchanged among those who had no liberty to speak;
and then eye asked of eye, 'What can he have done? He is
so gentle, so mild, so manly, that even these wretches, who
scarcely know the name of pity and respect, seem to feel both
for him.' There was, in truth, something in the countenance
of the new prisoner which, without asking for sympathy,
involuntarily enforced it. It was not amiability, though his
dark, soft, beautiful eye was full of a noble sweetness; it was
not resignation; it was not apathy; it was hopelessness, deep,
utter, immovable, suffering hopelessness. Very young, and
apparently not ambitious or revengeful, what crime could this
interesting stranger have committed to draw down 'the golden
foot' with such crushing weight on his devoted head? He
seemed utterly friendless, and even without the means of obtaining food; for, as the day advanced, no one came to see him, and
the officer who brought him had left no directions. He did
not, however, suffer from this neglect, for Madam Thief (most
wonderful to relate!) actually shared so deeply in the universal
sympathy as to bring him a small quantity of boiled rice and
water.

"Toward evening the Woon-bai, a governor, or rather mayor
of the city, entered the prison, his bold, lion-like face as open
and unconcerned as ever, but with something of unusual
bustling in his manner.

"'Where is he?' he cried sternly, 'where is he, this son of Kathay—this dog, villain, traitor! where is he? Aha! only one pair of irons? Put on five! Do you hear? five!'

"The Woon-bai waited till his orders were executed, and the poor Kathayan was loaded with five pairs of fetters; and then he went out, frowning on one and smiling on another, all white children of the prison watched his coun'enance and manner as significant of what was expected of them. The prisoners looked at each other, and shook their heads in commiseration.

"The next day the feet of the young Kathayan, in obedience to some new order, were placed in the s'ocks, which raised them about eighteen inches from the ground, and the five pairs of fetters were all disposed on the outer side of the plank, so that their entire weight fell upon the ankles. The position was so painful that each prisoner, some from memory, some from sympathe'ic apprehension, shared in the pain when he looked at the sufferer.

"During this day, one of the missionaries, who had see honored with an invitation, which it was never prudent to refuse, to the hut of the thief, learned something of the his'ory of the young man and his crime. His home, it was told him, was among the rich hills of Kathay, as they range far northward, where the tropic sun loses the intense fierceness of his blaze, and makes the atmosphere soft and luxurious, as though it were mellowing beneath the same amber sky which ripens the fruits, and gives their glow to the flowers. What had been his rank in his own land, the jailer's wife did not know. Perhaps he had been a prince, chief of the brave band conquered by the superior forces of the Burmans ; or a hunter among the spicy groves and deep-wooded jungles, lithe as the tiger which he pursued from lair to lair, and free as the flame-winged bird of the sun that circled above him ; or perhaps his destiny had been a humbler one, and he had but followed the goats as they bounded from ledge to ledge, and plucked for food the herbs upon his native hills. He had been brought away by a marauding party, and presented as a slave to the brother of the queen. This Men-thah-gyee, the Great Prince,

as he was called by way of pre-eminence, had risen, through
the influence of his sister, from the humble position of a fish-
monger, to be the Richelieu of the nation. Unpopular from his
mean origin, and still more unpopular from the acts of brutality to which the intoxication of power had given rise, the sympathy excited by the poor Kathayan in the breasts of these
wretches may easily be accounted for. It was not pity or
mercy, but hatred. Anywhere else, the sufferer's sad, handsome face, and mild uncomplaining manner, would have
enlisted sympathy ; but here, they would scarcely have seen
the sadness, or beauty, or mildness, except through the medium of a passion congenial to their own natures.

"Among the other slaves of Men-thah-gyce, was a young
Kathay girl of singular beauty. She was, so said Madam, the
thief, a burdle of roses, set round with blossoms of the cham-
pac tree ; her breath was like that of the breezes when they
come up from their dalliance with the spicy daughters of the
islands of the South ; her voice had caught its rich cadence
from the musical gush of the silver fountain, which wakes
among the green of her native hills ; her hair had been braided
from the glossy raven plumage of the royal edolius ; her eyes
were twin stars looking out from cool springs, all fringed with
the long tremulous reeds of the jungle ; and her step was as
the free, graceful bound of the wild antelope. On the subject
of her beauty, her grace and her wondrous daring, the jailer's
wife could not be sufficiently eloquent. And so this poor,
proud, simple-souled maiden, this diamond from the rich hills
of Kathay, destined to glitter for an hour or two on a prince's
bosom, unsubdued even in the desolation, had dared to bestow
her affections with the uncalculating loveliness of conscious
heart-freedom. And the poor wretch, lying upon his back in
the death-prison, his feet fast in the stocks and swelling and
purpling beneath the heavy irons, had participated in her
crime ; had lured her on, by tender. glances and by loving
words, inexpressibly sweet in their mutual bondage, to irretrievable destruction. What fears, what hopes winged by fears,
what tremulous joys, still hedged in by that same crowd of
fears, what despondency, what revulsions of impotent anger

and daring, what weeping, what despair must have been theirs! Their tremblings and rejoicings, their mad projects, growing each day wilder and more dangerous—since madness alone could have given rise to anything like hope—are things left to imagination ; for there was none to relate the heart-history of the two slaves of Men-thah-gyee. Yet there were some hints of a first accidental meeting under the shadow of the mango and tamarind trees, where the sun lighted up, by irregular gushes, the waters of the little lake in the center of the garden, and the rustle of leaves seemed sufficient to drown the accents of their native tongues. So they looked, spoke, their hearts bounded, paused, trembled with soft home-memories —they whispered on and they were lost. Poor slaves !

"Then at evening, when the dark-browed maidens of the golden city, gathered with their earthen vessels about the well, there, shaded by the thick clumps of bamboo, with the free sky overhead, the green earth beneath, and the songs and laughter of the merry girls ringing in their ears, so like their old home, the home which they had lost forever—oh what a rare, sweet, dangerous meeting-place for those who should not, and yet must be lovers !

" Finally came a day fraught with illimitable consequences ; the day when the young slave, not yet admitted to the royal harem, should become more than ever the property of her master. And now deeper grew their agony, more uncontrollable their madness, wilder and more daring their hopes, with every passing moment. Not a man in Ava but would have told them that escape was impossible ; and yet, goaded on by love and despair, they attempted the impossibility. They had countrymen in the city, and, under cover of night, they fled to them. Immediately the minister sent out his myrmidons— they were tracked, captured, and brought back to the palace.

" 'And what became of the poor girl ?' inquired the missionary with much interest.

"The woman shuddered, and beneath her scars and the swarthiness of her skin, she became deadly pale.

" 'There is a cellar, Tsayah,' at last she whispered, still shuddering, ' a deep cellar, that no one has seen, but horrible cries come from it sometimes, and two nights ago, for three hours, three long hours—such shrieks ! Amai-ai ! What shrieks!

"And they say that he was there, Tsayah, and saw and heard it all. That is the reason that his eyes are blinded and his ears benumbed. A great many go into that cellar, but none ever come out again—none but the doomed like him. It is—*it is like the West Prison*, she added, sinking her voice still lower, and casting an eager, alarmed look about her. The missionary, too, shuddered, as much at the mention of this prison as at the recital of the woman ; for it shut within its walls deep mysteries, which even his jailers, accustomed as they were to torture and death, shrank from babbling of.

"The next day a cord was passed around the wrists of the young Kathayan, his arm jerked up into a position perpendicular with his prostrate body, and the end of the cord fastened to a beam overhead. Still, though faint from the lack of food, parched with thirst and racked with pain—for his feet were swollen and livid—not a murmur of complaint escaped his lips. And yet this patient endurance seemed scarcely the result of fortitude or heroism. An observer would have said that the inner suffering was so great as to render that of the mere physical frame unheeded. There was the same expression of hopelessness, the same unvarying wretchedness, too deep, too real, to think of giving itself utterance on the face, as at his first entrance into the prison, and except that now and then he fixed on one of the hopeless beings who regarded him in silent pity, a mournful, half-beseeching, half-vacant stare—this was all.

"That day passed away, as others had done ; then came a night of dreams, in which loved ones gathered around the hearthstone of a dear, familiar home—dreams broken by the clanking of chains and the groans of the suffering ; and then morning broke. There still hung the poor Kathayan, his face slightly distorted with the agony he was suffering, his lips dry and parched, his cheek pallid and sunken and his eyes wild and glaring. His breast swelled and heaved, and now and then a sob-like sigh burst forth involuntarily. When the Tiger entered, the eye of the young man immediately fastened

16

on him and a shiver passed through his frame. The old murderer went his usual rounds with great nonchalance, gave an order here, a blow there, and cracked a malicious joke with a third, smiling all the time that dark, sinister smile which made him so much more hideous in the midst of his wickedness. At last he approached the Kathayan, who, with a convulsive movement, half raised himself from the ground at his touch and seemed to contract like a shrivelled leaf.

"'Right! right, my son!' said the old man, chuckling. 'You are expert at helping yourself, to be sure; but, then, you need assistance. So, so, so!' and giving the cord three successive jerks, he succeeded, by means of his immense strength, in raising the Kathayan so that but the back of his' head, as it fell downward, could touch the floor. There was a quick, short crackling of joints, and a groan escaped the prisoner. Another groan followed, and then another and another; a heaving of the chest, a convulsive shiver, and for a moment he seemed lost. Human hearts glanced heavenward. 'God grant it! Father of mercies, spare him further agony!' It could not be. Gaspingly came the last breath back again, quiveringly the soft eyes unclosed, and the young Kathayan captive was fully awake to his miseries.

"'I cannot die so; I cannot! So slow! so slow! so slow!' Hunger gnawed, thirst burned, fever revelled in his veins; the cord upon his wrists cut to the bone; corruption had already commenced upon his swollen, livid feet; the most frightful, torturing pains distorted his body, and wrung from him groans and murmurings so pitiful, so harrowing, so full of anguish, that the unwilling listeners could only turn away their heads or lift their eyes to each other's faces in mute horror. Not a word was exchanged among them—not a lip had power to give it utterance.

"'I cannot die so! I cannot die so! I cannot die so!' came the words—at first moaningly, and then prolonged to a terrible howl. And so passed another day and another night, and still the wretch lived on.

"In the midst of their filth and smothering heat, the prisoners awoke from such troubled sleep as they could gain amid these horrors; and those who could, pressed their feverish lips and foreheads to the crevices between the boards to court the morning breezes. A lady with a white brow, and a lip whose delicate vermillion had not ripened beneath the skies of India, came with food to her husband. By constant importunities had the beautiful ministering angel gained this holy privilege. Her coming was like a gleam of sunlight—a sudden unfolding of the beauties of this bright earth to one born blind. She performed her usual tender ministry and departed.

"Day advanced to its meridian, and once more, but now hesitatingly, as if he dreaded his task, the Tiger drew near the young Kathayan. But the sufferer did not shrink from him as before.

"'Quick!' he exclaimed greedily. 'Quick! give me one hand and the cord; just a moment, a single moment—this hand, with the cord in it—and you shall be rid of me forever!'

"The Tiger burst into a hideous laugh, his habitual cruelty returning at the sound of his victim's voice

"'Rid of you? Not so fast, my son; not so fast. You will hold out a day or two yet. Let me see'—passing his hand along the emaciated feverish body of the sufferer. 'Oh, yes; two days, at least—perhaps three; and it may be longer. Patience, my son. You are frightfully strong! Now, these joints—why, any other man's would have separated long ago; but here they stay just as firmly'—. As he spoke with a calculating sort of deliberation, the monster gave the cord a sudden jerk, then another, and a third, raising his victim still farther from the floor, and then adjusting it about the beam, walked unconcernedly away. For several minutes the prison rang with the most fearful cries. Shriek followed shriek—agonized, furious—with scarcely a breath between; bellowings, howlings, gnashings of the teeth; sharp, piercing screams; yells of savage defiance; cry upon cry, cry upon cry; with wild, superhuman strength they came; while the prisoners shrank in awe and terror, trembling in their chains. But this violence soon exhausted itself and the paroxysm passed, giving place to low, sad moans, irresistibly pitiful. This was a day never to be forgotten by the hundred wretched creatures congregated in the gloomy death-prison. The sun had never seemed to move so slowly before. Its setting was gladly welcomed; but yet the night brought no change. Those piteous moans, those agonized groanings seemed no nearer an end than ever.

"Another day passed—another night; again day dawned and drew near its close; and yet the poor Kathayan clung to life with frightful tenacity. One of the missionaries, as a peculiar favor, had been allowed to creep into an old shed opposite the door of the prison, and here he was joined by a companion just as the day was declining towards evening.

"'Oh! will it ever end?' whispered one.

"The other bowed his head between his hands. 'Terrible! terrible!'

"'There surely can be nothing worse in the West Prison.'

"'Can there be anything worse—can there be more finished demons in the pit?'

"Suddenly, while this broken conversation was conducted in a low tone, so as not to draw upon the speakers the indignation of their jailers, they were struck by the singular stillness of the prison. The clanking of chains, the murmur and the groan, the heavy breathing of congregated living beings, the bustle occasioned by the continuous uneasy movement of the restless sufferers, the ceaseless tread of the Children of the Prison and their bullying voices, all were hushed.

"'What is it?' in a lower whisper than ever, and a shaking of the head, and holding their own chains to prevent their rattle, and looks full of wonder, was all that passed between the two listeners. Their amazement was interrupted by a dull, heavy sound, as though a bag of dried bones had been suddenly crushed down by the weight of some powerful foot. Silently they stole to a crevice in the boards opposite the open door. Not a jailer was to be seen, and the prisoners were motionless and apparently breathless, with the exception of one powerful man, who was just drawing the wooden mallet in his hand for another blow on the temple of the suspended Kathayan. It came down with the same dull, hollow, crushing sound. The body swayed from the point where it was held by wrist and ankle till it seemed that every joint must be dislocated ; but the flesh scarcely quivered. The blow was repeated, and then another and another ; but they were not needed. The poor captive Kathayan was dead.

"The mallet was placed away from sight, and the daring man hobbled back to his corner, dangling his heavy chain as though it had been a plaything, and striving with all his might to look unconscious and unconcerned. An evident feeling of relief stole over the prisoners, the Children of the Prison came back to their places one by one, and all went on as before. It was some time before any one appeared to discover the death of the Kathayan. The old Tiger declared it was what he had been expecting ; that his living on in this manner was quite out of rule ; but that these hardy fellows from the hills never would give in while there was a possibility of drawing another breath. Then the poor skeleton was unchained, dragged by the heels into the prison yard and thrown into a gutter. It did not, apparently, fall properly, for one of the jailers altered the position of the shoulders by means of his foot; then clutching the long, black hair, jerked the head a little further on the side. Thus the discolored temple was hidden ; and surely that emaciated form gave suf-ficient evidence of a lingering death. Soon after, a party of government officers visited the prison yard, touched the corpse with their feet without raising it, and, apparently satisfied, turned away as though it had been a dead dog that they cared not to give further attention."

CHAPTER IV.

On the day after Mrs. Judson's first visit to the governor and the prison, Mr. Gouger's property, to the amount of fifty thousand rupees, was confiscated, and the officers, in passing, informed Mrs. Judson that they would call on her the next day. Taking advantage of this warning, she secreted as many articles of value as possible, together with considerable silver and Mr. Judson's manuscript translation of the New Testament. It was a hazardous thing to do, for if it had been discovered it would have caused her being thrown into prison—in which case she could no longer minister to her husband.

The following morning the royal treasurer, with the governor and another nobleman, attended by forty or fifty followers, came to take possession of their property in the king's name. She did not become in the least frightened nor lose her presence of mind, though evidently deeply affected at the thought of being deprived of all they had. She received them civilly, gave them chairs to sit on—quite a luxury to an Oriental—and placed her nicest tea and sweetmeats for their refreshment. Only the three officers, accompanied by the royal secretary, entered the house, the attendants being ordered to remain without.

(246)

Moung Shwa-loo, seeing the distress of the woman whom he had promised the prince to defend, felt very reluctant to lay his hands on anything in the house; yet he must make a show of confiscation, as he was compelled to report to the king. He sincerely apologized for the deed, and told her how painful it was to him to take that which was not his own. But the treasurer, ignorant of the circumstances that prompted this kindness of the governor, proceeded at once to business.

"Where are your silver, gold and jewels?" he inquired.

"I have no gold or jewels," she said; "but here is the key that unlocks the trunk containing the silver. Do with it as you please."

The trunk was opened, the silver weighed, and a note taken of the amount.

"This silver," she said, "was collected in America by the disciples of Christ to build a priest's dwelling and for our support while preaching the religion of Jesus. Is it suitable that you should take it?"

She knew the Burmese were averse to taking anything offered for religious purposes.

"We will state the circumstances to the king," said the treasurer; "perhaps he will return it. But is this all the silver you have?"

"The house is in your possession. Search for yourselves."

"Have you not deposited silver with some person of your acquaintance?"

"My acquaintances are all in prison. With whom should I deposit silver?"

The governor evidently suspected that she had concealed the articles; but he had gone as far as he was compelled to do by the king's decree, and quickly changed the subject by calling for the trunks and drawers. Neither he nor the treasurer touched these, but asked the secretary to accompany Mrs. Judson in the search. Everything he found nice or curious was presented to them, to decide whether or not she should be allowed to keep it. When the wearing apparel was produced, she begged them not to take that, as it would be disgraceful to carry partly-worn clothing into the presence of the king. They assented to this, and merely took a list—as they did also with the books and medicine By a cunning artifice, she also persuaded them that it would be improper to take her little work-table and rocking-chair, which had been presented her by friends in America; yet they appropriated everything that could be of service to his majesty and departed. She gave a sigh of relief as they passed out, leaving so many articles of inestimable value during the approaching hardships; but her eyes filled with tears to see her many little comforts and mementoes of friends and relatives borne away on the shoulders of Burman slaves.

The officers reported to the king:

"Judson is a true teacher. We found nothing in his house but what belongs to priests. In addition to this money, there are an immense number of books, medicines, trunks of wearing apparel, &c., of which we only took a list. Shall we take them, or let them remain?"

"Let them remain," replied his majesty; "and put this property by itself, for it shall be restored again if he is found innocent."

Mrs. Judson, by her continual entreaty, had prevailed on the wife of the queen's brother to intercede, through the queen, for Mr. Judson's release. As soon as the officers left her house she flew to the house of the queen's brother, anxious to know the result of her petition. But she was met by the cool answer:

"I stated your case to the queen; but her majesty replied, 'The teachers will not die; let them remain as they are.'"

Her hopes had been high; but this news was like a thunder-clap to her feelings, and she was, for a moment, almost in despair; for if the queen refused, who would dare to intercede before the Golden Face for a foreigner in disgrace? Sadly she turned away to return, with a heavy heart, to her home, two miles from the city, stopping at the prison to communicate her failure to Mr. Judson; but the gate was shut and she was harshly refused admittance. For ten days she was not allowed to enter again, but sent food for the white prisoners by Moung Ing. Yet she never ceased her efforts. Day after day, for seven long, weary months, she continued to importune some members of government to intercede with the king for the release of the prisoners. Among the members of the royal family she made many friends by these visits, who really desired to aid her; but their influence only assisted her by encouraging promises that preserved her from despair. The governor became very much attached to her, and would send for her if by any means she failed to visit him daily. He listened with eagerness to her descriptions of American manners and customs, arts and sciences. His wife also bestowed upon her a mark of affection by presenting her with a handsome Burman costume, such as the court ladies wear. She persuaded her to wear this while in the city, as it would tend to conciliate the people. Mah Po, a sweet, proud, but tender-hearted woman, and wife of a chief minister, often braved the anger of the king to give rice and eggs to the white lady, with which to feed the prisoners. Home and friends were forgotten by the faithful wife; self was forgotten. Not a fear possessed her as she trod alone the burning streets of that wicked heathen city, where pride and bigotry ruled. Her only thought was of a husband in chains and how to relieve him. She did not even shrink from the brawny frame of the Tiger, the cruel face of the spotted Thief, nor the hideous countenance of his leprous wife.

One day she was detained at home from some unavoidable cause, and consented to let Moung Ing carry the dinner to the prison, which she had formerly insisted upon doing herself, when allowed, in order to see with her own eyes how her husband fared. A happy thought struck her: she would make for Mr. Judson a mince pie, to remind him of home, doubting not that it would bring a smile to his face even in the midst of his misery. Her ingenuity in collecting material for this tempting dish, in such a country, must be equal to her perseverance in other things; but she at length succeeded to her satisfaction; and there was the old sparkle of girlish light in her eyes as she handed the dish to Moung Ing, with instructions to observe closely the teacher's countenance as he received it. Moung Ing had never seen the sumptuous tables of Plymouth and Bradford, but he conjectured that there must be something nice hidden under the snowy cloth, itself an unusual sight in the death-prison, and he could not restrain a smile as he passed it to Mr. Judson.

Lifting the cloth, the poor captive sat for a moment in mute astonishment at what he would have considered an impossible achievement in Ava. Then he thought of the devotion that prompted and the care that produced it. Visions rose up in his mind: a sweet face, framed in dark curls, peering through the half-open door into the gloomy death-prison; a delicate female form, standing like an enchantress, before the august tribunal of Burmese authority and fearlessly pleading for him; a faithful wife, two miles from the city, in her little home with her Burman maidens, planning pleasant surprises for him. Like a panorama these scenes passed before him; then a blank, an ocean voyage, a "home beyond the sea," father, mother and sisters; then, as he gazed into the depths of the dainty dish, a fairer picture. He was again, for the first time, at Bradford; his companions were discussing the prospects of the mission—he could, even now, hear their eager voices; a sweet girl, with maidenly grace and reserve, passes him a dainty morsel, like this, and in a modest manner invites him to partake; he feels her presence by his side, once more the flutterings of a youthful heart with its first love, and he reads again the verses in his plate. As in a dream, he lifts his hand to the dish; it is begrimed with perspiration and dust; a chain on his wrist rattles against the plate. The beautiful vision fades, and in its stead appear the dusty beams and rafters of the prison, the stocks, chains and dreadful bamboo. It was too much.

Bowing his head on his knees, he wept like a child, and thrusting the untasted dinner into the hands of his companion, he hobbled off to a corner to weep alone. That brave heart, that had for so long and so manfully withstood the cruelties of demons, is melted by the tender recollections of a faithful woman's love.

. . . .

The war down the river was now raging. To the surprise of the king, the terrible name, Golden Face had not conveyed the least terror to the hearts of the trained British soldiers; the invincible army that had departed with such assurance of success, had been dispelled like a cloud of thistle-down and feathers; and their golden war-boats crushed like gilded egg-shells beneath the iron keel of the British man-of-war. But another part of the Burman army, stationed in Arracan, under Bandoola, was having greater success, having sent three hundred prisoners to the capital at one time. His majesty, thinking that none but Bandoola understood the art of fighting foreigners, recalled him to take charge of the army sent to Rangoon. Arriving at Ava, he was received with great pomp and ceremony, the king and queen doing all in their power to honor him. The affairs of the war, and even of the kingdom, were given into his hands for the time.

Mrs. Judson had tried every resort hitherto for the release of her husband, but a new man having come into authority, she decided to apply to him, though several of her friends warned her not to do so, as it would likely remind him of the existence of the prisoners, and cause their immediate execution. But it was the only hope and she could not let the opportunity pass. Mr. Judson himself wrote a petition which she bore boldly to the great general. He received her very politely, heard the petition read by a royal secretary, and after inquiring several things of her in regard to the prisoners, he replied that he would consider the subject and invited her to come again. She was over-joyed at their prospect of success, and hastened to bear the news of her reception to Mr. Judson. Both now considered that the time of release was near at hand; but the governor was amazed at the indiscretion of his prisoner and his wife, and said he feared it would cause their death which he would be powerless to prevent.

After a day or two Mrs. Judson returned to the pavilion of the general with a valuable present. Ban-doola was not at home; but his wife, after receiving the present, reported that he was very busily employed in his preparations for the war, and had said when he should have regained Rangoon, and expelled the Eng-lish, he would return and release all the prisoners.

That destroyed every hope of release before the ter-mination of the war, and all that could now be done would be to make the prisoners as comfortable as the jailers would allow.

Through the influence of this untiring woman, the prisoners were allowed to come out into the open air and hobble about the yard as best they could with their fettered feet, and rest, at times, under an open shed, but always attended by a keeper. By the help of Moung Ing, Mrs. Judson erected a little bamboo room in the yard and obtained permission from the governor to let Mr. Judson stay in there where she could minister to him. Hitherto they had been allowed to speak only in

Burman, but as soon as this restraint was removed, Mr. Judson inquired for the manuscript copy of the New Testament which had cost him so much labor. It was found safely hid away at home, where it had been concealed from the officers, and fearing it might be injured by mold or destroyed, they sewed it up in a pillow and kept it in the little room.

By making presents to the jailers Mrs. Judson often obtained the privilege of coming to the little room and spending two or three hours a day with her husband. This was an inexpressible joy to them, and they enjoyed each other's society more than did the king and queen in the golden palace, harassed by defeats in war. On these occasions Mrs. Judson left the house and teaching of the little girls to Moung Ing, who showed great attachment for them.

CHAPTER V.

—Mrs. Emily C. Judson.

THERE came a time when the angel visits to the palace ceased. For twenty days the governor sat in solitude because his fair entertainer was absent. The government for once, had a respite from daily appeals in behalf of condemned foreigners. The jailers now received no more presents, and, as a consequence, comforts were withdrawn, and the prisoners more frequently confined within the prison. Moung Ing came every day with food and reported the condition of his mistress.

Mr. Judson, during this time, suffered mental agony and suspense, with which his former bodily tortures could not compare. A crisis was approaching, at the very thought of which every Christian mother's heart must bleed in sympathy for the lone young wife in that savage country. Assisted only by a Portuguese nurse, she passed through the terrible trial and all was well.

On the morning of the twentieth day after her confinement, the prison door was opened, and the anxious father summoned from his gloomy corner to meet his loved ones. There in the door-way stood, what was to him, the loveliest scene of his life. His faithful Ann, clad in the rich dress, the present of the governor's wife. "Her dark curls carefully straightened, drawn

(255)

back from her forehead, and a fragrant cocoa blossom drooping like a white plume from the knot upon the crown; her saffron vest thrown open to disclose the folds of crimson beneath; and a rich, silken skirt, wrapped closely about her fine figure, parting at the ankle and sloping back upon the floor.   .   .   .
Behold her standing in the door-way (for she was never permitted to enter the prison), her little blue-eyed blossom wailing, as it almost always did, upon her bosom, and the chained father crawling forth to the meeting." IIis companions who were chained with him, all shuffled simultaneously towards the door. The trembling father took the tiny form into his arms and gazed into the tearful blue eyes with such feelings as can be rarely experienced by parents in a civilized land. They called her Maria, a child of sorrow, and so her life proved how appropriate was the name. Born in sorrow she never knew a well day, and the mother's love was only stronger for the poor little creature that always moaned even when asleep. The scene of the meeting was so affecting that even the Thief burst into tears, and the Tiger, to stifle the faint feeling of tenderness welling up in his own savage bosom, rattled on the door, and ordered them to part, and the door was shut.

"Go, darling infant, go;
Thine hour has passed away;
The jailers' harsh, discordant voice
Forbids thy longer stay.

"God grant that we may meet
In happier times than this,
And with thine angel mother dear
Enjoy domestic bliss."

A vision of the " white mamma " again in the prison-yard once more stimulated the jailers to a hope of reward, and they allowed the prisoners to come out into the prison enclosure, as formerly, and Mr. Judson to rest in his little bamboo room, visited as often as possible by his ever-busy wife, who now must care both for him and the child.

Mahree, though scarcely more than a child at her adoption, had grown wonderfully during the seven months since then, and gladly assumed the office of nurse. Moung Ing, with almost a father's care, overlooked the affairs of the little family, filling Mr. Judson's position as near as it was possible for any one to fill it. His devotion to the winning, black-eyed lass, Mahree, and to the puny babe, was something remarkable. He also taught Mahree and Abbe in the absence of Mrs. Judson, and made himself an indispensable member of the family.

It was only for a short time that affairs were permitted to remain thus bright and hopeful. A royal messenger suddenly arrived in great haste, and announced in the palace the total defeat of Bandoola and the destruction of his magnificent army of invincibles. The king was dumb with silent, stupefied amazement. The queen smote on her breast and ran wildly about the palace, crying, "Ama! Ama!" The invincible Bandoola was defeated. Who could take his place? The English were proceeding steadily up the river, already as far as Prome, and the common people were whispering of rebellion if forced to raise another army from their resources, for as yet not a rupee had been taken from the royal treasury. All the spite was taken

17

out on the prisoners. They were seized in the yard, and having their ankles enclosed in five pairs of fetters, were hurled again into the inner prison and the bamboo passed between their legs, resting on one foot, while the other foot, with its fifteen pounds of iron added to the pole, almost crushed it into the ground. The little bamboo room was torn down, and one of the keepers carried the pillow and mattress to his own shed.

Herded thus together and bearing the additional fetters, the condition of the prisoners was now worse than ever. Night came on. A whisper went around that they were to be led out to execution in the morning. The keepers outside the door sharpened their long, flashing knives, and brandished them about to show how gladly they would perform their task. But why need the prisoners fear? Death was preferable to such a life as this. Mr. Judson sat musing. He regretted that he was not allowed to bid his wife and child farewell. Death in itself would be desirable. His faithful companion would no longer be subject to care on his account, but with her child, under the faithful care of Moung Ing, she could escape to the approaching British line and find safety. It would be better for her and better for the child. Then he thought of the pillow containing the precious manuscript, and wondered if it would ever be found and rescued. The long night dragged heavily by. The solemn hour of three drew near, the hour when all executions took place, and when they had seen so many of their fellow-prisoners led out at the sound of the watch-gong. The prisoners prayed, Mr. Judson leading, then all prayed separately. The hour was near. Not a breath could be heard. Not a chain rattled.

"Yoang! yoang! yoang!" three times sounded the deep-voiced gong in the palace yard. They were all in readiness, but not a keeper stirred. An hour passed, and yet no sign. Could they have been deceived? A faint glimmer through the cracks on the eastern side, and they knew day was at hand, and they were spared, at least till another night. The door opened and the Tiger entered, cordially poking all whom he passed and kicking those at his feet. He chuckled the white prisoners under the chin, and in answer to their questions replied:

"Oh, no; I could not spare my children yet, just after taking so much trouble to procure them fitting ornaments." Here he gave the bamboo such a kick that the chains rattled and the five pairs of fetters crowded together, pinching the flesh between, till they almost screamed with pain.

At this period a pakan-woon who had suffered the disgrace of being thrown into prison by the king, now offered his services to lead another army against the British. His offer was accepted, and he was commissioned as general of the new troops collected. He was a violent enemy of all foreigners, and it was to him that the prisoners owed their return to torture.

As soon as Mrs. Judson heard of the confinement of the prisoners and their additional fetters, she went at once to the governor's house. He was away, but left word if she came that she must not ask the removal of the fetters nor the release of the prisoners, for it could not be done. She went to the prison, but was refused admittance. All was still as death within. Not a rattle of a chain disturbed the oppressive silence. She could not rest without making one effort for their comfort, and she determined to see the governor and at least learn the cause of the new torture. So she returned to the city that evening at an hour when she knew he was always there. He was sitting alone in the audience chamber, and received her in silence, his face showing a feeling of shame mixed with affected anger at the intrusion. She began without ceremony:

"Your lordship has hitherto treated us with the kindness of a father. Our obligations to you are very great. We have looked to you for protection from oppression and cruelty. You have in many instances mitigated the sufferings of those unfortunate, though innocent, beings committed to your charge. You have promised me particularly that you would stand by me till the last, and though you should receive an order from the king, you would not put Mr. Judson to death. What crime has he committed to deserve such additional punishment?"

The expression of his face when she entered, changed as she began to plead, and he showed the true feeling of his heart for her and her suffering. Covering his face with his hands, he wept like a child.

"I pity you, Tsa-yah-ga-dau," he said. "I knew you would make me feel; I therefore forbade your application. But you must believe me when I say I do not wish to increase the sufferings of the prisoners. When I am ordered to execute them, the least I can do is to put them out of sight. I will now tell you what I have never told you before—that three times I have received intimations from the queen's brother to assassinate all the white prisoners privately; but I would not do it.

And I now repeat it, though I execute all others I will never execute your husband. But I cannot release him from his present confinement, and you must not ask it."

She now understood the old man better than ever and placed more confidence in his promises. But she must depend upon herself and Moung Ing to make the prisoners as comfortable as possible.

Mah Po, though the rich lady of a court minister, often traversed the two miles of dusty road to the mission-house, carrying provisions and helping Mahree to care for the feeble babe while its mother sped away to the prison.

A month's confinement in his densely heated and loathsome apartment, threw Mr. Judson into a raging fever, from which, death, in such a place, was inevitable. Sometime before, a new prisoner had appeared in the enclosure in the form of a lion in his cage. The lion had been a favorite pet of the king, but some of the refugees from the destroyed armies reported that the British displayed a lion on their standard, and they were sure that the success of the foreigners was due to the lion in the palace, which they thought beguiled the king's heart. It was therefore sent to the death-prison as condemned to die, yet the king commanded that he should not be executed without his orders. The queen's brother, who did most of the mischief connected with the prison, left orders that the beast should not be fed— which would insure his death, even without the king's order. So, day after day, the huge creature stood in his narrow house, roaring horribly, or madly dashing himself against the bars. It was even a worse sight than the death of the poor Kathayan to see the royal monster pining away, the tawny skin hanging from his gaunt sides, and his mad eyes glaring in their sunken sockets. At length, however, his majestic strength succumbed to the ravages of hunger, and he was carried out, a sack of dry bones, to be thrown into the gutter, there to await the inquest of the government officers. Mr. Judson thought the vacant cage would make an airy couch for him in his illness, and, through the earnest pleading of his wife, the governor allowed him to be removed there. Even this change, however, did not have its desired effect, and it seemed that he must die.

Mrs. Judson brought Moung Ing with her to the city, and they erected a little bamboo room in the governor's yard opposite the prison gate. She now importuned the governor to let her bring Mr. Judson into the little room, where she could stay with him and nurse him through his sickness. He refused, saying it was impossible.

Nothing daunted, she renewed the request so incessantly, day by day, that his patience was exhausted and he gave her the desired permission, with a written order to the jailers to allow her to pass freely in and out of the gates. She was now happy. With the assistance of Moung Ing, she brought the sick man out of the cage and placed him in the little room, which was to him a palace, in contrast to the filth of his former abode. The medicine chest was now brought, and Mrs. Judson, having sent for Mahree and the child, took her station by the sick-bed, while Moung Ing took charge of affairs at home and brought their daily provisions.

One morning, two or three days after their removal into the little room, Mrs. Judson came in with her husband's breakfast; but he was so ill from the effects of the fever that he could not eat. She sat down by the mattress to soothe him as much as possible by bathing his burning brow and speaking gently to him. Mahree had been sent home with the child, in company with Moung Ing, who brought their breakfast—so they were entirely alone.

Suddenly a messenger came rushing in, in great haste. "Tsa-yah-ga-dau!" he cried. "The governor wishes to see you immediately."

Much wondering what could be the cause of this hasty summons, and suspecting that something fearful was about to happen, she arose quickly, and telling Mr. Judson that she would return as soon as she found what the governor wanted, she departed with the messenger.

The old man was in an unusually pleasant mood and soon put her fears to flight. He wished to consult her about his watch—an uncommon novelty in Burmah. He drew her out on the various beauties of its design and the wonderful workings of its wheels, holding her in pleasant conversation for half an hour. At length she excused herself, saying that Mr. Judson was very unwell—not able to eat his food—and she must return to give him his medicine. Passing out the door, she was met by a servant with a ghastly face, who informed her that the white prisoners were carried away, he knew not whither. The news so stunned her that she could not believe it. Returning to the governor, she inquired if it was true. He replied that he had just heard it through the same messenger, but did not know what had become of them. She then ran hastily into the street to see if she could see them, before they got out of sight; but she saw nothing of them. She then ran from street to street, inquiring of all she met; but no one would give her an answer. Crossing another street, she found Mah Po, who seemed also excited, and who informed her that the prisoners had been taken toward the little river, and that they were to be carried to Amarapura, the former capital, six miles away. She then ran to the little river; but seeing no sign of them, concluded that the kindly old woman had deceived her, and that something worse had happened; but some friends of the foreigners whom she had sent to the place of execution returned and said they were not there, so she returned to the governor to try and find the cause of their removal and what was intended by it. The old man told her that he had had no intimation of the intention of the government to remove them till that morning, and that he had only learned since she went out that they were to be carried to Amarapura. "But for what purpose," he said, "I know not. I will send off a man immediately to see what is to be done with them. You can do nothing for your husband; *take care of yourself.*" The Pakan-woon had instituted great cruelties in the city and the governor advised her not to go on the street alone. But he knew not yet the indomitable spirit of the woman.

She had built in addition to Mr. Judson's room, a little apartment for herself, Mahree and the child, in the governor's enclosure. Going out from the audience chamber, she sank down in her rocking chair that Moung

Ing had just brought from home. For awhile she was almost in despair. It seemed that her heroic nature was, for once, conquered. The prison gate, where she had so often knocked for admission, was standing open, but no one was within that she wished to see. Life now had for her no object. For seven months she had contrived day and night, how to make her husband comfortable. She had daily trod the streets, from door to door of the members of government, pleading for the release of the prisoners. When they had been thrown the last time into the inner prison, and even Moung Ing denied admission with food, she had come, and waiting patiently without till night, when the earth-oil lamp was lighted and then obtained permission to bear in the long delayed repast. Night after night, for months, had she been thus forced to wait, and then go home alone at nine o'clock in the night when the fierce jackal prowled by the way-side and more savage men thronged the streets. The long two miles were unheeded, the dangers were not thought of; only how could she best contrive for the comfort of the prisoners. Now they were gone; what could she do? Mr. Judson was sick in bed, and unable to eat. Could it be possible that the inhuman wretches had driven him away in that condition? The thought was maddening. Springing up she went to the governor and told him that she was going to Amarapura in search of her husband. He was shocked at the very thought of such a thing. What, a female encounter such a journey in such weather! It was impossible. She could not live through it. Then the country was filled with robbers, the result of the war. She should not think of such a thing. But she replied undaunted, that her place was by her sick husband and she would go to him, let come what would. Seeing her determination, he begged her to wait till night, a more pleasant season for traveling, when he would send a man with her to open the gates. But she refused to wait. Mr. Judson might die during that time. Returning to her house out of town she had Moung Ing and a servant to carry two or three trunks of the most valuable articles to deposit with the medicine chest in the care of the governor. She then committed the house and premises to Moung Ing. He insisted on going with her, but she said she would take the Bengalee cook who could serve her as well there, but who could not be entrusted with the house. Thinking that perhaps by being close by he could use his influence with the governor to better advantage, he consented to remain. She then took the cook, Abbe, Mahree and the child, and procuring a boat, set out through the burning sun toward Amarapura.

Mahree, with her daily care of little Maria, and watching her "white mamma" in these unselfish labors of love, began to have some conception of life with its awful responsibilities, and resolved to emulate the example of her teacher, and follow her path to a noble womanhood. Mrs. Judson was thinking of her sick husband driven in chains over the burning sands; the child was sleeping in her arms; Abbe was thinking over the mysteries of the alphabet; the cook looked on in compassion; and thus they toiled on to the "Never-to-be-forgotten place."

CHAPTER VI.

As soon as Mrs. Judson had gone from the little room to answer the governor's call, a band of men rushed into the prison-yard and began to bind the white prisoners, two and two. One of the jailers ran hastily into Mr. Judson's room, and seizing him by the arm, jerked him roughly from his couch, sick as he was; then stripping him of his clothing, all except shirt and pants, drove him forth bare-headed and bare-footed into the prison-yard where the others were waiting. He was now tied to one of these, and a slave holding the rope that connected each couple, they were driven out on the shimmering plain, the lamine-woon riding alongside on his horse. It was now May, the Tropical Summer. Since June of the year before, they had been confined to the darkness of the death-prison or protected by the shade of the open sheds. Consequently their skin was tender. On their first touching the plain the heat almost withered them. Not a tree was to be seen, only the far-stretching waste of shining gravel. The sun was almost to the zenith, shining perpendicularly on their bare heads. Their necks, faces and hands were soon blistered red, and burning painfully. The sand and gravel were so hot that every step caused them to shrink and hesitate to take another except when prompted by the continual goading of their drivers. Mr. Judson, having taken no food that day, and burning with fever besides, was scarcely able to stand, much less to undertake such a journey on foot. By the time they reached the little river, only a half mile distant, the soles of his feet were solid blisters, and he longed to throw himself into the water and end his miseries, only the sin of such an act preventing. When they had proceeded four or five miles the skin was entirely gone from their feet, and the flesh was horribly lacerated by the sharp gravels on which they left their bloody tracks gleaming behind them and almost hissing with the heat. Mr. Judson here begged the lamine-woon to let him ride his horse a mile or two, as he was completely exhausted. That dignitary's only reply was a scornful, withering look, such as he would have bestowed upon a dog. He then asked Captain Laird, his fellow-prisoner, to let him rest one hand on his shoulder, as he was sinking fast. The Captain, who was a robust, healthy man, readily granted the request for a mile or two, but his own feet were worn out, and he was unable to assist him any further. Mr. Gouger's Bengalee servant overtook the party at this point, and seeing Mr. Judson's distress, tore off his own head-dress, and giving half to his master and half to Mr. Judson, wrapped it instantly about his feet, then offered him his own shoulder to support him the remaining part of the journey. Had it not been for the prompt interference of this humane heathen he must have perished by the way-side. The Greek who had been confined at the same time was taken out of prison that morning strong and vigorous, but being of corpulent frame his strength gave way, and he fell almost dead. The drivers beat him and dragged him through the sand till they were weary themselves, then procuring a cart, hauled him the remaining. two miles to the court-house of Amarapura. He was helpless and breathing very heavily when taken from the cart and laid on the ground; and in about two hours expired in great agony.

Reaching the court-house the prisoners could stand no longer, and sank on the ground completely exhausted. Leaving them in charge of their drivers, the lamine-woon went before the magistrates to see what was to be done with them. He received the intelligence that the Pakan-woon had ordered them conveyed on to Oung-pen-la, four miles farther, there to be confined in a dilapidated prison and burned alive at his order. The lamine-woon then went out, intending to proceed with them to Oung-pen-la that night, but finding the Greek already dead and the others unable to move, he decided to let them remain till morning rather than exert his slaves in trying to drag them. They were allowed to crawl under an old shed and lie during the night, without any covering or accommodation of any kind. The lamine-woon's wife, prompted by curiosity to see the white men, visited the shed, and her compassion was so excited that she brought them some fruit, sugar and tamarinds for their refreshment. Weary and hungry as they were, never had repast been so like a banquet to them.

In the morning, as they were still unable to walk, carts were provided and they were conveyed by that means to their destination. Hitherto they had been totally ignorant of their future fate, but when they arrived and saw the ruined prison without cover to shield them from the sun, there was no longer any doubt, and they began preparing themselves for a living cremation; and not until they saw slaves mount to the roof and begin repairing it with leaves, did they think any respite would be granted them. They were lying under the shadow of the crumbling walls without, almost dead. Mr. Judson's fever, now raging more fiercely, and added to the excessive temperature, with the fatigue and violent headache resulting from the motion of the cart, was a torture from which death by fire would have been a desired relief. He lay there thinking of Ann. What would she think when she returned from the governor's room and found him gone? a scene from which he now saw the old man sought to spare her the sight. What would she do? Follow? He hoped she would not. Lying thus, verging on delirium, almost unconscious of his surroundings, his eyes dim with dust and fever, he saw, as in a dream, a distant vision on the plain; almost immovable; yet the radiation of the sand caused it to show a quivering motion. It was seemingly without form, like a phantom. Could it be that he had already lost his reason and this was some myth of his disordered brain, or was it a mirage? Neither. Still nearer it approached, its motion now being perceptible. It dissolved itself into two forms; a yoke of buffaloes, their heads almost on the ground. Then another form, a native driver walking beside, and goading them with an iron-pointed bamboo. Now the motion and bulk of a cart in the rear. Its wheels, made simply of round boards with holes through them, in which the axle was thrust, without any hub what-

ever, were allowed to flap from a sudden incline to a
brief perpendicular and then a more sudden incline in
the opposite direction, causing the vehicle to careen
from side to side of the road like a ship in the trough
of the sea. Now the screaking of the wheels could be
heard, and several occupants indistinctly seen as they
clutched the sides to save themselves from being thrown
out. In front of the prison the mysterious carriage
halted. A man descended from the rear end. It was
his Bengalee cook. The sick man started from his
death-like stupor as if he first credited the reality of
the vision. Then out came Mahree and Abbe; then—
could it be true?—his own faithful Ann, her babe on
her bosom. Rushing to him she knelt at his side

"Oh, why did you come?" he said reproachfully,
though feebly. "I so hoped you would not. You cannot live here."

Kissing him and brushing the dust from his face
with her apron, she replied:

"And where should I be but at my husband's side?
Could I stay behind and know that you were here suffering, perhaps dying, and no one to minister to you?
If I cannot live here, I can die here, and that with
better satisfaction than I could live away from my
beloved. But we cannot remain here; I will see the
jailer."

Placing the child in the arms of Mahree, she boldly
approached that savage-looking personage, who was
standing aside giving orders to the men on the roof.
Association with such men had long since deprived her
of fear. She began as if talking to the governor of the
north gate, by inquiring if she might erect a little bam-

boo house for herself and child, in order to care for her sick husband.

"No," he replied gruffly, "it is not customary."

"Then," she said, "will you not please procure for me shelter for the night, when on the morrow I can find a place to live in?"

He looked at her then for the first time. Her beautiful face and pleading manner seemed to melt him, for he conducted her to his own house, two or three hundred yards away. It contained only two rooms, one of which was occupied by his own family, the other, half full of rice-straw, dust, and vermin. He pointed to this, then went back to superintend affairs at the prison. Here she brought the children, and spread a mat on the paddy which was to be their bed for the next six months. She now made some tea for herself and the prisoners, which was all that could be obtained that night, and after they were locked up in the rickety old building, she returned to the little grain-room to try to rest.

This was to the prisoners the most horrible night of their experience. They were so stiff in every limb that they could scarcely turn, and their feet, without a particle of skin on the soles, of course rendered standing impossible. At dark they were sent to bed in the familiar couch, the stocks. Lying flat on their backs they now tried to obtain a little sleep. Suddenly they became conscious of a slow motion about their feet. The keepers were all in a shed without; what could it mean? The stocks were certainly rising slowly and majestically towards the roof. Reaching the height at which they were so accustomed to see the bamboo at the Let-ma-yoon, it rested and left them suspended as if it was thought they could sleep only in that position on account of their former custom. The stocks were not so bad, but it was what followed. The mischievous rogues had raised the wonderful contrivance by means of a crank on the outside, and could be heard enjoying the fun due to their mechanical skill. Now the mosquitoes swarmed in from the stagnant waters of the rice-fields and settled in great hordes on their suspended feet. They tried in vain to reach up to drive them off, but were forced to lie there and feel the hundreds of voracious bills thrust deep into their raw and bleeding soles. Squirming and beating the air, they could stand the torture no longer, and cried loudly for pity from the guard without. The good-natured fellows enjoyed the yells for awhile, then kindly lowered the stocks, about midnight, within a foot or two of the ground, where the enemy could be more successfully encountered.

Such are the sufferings of those who would preach the gospel in a heathen land.

CHAPTER VII.

On the next morning, rising from her couch of straw at the first appearance of day, and leaving the weary children still asleep, Mrs. Judson went into the village in search of food to prepare for the breakfast of the prisoners, knowing that they had been without food most of the day before. But there being no market, she almost despaired of procuring anything nearer than Amarapura. She found, however, that Dr. Price's servant had brought some cold rice and curry, and some one else a cup of tea, from which she managed to prepare a meal, depending for dinner on some dried fish brought by Mr. Gouger's servant. This gave her time to send to Amarapura for other provisions. The prisoners, on account of the lacerated condition of their feet, were unable to move for several days. Mr. Judson's fever was, of course, much increased by the journey, and it would require the closest attention from his faithful nurse to preserve his life. She now thought of trusting little Maria solely to the care of Mahree, and giving her attention to her husband.

After carrying the food to the prison she returned to her lodging to see after the children and arrange the little

(271)

room to be as comfortable as possible. Maria, who had never known a well day since her sorrowful birth, was crying pitifully as she entered. Abbe was sitting beside her on the mat endeavoring to quiet her, and poor Mahree, on her couch of straw in the corner, was tossing to and fro in feverish agony. Going near to ascertain what ailed her, she found the child's body already covered with the eruptions of that fearful disease, the small-pox. Here, indeed, was a trial; a child always sick, and demanding a mother's care both night and day; a helpless husband in chains, who had to be ministered to every hour, and a case of the small-pox in her own room. She had been vaccinated, so she did not fear the disease for herself. With a needle she inoculated the other two children. Abbe, as a consequence, escaped, but it did not take with Maria. No physician was to be had. Dr. Price was in the stocks, and could only advise in regard to inoculation and diet, as he had no medicine.

The care-worn mother could now be seen almost hourly going to and fro from the hovel to the prison, with her child in her arms, ministering to her two patients. In a few days Maria was also seized with the small-pox, and she was forced to leave her with Abbe when going to the prison. The jailer, fearing his children would take the disease, brought them to be inoculated, and her fame soon spread so that almost every one in the village, old or young, came to undergo the operation; all these things added to her already pressing duties. By incessant watchings and skillful nursing, Mr. Judson's fever was conquered and he began slowly to regain his health. The children were also rescued from the usually fatal effect of their disorder, and began to recover.

Their prospects now seemed brighter. The Pakan-woon who had ordered the foreigners there, and who intended to witness their sacrifice, was found guilty of embezzling public money and executed without even a trial. The jailer having no further order in regard to the prisoners, kept them in confinement, though not so closely as formerly, a shed being erected under which they were allowed to rest during the day, but they were shut up in the cell at night.

However, the lives of her dear ones were only spared to Mrs. Judson through the sacrifice of her own health. Incessant watching for four months had sapped her constitution to such an extent that she was completely prostrated just as the others began to revive. A disorder, peculiar to the country, and nearly always fatal, seized upon her, when she and the whole family must have perished had it not been for the faithfulness of the Bengalee cook, who forgot his caste and served them devotedly, even without pay. Mrs. Judson knew she could not long survive in that condition without medicine and more wholesome food; so procuring a cart she set out for Ava to obtain the medicine-chest from the governor. Reaching the city, she had such a violent attack that she expected to live only a few hours, and her only anxiety was to get back to the prison to die by her husband and child. After some difficulty, having obtained the medicine-chest, she managed to get at the laudanum, and by taking two or three drops every hour she gained strength to crawl on board a boat, being too weak to stand. She could only go within four miles of

A Karen Mission House.

her destination in the boat, the remaining distance to be traveled in that painful conveyance, a cart. It was during the rainy season, when the whole sandy plain was a lake of soft mud. The laboring oxen crept along at a snail's pace, floundering in the mud up to their sides. Sometimes the wheels would rise within two or three inches of the surface of the ground and waddle along on firm ground for a few yards, then suddenly drop almost from sight, the body of the cart striking the mud with a splash, and dragging behind the team after the manner of a canal boat, the sick occupant feeling that almost every moment would end her misery before even seeing husband and child.

The kind-hearted cook came out to assist her from the cart as it drew up before the jailer's door. But instead of the buoyant figure leaping to the ground and rushing to meet her husband, as on a former occasion, he saw a haggard, emaciated form, struggling to raise herself from the bare floor of the cart where she had been compelled to lie the whole of the way from the river. He assisted her gently to reach the door, when she crawled feebly to the mat on the straw, and fell completely exhausted. For the next two months she lay thus, lingering between life and death. In her moments of painful consciousness she forgot her own afflictions and only seemed to regret that she was unable to minister to her husband and children as before. Mahree, though convalescent, was not yet able to resume the care of Maria, who was now the greatest sufferer of all. Throughout the long nights the child would cry pitifully for that nourishment which the mother's breasts could no longer afford. The jailer, weary with her cries, at length allowed Mr. Judson to come out of the prison, his feet still tender from former wounds and bound with shackles, and hobble about the village with the child in his arms, begging nourishment for her from those mothers who had young children. The cook did all in his power to serve them. Often he went without food himself for a whole day, in his efforts to provide something palatable for his sick mistress and fettered master.

But afflictions do not last always. Just as Mrs. Judson began to recover, good news was heard from down the river. The English had destroyed every army that had been sent against them, and having captured city after city, were marching steadily towards the capital. The king, finding his name no longer so terrifying, now began to sue for peace, which was granted only on condition that all white prisoners should be released.

One morning joyful Moung Ing appeared at the prison and announced a message from the governor of the north gate that an order had come from the palace for their release. The order arrived in an official form that evening, and they began preparations for returning to Ava. The avaricious jailers sought to retain Mrs. Judson, insisting that her name was not included in the order, and that she should not go. But by threats and promises, and consenting to leave the remainder of the provisions last procured from Ava, she was reluctantly allowed to depart. Mr. Judson was carried to the court-house at Ava to act as interpreter. The rest of the family, under the charge of Moung Ing, returned to their own house out of town. Here it was found that he had managed affairs almost as well as if Mr. Judson had been there, and what was most gratifying of all, he had rescued the manuscript copy of the New Testament. On the morning when the prisoners had been sent to Oung-pen-la, he went to the jail-yard and found where Mr. Judson's pillow had been torn open and the roll of cotton carelessly thrown away. He picked it up and carried it back to the house as a relic, ignorant of its valuable contents.

The next day Mr. Judson received twenty ticals from the government, with instructions to proceed down the river to the Burmese camp at Maloun, there to act as interpreter for the English embassadors. The governor gave him permission to stop at home a few moments, as it was on his way, and let Mrs. Judson provide his clothing and food for the trip. All fear and anxiety was now removed, and they hoped soon to see peace in the country.

Mrs. Judson's health, which had not been fully restored before leaving Oung-pen-la, now began to decline, and in a few days she was attacked with the spotted fever. Knowing the nature of the disease, and her own shattered constitution, she had no hope of recovery, and her greatest anxiety was for Maria who would be left till her father's return. But God never forgets his people. The day she was taken sick a Burmese nurse appeared and offered her services, which were thankfully received. The woman would give no name, simply saying that she had heard of the teacher's illness and had come from afar to see her, and that she was a Christian. In a few days the fever had assumed a violent form, and it seemed that it would be impossible to arrest the disease. Dr. Price, on his release from prison, heard of her illness and hastened to see her. He said her condition was the most distressing he had ever seen, and he did not think it possible for her to live many hours. He ordered her head shaved and her feet covered with blisters, instructing the nurse to endeavor to persuade her to take some nourishment, which she had refused to do for two or three days. She became unconscious, and the Burmese neighbors came in to see her die. She fell into a deep stupor and they whispered, "She is dead; and if the King of Angels should come he could not recover her." Finally the crisis was passed and she opened her eyes, bright with the light of reason, for the first time in many days. The first thing she saw was the faithful nurse bending over her entreating her to take a little wine and water. She drank the stimulant and then lay listlessly gazing into the nurse's face. At length she asked abruptly, "Nurse, who are you?"

"A friend to you, teacher," she replied evasively.

"But your name?"

"Pray, teacher, do not ask me to tell that, it would endanger both our lives while in the Golden City. I will tell you all when the proper time comes."

"Have I not seen you before?"

"Once."

"Where?"

"In Bengal."

"In Bengal?"

"Yes, teacher; but you must not talk any more now. Dr. Price told me to keep you quiet. I will go see after the child and let you sleep."

In a day or two she so far revived as to become more sensible to her surroundings. A servant came one night and said Mr. Judson had returned and they had carried him on by, to the court-house. She sent him in town to watch and see where they carried him. He returned next morning with the intelligence that he saw his master conducted from the court-house towards one of the prisons, and it was reported that he was to be sent back to Oung-pen-la. The simple mention of that horrid place, in her present weak condition, was almost a death-blow. Mr. Judson sent back to Oung-pen-la, and she not able to follow him! What must be the consequences? She lay for some time completely stunned by the shock, then having regained sufficient composure, she sent for Moung Ing and told him the circumstance, begging him to go in search of Mr. Judson and to plead with the governor to use his influence once more in their behalf, as she was unable to go. Moung Ing promised to find him if possible and bring him back home.

Mr. Judson, on his way to Maloun, had been exposed to the damp nights, and the heavy atmosphere of the river, which threw him into a fever equally as severe as the one endured in prison, and which came near ending his life. Reaching the camp he lay in a damp tent for several weeks, and explained the papers that were brought him until he became unconscious and insane from his sufferings. When he came to himself he was lying in a room on a mat suspended from the rafters. Suddenly, without a minute's warning, he was placed in a boat and sent back to Ava with the communication to government: "We have no further use for Yoodthan; we therefore return him to the Golden City." He arrived in the night and the guards conducted him past his own door to the court-house. A feeble light was burning within, and he begged the guards to let him go in for a moment and see if all were alive. They refused. He pleaded, threatened and tried to bribe them, all to no purpose. They showed some regard to his feelings, however, and said they had been ordered to take him immediately to the court-house, and dared not disobey lest their own lives should be forfeited. There was no one at the court-house who was acquainted with him, and the presiding officer having read the communication, and not knowing what to do with him, asked the attendants from what place he had been sent to Maloun.

"From Oung-pen-la," they replied.

"Then let him return thither," said the officer. He was then hurried away to an obscure shed to await conveyance to Oung-pen-la Next morning Mrs. Judson had sent a servant in search of him with food but he could not be found. After looking for him all day, Moung Ing approached the shed near night, and, to his joy, saw the object of his search crouching in a corner. After their greetings were over, Mr. Judson's first inquiry was:

"How are my wife and child?"

"The child is as well as she usually is," answered the Burman evasively, "and your wife is very anxious about you, bidding me make application to the governor once more for your release."

"Just like her," said Mr. Judson, "always thinking of me first, no matter what her own troubles may be.

But go quickly, Moung Ing, go quickly to the governor
and state our case plainly before him. He has always
befriended us and will not refuse to do so now. Tell
the Tsayah-ga-dau to have courage one day longer. Go
now to the governor."

Left alone, he began to ponder with himself.

"Did he not evade my question in regard to my wife's
health? His expression was peculiar and he hesitated
to speak of her. He said the child was well, but he did
not say it was so with her. Can it be that she has been
suffering?"

Revolving such thoughts in his mind, doubting, hoping, fearing, he passed another night in the shed. Early
next morning the governor sent for him, and he found
that the kind old man had placed himself as security
for the prisoner and thus obtained his final release from
the government.

"And now," said the governor, when he had told him
of his freedom, "go to your wife, for I know you are
anxious to meet her. As soon as possible bring her to my
house where you both shall have a home as long as you
stay in the Golden City."

He forgot his maimed ankles and tender feet, as, with
a step fleeter than he had used for two years, he passed
through the streets to his own house. All was still.
The door was half ajar. Passing into the front room he
saw the Burmese nurse with his wan child in her arms.
Though with all a father's affection for the little one,
he was too anxious to know the fate of her mother to
stop and caress her. Entering the next room a wretched
sight met his gaze. Lying acoss the bed, as if she had
tried to arise and had fallen, lay the form of his wife,

but so altered and emaciated that he would have scarcely recognized her elsewhere. The face that had once been so fair and round, was haggard, pinched and white. The glossy black curls that had so beautifully adorned her shapely head were gone, and a closely-fitting cotton cap took their place. His own bodily sufferings had been light compared with the mental anguish he experienced on seeing her thus. Bending sorrowfully down to kiss her sleeping face, a tear-drop fell from his brimming eyes upon her wasted cheek. It aroused her. She opened her eyes and looked him joyfully in the face. He clasped her in his arms, and there we leave them. A scene too sacred for strangers to behold.

CHAPTER VIII.

—Moore.

THE government had several times broken off the negotiations pending between them and the enemy, but at length, even the proud heart of the king was humbled by the near approach of the English, and he agreed to their stipulations, surrendering all prisoners, and ceding to England a considerable portion of his territory, and promising to pay large sums of money besides. The missionaries had rendered invaluable service in the transactions of peace, and the king, sensible of their service, invited them to remain at Ava as citizens. Dr. Price accepted the invitation, but Mr. Judson, partly for the sake of his family, and mainly because he thought he could be more useful elsewhere, made arrangements to depart, at the earliest convenience, for the English camp.

It was on a cool, moon-light evening, when, with his family, and property, in six or eight of his majesty's golden boats, he launched upon the broad, placid bosom of the Irrawaddy, and turned his back once more upon the golden city. His wife was by his side, and little

Maria in his arms, while Moung Ing followed behind in another boat with Mahree, Abbe, the Bengalee cook, and the Burman nurse, who begged to stay with the teachers always.

A boat-ride by moon-light is pleasant under almost any circumstances; with your loved one by your side it is peculiarly delightful; but under present circumstances, who can appreciate it! There was to the missionaries a delicious thrill of joy, such as can only be experienced by those who have come up through great tribulations. Only a delivered captive can properly estimate the depth of the meaning of that simple word —*free*. Free from the frown of the haughty king; free from the horrible scenes of the Let-ma-yoon; free from the oppressions of Oung-pen-la; this night is the most blissful of their life. Said Mr. Judson afterwards, "I can never regret my twenty-one months of misery when I recall that one delicious thrill. I think I have had a better appreciation of what heaven may be ever since."

The reception of a white lady was an unusual occurrence in an English camp, especially in that country where they had never seen a white female. Mrs. Judson's fame had gone before her, and the English general, Sir Archibald Campbell, made extensive preparations for her accommodation. He had a tent erected for her, larger than his own, and with the agreeable addition of a veranda; and his own son was sent forth, with an escort of staff officers, to meet her. Both she and her husband were greatly endeared to Sir Archibald for his fatherly kindness, manifested in many instances during their stay at the camp. Henry Havelock, a young assistant-adjutant-general, whose famous career as a soldier began with this war, and who shall after-wards figure prominently in our story, was one of the offi-cers who met and escorted the missionaries to the camp.

A few days after, General Campbell gave a magnifi-cent dinner to the Burmese commissioners who had been sent down from the palace to complete negotiations for peace. The whole camp was turned into a scene of gorgeous display, with such a profusion of gold and crim-son, and floating banners as would put to shame even the gaudy parades of the Great White Elephant on gala days, in the golden city. A bountiful table was spread in a broad pavilion erected for the occasion. When the hour arrived for dinner the whole company marched in couples to the music of a band, towards the table, the general walking alone in front. Opposite the tent with the veranda the whole procession halted, the music suddenly ceased, and the general entered the tent, re-appearing in a few moments with Mrs. Judson on his arm, much to the discomfort of the conscience-smitten commissioners, who realized that they were now in her power if she should show herself at all vin-dictive. The general led Mrs. Judson to the table and seated her at his own right hand, while the commis-sioners shrank into their seats abashed. They could not have exhibited greater fear if suddenly called upon to stand before the golden face. General Campbell began to suspect the cause of their uneasiness which afforded him great amusement.

"I fancy these gentlemen must be old acquaintances of yours, Mrs. Judson," he remarked, "and, judging from their appearance, you must have treated them very ill."

Mrs. Judson simply smiled as she glanced at the terrified group, who, although unable to translate the remark spoken in English, suspected that they were the objects of it.

"What is the matter with yonder owner of the pointed beard?" continued the general, "he seems to be seized with an ague fit."

"I do not know," she said, fixing her eyes mischievously on the trembler, "unless his memory may be too busy. He is an old acquaintance of mine, and may probably infer danger to himself from seeing me under your protection."

"How so?"

"When Mr. Judson was in the death prison, sick with fever, stifled with the loathsome air, and bound with five pairs of fetters, I walked several miles to this gentleman's house to ask a favor. I went soon in the morning, but he held me waiting till noon before hearing my request, and then roughly refused it. As I was turning sorrowfully away, his avaricious eyes were attracted by the silk umbrella which I carried, and he rudely snatched it from my hands. I begged him to restore it, pleading that I could not buy another as my money was at home, and it would endanger my life to walk through the heat of noon without one, but he would not listen. I then begged that he would at least give me a paper one instead, to protect me from the scorching heat. He laughed scornfully as he looked on my wasted form. 'It is only stout people that are in dan- of sunstroke,' he said, 'the sun could not find such as you.' He then shut the door in my face and turned me away to walk the long distance with no protection except my bonnet."

The officers, who had been listening to this narrative of brutality, could not restrain an outburst of indignation at such treatment. The poor Burman sat in his seat, his features tortured with fear and great drops of perspiration oozing from his deathly-pale face, while his body trembled like an aspen. Mrs. Judson felt nothing but pity for him, and remarked softly in Burman that he had nothing to fear. Sir Archibald now turned the conversation, and tried in every way to render his guests comfortable; but their own consciences smote them too heavily, and they were glad when an opportunity was presented for them to escape the presence of those whom they had so shamefully treated.

The fortnight which the Judsons spent at the English camp was the happiest period of their lives; but Mr. Judson was anxious to once more resume his work, from which he had lost so much time. After bidding a reluctant farewell to the fatherly general and his courteous officers, they departed, and after a little more than two years' absence landed again in Rangoon.

.   .   .   .

Before taking our final leave of the British camp, we must not omit to notice one event, which was not the least important incident of the occasion, at least to two of the parties concerned.

During the two years that have passed since Mahree, a shy, black-eyed lass, entered the home of Mrs. Judson, she has rapidly developed into a full-grown young lady. The small-pox, instead of retarding, by a lucky turn, had advanced her growth; nor had it left a single mark to disfigure her face, which was now as beautiful as that of the unfortunate princess of Kathay.

Added to her physical charms was that modest Christian disposition, imbibed from so long a contact with the "white mamma," whom she considered a perfect ideal of true womanhood. Her education had not been neglected even in all their trials and sufferings; while her devotion to the feeble child and daily participation in Mrs. Judson's heroic efforts for the comfort of the prisoners rendered her peculiarly well qualified for the scenes in which she should afterward engage.

Robert Stuart, one of General Campbell's staff officers, and a companion of Havelock, became very much enamored of the beautiful Burman maiden, and, conscious of her rare accomplishments, resolved to win her for his wife During the two weeks of her stay he often sought her presence, as she sat alone under the open veranda with the child in her arms. At first she was rather shy of his presence, never before having seen a young Englishman, especially a soldier. But as he seemed to direct his attention mainly to the child, and hinted no intimation of his intentions, she gradually lost her reserve, and began to expect, then long for his coming—feeling disappointed if he did not appear. He gave her interesting accounts of life in England and told racy stories of his college life with his chum, the studious, noble-minded Havelock, and of their high ambitions in going to India as soldiers. Then, at intervals, he drew from her the tragedies of Ava and Oung-pen-la, with some of the mysteries connected with her own origin.

It was not long till he could tell, from the glad light that shone in her eyes whenever he approached, that his love was in some measure reciprocated.

It was the evening before the Judsons were to return to Rangoon that the two were sitting, as usual, before the tent at twilight. The time was one when sentiment is always the strongest. The moon was peeping shyly through the thick boughs of the cypress and mango trees that surrounded the camp; lights were beginning to glimmer in the tents along the shore, and to be reflected from the steamer in the quiet waters below. Crickets and katydids began their serenade, and from one of the tents floated a soft Scottish air, the melody of the Highlands.

The lovers sat in silence. Their conversation had several times approached the subject nearest the heart of each; but she, though not seemingly displeased, had artfully managed to change the subject each time before it reached a point, and he had not the courage to press it. Such a strange thing is love! Even a brave-hearted soldier, who could unflinchingly withstand the terror of the Golden Face, is overcome in the presence of a modest Burman girl. But knowing this to be his last opportunity of meeting her, he made a great effort to break the embarrassing silence, and falteringly told her his feelings from the time he first saw her, and how the passion had grown upon him till he could no longer think of living without her. But he was struck with astonishment and consternation at the manner in which she received his confession. Springing to her feet, she clasped the child in her arms, exclaiming:

"Hush! You must not talk so; indeed you must not." And before he could detain her, she rushed into the tent to Mrs. Judson's apartment.

Much wondering at this unexpected freak, he sat for some time, waiting to see if she would not return. Then, in bitter disappointment, he strode away. He went to his own tent, but he could not rest. Even the music of the band gave him no relief. Coming out again, he wandered for hours on the river bank in front of the tents, kicking the turf into the water and muttering to himself, "What can the silly girl mean? She certainly could not intend that for a flat refusal. I am satisfied she loves me; and yet she knows this is the last opportunity. Perhaps she may reconsider and come out again.'

So he lingered in front of the veranda till the lights were extinguished and he knew all had retired. He then entered his own tent, where he lay tossing restlessly till morning.

Ah! young man, you need not have been surprised at that singularity of feminine behavior. I expect they all do that way, judging from what the novelists say. Milton pictures Eve as running from Adam the first time she saw him, though she loved him better than life. It was not artfulness, but nature. That shy girl had never mingled with belles of civilized society, to learn coquetry. But it looks sweet, after all, does it not? There is a philosophy about it that even Plato could not explain; a feeling, even amid a man's disappointment, that she appeared better for the action, and he is more fired with a resolve to conquer or die.

Within a few days after the departure of the missionaries, Havelock was ordered to Rangoon with his detachment to hold that city till the Burmese government should pay the war debt. Sir Archibald, himself, was to depart in a few days with the main army to Bengal. Stuart begged to be allowed to remain with his command in Rangoon for awhile, as he did not wish to be separated from a part of his forces under Havelock. There was a twinkle in the good-natured general's eyes as he suspected the true reason of the request, but it was kindly granted, and the two officers were left in charge of the city which guarded the entrance to all Burmah.

CHAPTER IX.

Maiden ! with the meek, brown eyes,
In whose orbs a shadow lies
Like the dusk in evening skies !

.   .   .   .   .   .

Standing, with reluctant feet,
Where the brook and river meet,
Womanhood and childhood fleet !

—Longfellow.

On his arrival at Rangoon Mr. Judson found the little church of eighteen scattered in every direction by the war. Moung Shwa-gnong had gone into the interior and died with the cholera, and only four of the original membership, including Moung Ing, could be found. Messrs. Wade and Hough had narrowly escaped with their lives, being already under the knife of the executioner when rescued by the British. Their brave wives disguised themselves, and joining them they proceeded to Calcutta to await the issue of the war, and were now ready to join Mr. Judson in whatever place he should establish the mission.

The English government, recognizing the value of Mr. Judson's services, offered him a salary equivalent to three thousand dollars to act as interpreter for them; but he refused, as he had "no time to make money." But as his services were to some extent indispensable, he consented to accompany Mr. Crawford, the commissioner of the East India Company, on an expedition to choose a suitable site for the capital of the ceded Burman provinces, now British Burmah. He did not now

(295)

so much dread to leave his family alone, since they would be under the protection of the English garrison. So intrusting them to Moung Ing he sailed with the commissioner. They selected a high, beautiful promontery at the mouth of the Salwen river. In honor of the Governor-General, Mr. Crawford named the site Amherst. Here it was proposed to found a city in which a garrison should continually reside, an asylum for those oppressed by Burman despotism, and a place where no restrictions should interfere with religious liberty. Mr. Judson at once concluded that this would be the most suitable place for his mission, as Rangoon would be again under the power of the Golden Face when the English should vacate the city for this place. Besides, the free government would draw a large population and render circumstances remarkably favorable for missionary labor. His hopes of the future were now brighter than ever before. Here he would bring his wife and child, with the faithful disciples left at Rangoon, and take possession of the new city in the name of the Lord of Hosts.

   .   .   .   .

It was the evening after Mr. Judson's departure. The three remaining disciples in the city had just been at the mission-house, and before they left Moung Ing had gathered them in the room with the family and himself conducted the evening worship; after which they enjoyed a few moments of delightful conversation concerning the goodness of God to his creatures, and the accompanying joy of trusting in him. Mrs. Judson, whose recent sufferings so well qualified her for an understanding of such things, led in the conversation. It was a delightful hour. The Burmese nurse from Bengal also testified of the unbounded mercy that had saved her and given her so much happiness. Moung Ing saw her face aglow with light, and he covered his face with his hands, not altogether because he was affected by what she said, but because in her eye he saw a gleam that recalled a tender recollection of the past—a memory which he had tried to forget. She, too, had often started at some expression of his, but neither could explain the mysterious sympathy that existed between them.

Moung Ing, engaged in his duties generally in silence, often had thoughts and feelings that no one would have suspected in him. From the time when the two little Burmese girls were brought to Mrs. Judson, he had shown for them a fatherly devotion, especially for Mahree, toward whom he felt strangely drawn. Though having undergone hardships innumerable during the past fifteen years or more, the old affections of earth still clung to him, and his strong heart had in it a place of sympathy for every one in distress or deprived of friends. One day, while alone with Mrs. Judson, he astonished her by asking:

"Teacher, did you ever notice, or fancy, any resemblance between Mahree and your nurse?"

"Why, no, Moung Ing," she replied, "why do you ask?"

"I don't know what it is, teacher, but something moves me strongly whenever I see them together. I wish I knew her history."

"I have asked her for that repeatedly," said Mrs. Judson, "but she refuses. She says I should recognize

her if I knew it, as I have once heard it, and she wishes
not to be known yet."

"Please ask her one question for me," he said.
"Whether she ever had a child?"

He then went about his duties, leaving her wondering
at his strange question. Presently the nurse came to
bring her some tea—this was while at Ava. After drink-
ing the beverage, Mrs. Judson looked her in the face
and inquired:

"Nurse, did you once have a child like my little
Maria?"

The poor creature's eyes filled with tears and she
trembled painfully as she said:

"O, teacher, would you kill me by continuing to ask
about my past, so sad and dark? I did once have a
little daughter as lovely as the sun ever saw, but please
do not ask me more now. I will tell you all some
day."

. . . .

Twilight was slowly creeping over the land. The
little company had dispersed from the mission-house.
Moung Ing was overlooking the preparation of supper.
Mrs. Judson had just gone toward the clump of mango
trees, in the yard, with a pail of water with which to
sprinkle some flowers which she had lately planted
about little Roger's grave. Mahree was sitting on the
veranda, rocking back and forth, with the child in her
arms, and singing a lullaby which the nurse had taught
her. Her own voice and the noise of the rockers on the
boards prevented her from hearing a quick, military
step approach the veranda. A hand was laid upon the
back of her chair, and looking up, she was startled to

see the tall, handsome form of Robert Stuart at her side.

"Ah! my bird, I have caught you at last," he said as he clasped her hand and seated himself on a bench by her side.

At first she showed some inclination to run away, but the child was sleeping and he held to her hand. So she quietly submitted to her fate, her eyes drooping and her bosom heaving.

"Mahree!" he said passionately, "I want to know why you treated me so cruelly the other night at the camp. For mercy's sake, if you have any pity in your soul, or any tenderness in your heart, do not again torture me by such a rebuff. A plain refusal would not have been so painful as an act that thus held me in suspense. Do tell me candidly, the feelings of your heart for me. Will you not?"

"Robert," she said softy, and a faint flush tinged her brown cheek as she spoke his name with trembling lips. His heart gave a great bound as she continued: "I have not been insensible to your attentions. In fact, I fear I did wrong by allowing you to go so far, but it was really a pleasure to me, though I knew nothing could come of it, and hoped you would not think seriously of wedding a nameless heathen girl. I can only justify myself in that I never thought you would declare yourself, and that you would never see me again after I left the English camp. But since you have shown this earnestness in coming so far to see me, and have asked me for a candid answer, I reply, I do love you, but I wish, for the sake of both, it was not so. We can never marry."

"Say not so, Mahree," he interrupted, "having acknowledged that you love me, nothing on earth shall prevail to keep us apart. I will overcome every obstacle. Tell me one reason why you cannot marry me."

"The first and greatest," she said, "is that I intend to be a missionary. Since I have been with my white mamma I have been made to feel the importance of the work, and her noble example has so influenced me that I cannot sacrifice the Lord's work for my own pleasure. She can love and labor, too, having her husband with her. That I could not do, you being a soldier and engaged in an entirely different occupation. That is why I regret we ever loved."

"I understand your excuse, Mahree, and I love you better for it; but when you know more fully my mission in the Indian army you can no longer cling to that. It is not for the glory of a soldier's fame that Havelock and I entered the service We, too, are missionaries; and, though in somewhat a different sense from the ministers, our influence is none the less felt, and will go equally as far in disseminating the grand truths of Christianity. With our troops, we are to be stationed at various posts, there, by military authority, to restrain lawlessness, and by Christian influence, to encourage religion. Our regiments are composed of God-fearing men, and we gather them together every day for prayers, and hold public worship in Havelock's tent every Sunday. It is not necessary that we should go to a zayat and teach, to be missionaries. While our work is not aimed directly to the natives, it indirectly bears upon them through the conduct of our orderly bands. Could you not be a missionary in the camp, and aid me in that enterprise, equally as important as any?"

"I confess," she replied, "that your words have caused me to see things in a new light. My convictions stagger between the prospects of the field I had in view and the one you suggest. Perhaps you have chosen the best way. I can't tell. It is so different from anything I had ever dreamed of. I must have further time to consider. But, even then, another barrier arises which you cannot surmount, nor I, as yet."

"What is it?"

"I will not wed while there exists such a mystery in connection with my origin. I am a nameless girl."

"I can remove that difficulty," he said.

"How?"

"By giving you my own name."

"No," she replied, "that does not remove it. I love you too much to have it said in India that you have married a pariah, a waif of the jungle. I shall never marry till the mystery is solved."

"But is there no clue to your identity? The man who brought you to Mrs. Judson, does he not know something?"

"Nothing more than he told her. He said, as his wife was insane, all must depend on the contents of the little casket which is now locked away in the trunk."

"When may it be opened?"

"When I am of age, they say."

"Are you not that now?"

"No one knows my age, but it is more than they think. I was small when carried to the mission house, but I know I was at least sixteen then, and it has been two years since. But I shall quietly wait till mamma thinks me old enough. I could not leave her and little

Maria now," and she drew the sleeping child closer to her bosom.

Robert sat for a few moments in silence, musing sadly and gazing thoughtfully into the fair face of the maiden. Presently she remarked:

"There has always been something strange connected with me. I have not been as other girls. One of my first impressions was a great horror of water. They used to carry me out on the Irrawaddy in the king's boat, but I always shrank from looking at it and shivered when brought near, though I have since overcome the feeling. I know I was but an infant, but I have a vague, indistinct recollection of crossing the sea once, and of being brought to this very house in a white man's arms. Then all is blank for several years, till I was carried to the Golden City. Even then I thought as in a dream I had seen the king's palace before. Of course it is not so, but is it not strange those things should come over me?"

"It is indeed," he said, "and there must be something behind it all. But if this difficulty is to prevent our union, I will remove it at any cost. Nothing shall stand between us, though I see no reason why this should. I would value you as highly as I would if I knew you were the daughter of the Golden Face himself."

"How would you remove it?" she asked.

"I would seek the white teacher who brought you here."

"Where would you seek him? He is a restless wanderer, and has long since left Burmah."

"I will inquire of his father in Bengal. I will give up my command and search the earth or find him.

You do not realize the determination of a man in love when he sees the object of his desire about to escape him. I will marry you, Mahree, within the next six months, and all shall be clear. God will help me to find Felix Carey. But there, the bugle calls me to camp. I must go. May I not kiss you good-night?" he asked as he rose to his feet.

"No," she said, "not yet. We can only be friends till then. I shall still love you and pray for you, but we will not speak of this again till all is known. Do you think we should?"

"Perhaps it is best as you say," he answered, "but I will at least kiss the child."

Bending over, he kissed the wan cheek of the little sleeper, and clasping for a moment the hand of her fair nurse, he hastily departed in the direction of the gunboats, leaving Mahree to ponder in silence the strange, new thoughts that had been suggested.

It was now growing dark, and Mrs. Judson came in from the grove, her pail in her hand. Stopping in the veranda, she imprinted a motherly caress on the cheek both of Mahree and the babe. She noticed that the girl seemed agitated, but not having heard of the new arrivals she could not divine the cause. Passing into the room she lighted the lamp, and sitting down at her desk, began a letter to her husband's brother in America, telling him of the horrible scenes through which they had come, and explaining the two years of silence.

.   .   .   .

Mr. Judson returned highly elated with the prospect of a mission at Amherst, and upon relating his views to his family and the disciples, all were of his opinion and readily proposed to proceed there at once. A gun-boat, with a detachment of soldiers, was to depart from Rangoon for that place in a few days, and when it sailed it carried the missionaries and all the native Christians.

The spot selected was entirely a jungle as yet, without a single house, but on the arrival of the troops and missionaries, three hundred Burmans were already on the ground, and reported three thousand on their way in boats. The missionaries took up their temporary residence in the tent of an English officer till a house could be erected.

BOOK SIXTH.

CHAPTER I.

THIRTEEN years have passed since the missionaries first landed in Burmah. Yet, after all this time, it seemed that they were just now to begin their labors. The field was open, the language acquired, the New Testament translated, and all things ready. They anticipated great results from the effects of the war, which had seemed so disastrous to their cause while it lasted. Now the storm was over and the rainbow of promise spanned the heavens in resplendent glory.

But before beginning their work, Mr. Judson was once more called upon to assist the English Commissioner, Mr. Crawford. He had been appointed envoy to Ava to negotiate a commercial treaty with the king, and desired Mr. Judson to accompany with as interpreter. The latter refused for some time, being unwilling to leave for a moment the work so much requiring his attention. But, prompted by a sense of obligation to the English officers for their kindness, and receiving a promise from them that they would use every endeavor to have inserted a clause allowing religious toleration in all Burmah, he consented to go. He expected the new missionaries, Wade and Hough, to be there by the time he returned, and then the work could go forward rapidly.

His parting with his wife was less painful this time than it had ever been to either before. Though about to return to the scene of his former sufferings, he would be under the protection of powerful friends whom the monarch dare not offend; and she, too, would be surrounded by courteous officers, who respected her little less than their queen herself.

It was sunset, and his boat was waiting at the mouth of the Salwen, Mr. Crawford already aboard. He took an affectionate leave of all the family, his wife accompanying him as far as the little grove, half way to the river, he bearing the child. There, in the shade of the mango trees, they knelt and prayed. Rising, he laid the little one tenderly in her mother's arms, embracing them both.

"You must write me every week, Ann," he said. "You know how unpleasant it will be in the presence of the haughty, stubborn king for four or five months, and in sight of the dreadful Let-ma-yoon, even though now safe from its power. Let me know regularly of your health and the condition of dear little Maria. Poor child!" he said gently as he kissed her pure, white lily cheek, "she is indeed a child of sorrow; born in grief, and nurtured amid scenes of torture. But her little face is growing brighter, perhaps she even feels our happiness in release. Moung Ing will care for you.

Do not be anxious on my account as I shall write regularly of our progress at court. Good-bye."

Another kiss and he was gone. Six months was a long time to the waiting wife, but she would not be idle, and she resolved to surprise him on his return, when he should see what had been accomplished in his absence. Watching him till his retreating form was lost in the yet untrampled sedge of the river's border, she turned and clasping the child more closely on her breast, went back towards the tent. See her as she approaches, beautiful, even now, after all her sufferings. The short, black ringlets are once more beginning to crown her head. True, the flush of girlhood has faded from her cheeks, and they are white, very white; yet there is an angelic sweetness there; and her earnest dark eyes betray a depth of soul which only the hand of God can give, made more "perfect through suffering." Her step is not so elastic as formerly, and that form which braved the heat of the scorching plains, the taunts of heartless jailers, bearing the burden of the child on her bosom while ministering to a sick husband in prison, and facing the Burman Lion in his golden den—is now slender and delicate. She seems, withal, a flower too pure, too tender for earth, much less a savage country, in the jungle at that. Yet her mind is filled with designs for advancing God's cause among the heathen, and bravely she will attempt to execute her plans.

.   .   .   .

In an incredibly short time she and Moung Ing had erected two bamboo school-houses. In one of these Moung Ing gathered ten Burman children whom he undertook to instruct, while she made arrangements to begin a female school in the other, in which she gathered the converts every Sunday morning for worship.

The next thing was to have a home. So she began the erection of a roomy dwelling, sufficiently large to accommodate both her own family and the natives who had come with them from Rangoon.

One room was designed especially for Mr. Judson's comfort. She arranged everything just as she knew, from experience, he would like it; the table, the wardrobe and the study-corner. Here she made a window fronting the river and sea, overshadowed by a large tamarind tree. While engaged in this work of love, Maria's health began to decline, and it seemed, in spite of the mother's devoted watchfulness, that the feeble spark would be extinguished. Mahree and the nurse often besought her to take more rest, assuring her that they would care for the little one, but she could only be content beside the cradle. The infant was more dear to her for the very trials that had made its life so sad, and she would spare no effort to preserve that life in hope of a brighter future. Her faithfulness had its reward, and she soon had the satisfaction of seeing the crisis safely past, and the child beginning to improve. She now intrusted her to Mahree part of each day while she superintended the completion of the house.

Mr. Judson had heard from her regularly in regard to the child. His last letter from her was hopeful. She says:

"I have this day moved into the new house, and, for the first time since we were broken up at Ava, feel myself at home. The house is large and convenient, and if you were here I should feel quite happy. Poor little Maria is still feeble. When I ask her where papa is, she always starts up and points toward the sea. The servants behave very well, and I have no trouble about anything except you and Maria. May God preserve and bless you and restore you again to your new and old home, is the prayer of your affectionate Ann."

That was the last she ever wrote. Comfortably situated now in the new house, her child saved through her unwearied attentions, the anxiety which had stimulated her so far was now removed, and she failed like a runner who, forgetting everything behind him, expires as his hand touches the goal. Wakefulness and anxiety had undermined the frail constitution, and the old fever of Oung-pen-la returned. She could no longer resist its ravages, and as she lay in her room in the new house she knew she could never rise again. She only wished now to see her husband and the new missionaries established in the house she had so lovingly provided. Even then she did not repine. But it was, oh! so hard to leave little Maria, and not a parting word to the distant father, who never suspected her sickness. The English officers were very kind to show every attention in their power and to provide anything they had for her comfort. The attack was violent and her mind often wandered in her delirium. In a day or two the friends knew all hope was gone. Moung Ing was unwearied in his devotions. He could not bear the thought of the teacher returning to his home and finding his loved one gone. All night he and the Burmese nurse watched by the sick-bed. Mahree and Abbe, by turns, nursed the child, or brought water and medicine to the nurse; and the disciples who had come with

them from Rangoon, Mah-Men-la and Mah-Dokè, rendered loving assistance.

She had now been delirious for several days; the
nurse had gone out to order some broth, requesting
Moung Ing to watch in her absence. He took his place
by the bedside. On looking at the sufferer, he saw her
eyes fixed steadfastly upon him, and that they contained the light of reason, which often returns just
before the spirit's departure. She spoke. Bending
over, he heard her call for Mahree. He motioned to
the girl, who was at a window on the other side rocking the cradle. She stepped softly to the bed.

"What is it, mamma?" she asked gently.

"The little casket, Mahree, in the trunk.   Bring it
to me."

When it was brought, she motioned Mahree to sit
on the bed beside her.

"You are now old enough," she said, to understand
the mystery of its contents. Take the little key from
round your neck and open it, that I may see also."

Moung Ing had stolen away and was rocking the cradle, lest the child should awake and disturb its mother.

With trembling hands Mahree drew forth the little
key. Now she should know the mystery of her life,
and whether she should marry the man she loved. The
lid flew open. Lying within, on a piece of cotton, was
a child's bracelet, small and beautifully set—such as
she had seen only on the children of the royal family.
Within was inscribed the name

MANOHARA.

The girl gazed in mute astonishment, no nearer a
knowledge of her identity than before. Mrs. Judson

reached forth her hand and took it. While she was looking at the inscription, Mahree found a faded paper in the bottom of the box.

"See here, mamma!" she said breathlessly.

Unfolding it, they read:

"TAKEN FROM THE GANGES, ABOVE BENARES, NEAR THE GROVE OF SORROW, WHERE HER MOTHER HAD THROWN HER TO THE SACRED CROCODILE.   FELIX CAREY.

"MARCH 4TH, 1808."

"Ah!" said Mahree; "now I understand why I feared the Irrawaddy, and my dreams of the sea. But what can it mean? I am a Burman, and Burmese women are not allowed to leave the country. What was my mother doing on the Ganges? Then, oh, dreadful deed! how could she be so cruel? But even yet I do not know who I am."

"There is only this clue," said Mrs. Judson, as she looked at the bracelet. "Only the daughters of the palace are allowed to wear such spangles as this. You are a princess, and must have been spirited away by some envious person, who feared for you to live, or else stolen for your beauty or because of hatred for the king. I confess I do not understand it. Call Moung Ing. He has been about the palace during Mr. Judson's imprisonment, and may be able to judge something of the circumstances."

Mahree motioned him to come.

Mrs. Judson handed him the bracelet. A violent tremor seized the strong man as he took the little relic. He read the inscription, then eagerly clasped the paper. Reading it, he fell on his knees.

"Thank God for this day!" he cried. "My child; my own sweet Manohara! I am your father!" and he clasped the wondering girl in his arms. It was some time before he could compose himself sufficiently to speak. Then, drawing himself up, he looked Mah-ree in the face.

"The very image of your beautiful mother the day I married her," he said, "why had I not seen it before?"

"Teacher," he said, turning to her, "you do not understand it all, neither does she. My name is not Moung Ing. I am Mekara, whom they sought at the death of Min-der-a-ge Praw. I was his oldest son, and heir to the throne of Burmah. I refused to worship Buddha and he drove me from the country. With my wife and child I went to India. While in the woods a Brahmin told me that my poor wife had thrown herself and child into the Ganges. I have since mourned them as dead. My child is found, and this paper leads me to hope her mother may yet be living. God grant it may be so!"

"Let us bless Him for His goodness and praise him for his mercies so far," said the sick woman fervently. "I bless you both, my children."

Moung Ing sprang to his feet.

"A light dawns upon me!" he cried. "Call the nurse, Manohara; call the nurse quickly!"

Filled with astonishment, and trying to conjecture what further developments awaited, she rushed out of the room. When she had gone, Mekara sat down, though so much agitated he could not be still.   .

"Teacher," he said, "do you not remember, I asked you once if you had ever traced any resemblance in the face of your nurse to Mahree, and requested you to ask her if she ever had a child? What was her reply?"

Now a new light gleamed in the eyes of the dying woman.

"Now I understand her strange behavior," she replied. "Yes, I asked her, and it agitated her greatly. She acknowledged she had once had a child, but begged me not to inquire further, and she would tell me all some day. Now I recall the time I met her in Serampore, and the sad story she told me there. But she is coming; let us see further."

Manohara, girl-like, could not keep the secret, but breaking into the kitchen she excitedly told the story of the golden bracelet to the nurse, who threw down her pan at the mention of the name MANOHARA, and clasped the now doubly-astonished maiden wildly about the neck. Then taking her hand, without a word of explanation, broke with her to the sick-room.

"Teacher!" she cried, drawing something from her bosom, "Mekara! I am Mahdri. See the companion to the little bracelet!" and she held it up.

With one bound Mekara had them both in his arms, and a happier trio never was seen.

Suddenly Manohara exclaimed:

"Look, papa, mamma! my poor, dear white mamma is dying. We have excited her too much!"

They turned to the bed. It was, indeed, too true. The excitement had again thrown her into delirium. She lay on one side staring with vacant eyes and talking incoherently to herself. Mahdri hastened to bring the broth, and Mekara applied all the restoratives at his command, but seemingly without avail. She was sinking rapidly. In a few moments Mahdri returned, followed by the other members of the household. The sufferer lay moaning with pain and burning with fever. Once the light shone in her eyes. A faint smile stole over her face as she looked upon her tender nurses.

"All is well," she said feebly. "I am glad I see my beloved Mahree united to her father and mother, and to think they are the ones who have been so faithful to me. May you be happy. I wish I could be with you longer to enjoy your happy meeting, but it is not the will of Him who calls me. May we meet again where there will be no more rude parting."

Again unconsciousness, and they thought all was over. But no; in her wanderings she is heard to whisper:

"Oh, the teacher is long in coming. The new missionaries are long in coming. I must die alone and leave my little one. Tell the teacher the disease was most violent. Tell him I could not write. Tell him how I suffered and died. Tell him all you see."

Her voice sank to the faintest breathing. The rattle was heard in her throat; her eyes closed wearily, and she seemed insensible to all earthly objects. The women were weeping. Poor Mahree and Abbe sobbed bitterly. She had done so much for them, and they loved her so. Now another mourner breaks in. From the neglected cradle comes a faint cry. The mother's eyes open anxiously; her lips struggle to speak, and she feebly motions her hand in the direction of the cradle. Mahree understands, and brings the little one, laying her by her mother's side. The mother's hand creeps softly over the little form.

"Mahree," she whispered, "be kind to my darling Maria—indulge her in everything till her father comes home—precious, precious baby!"

Again the lethargy. Mahdri stoops and whispers to her. Again her lips open and she speaks her last words on earth: "I AM QUITE WELL, ONLY WEAK." A brief interval of heavy breathing—an exclamation, "Amai-ai!" in the Burmese language, and all is over.

> "She made a sign
> To bring her babe—'twas brought and by her placed.
> She looked upon its face · . . and laid
> Her hand upon its little breast, and sought
> For it with look that seemed to penetrate
> The heavens. . . . . . .
> 'God keep my child!' we heard her say and heard
> No more ; the Angel of the Covenant
> Was come, and faithful to his promise, stood
> Prepared to walk with her through death's dark vale."

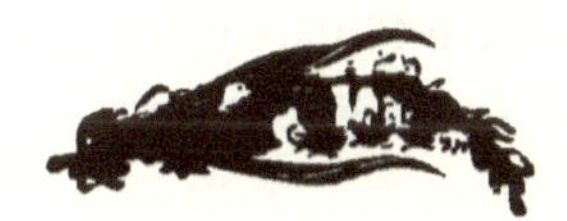

CHAPTER II.

" He comes! he comes!
The wearied man of God, from distant toil.
His home, while yet it seems a misty speck,
His glance descries,—half-wandering that the step
Of his beloved glides not o'er the heath,
As wont to meet him.

" Ah ! what heathen lip,
In its strange language, told him, that on earth
Nothing remain'd which to his throbbing heart
In that hour's desolation he might press,
Save that poor, famish'd infant.   Days of care
Were measur'd to him, and long nights of grief
Weigh'd out,—and then that little moaning one
Went to its mother's bosom, and slept sweet
'Neath the cool branches of the Hopia tree."

—*Mrs. Sigourney.*

A COMPANY of British soldiers, and many natives, stood with bared heads beneath the shade the Hopia tree, while Burmah's soil closed over the body of her first Christian martyr.   Mckara conducted the funeral in a very impressive manner.   The grave was closed, a " small rude fence " placed around " to prevent it from incautious intrusion," and all departed in silence and in sadness.

The officers conferred together as to the best means of informing the bereaved husband of his unexpected loss. Captain Fenwick wrote as follows to a friend in Rangoon :

" I trust you will be able to find means to inform our friend of the dreadful loss he has suffered.

.   .   .   .

(316)

"I shall not attempt to give you an account of the gloom which the death of this most amiable woman has thrown over our small society. You, who were so well acquainted with her, must feel her loss more deeply ; but we had just known her long enough to value her acquaintance as a blessing to this remote corner. I dread the effect it will have on poor Judson. I am sure you will take every care that this mournful intelligence may be opened to him as carefully as possible."

Worn out with the vexatious affairs of a haughty court, and the obstinacy of the proud young monarch, Mr. Judson was longing for the quietude of his own new home in the yet wooded city. It seemed that the time spent at the capital had been wholly lost, for the king obstinately refused to grant religious toleration to his subjects. Then it seemed that only once a week was not often enough to hear from home. It has been now more than a week, and Ann has not written. He is growing impatient. But then her last letter was cheering and all must be well. She is only too busy to write. With such reflections he sought to console himself. Ah, there comes a friend with a letter; now he will hear from home. But the man's countenance is sad and as he hands the letter to Mr. Judson, with the black seal upon its back, he kindly seeks to prepare him for the distressing news it contains, by saying:

"I am sorry to inform you of the death of your child."

Then it has come to the worst. The poor little sufferer has at last been relieved from her life of pain. It is hard to bear, to think her father should be away. But God knows best. His will be done. Sadly he breaks the seal to learn the particulars. He reads a few lines. A horror of great darkness comes over him

Can it be possible he has been deceived? Again he reads the dreadful words:

"My Dear Sir :—To one who has suffered so much and with such exemplary fortitude, there needs but little preface to tell a tale of distress. It were cruel indeed to torture you with doubt and suspense. To sum up the unhappy tidings in a few words, *Mrs. Judson is no more.*"

He staggered as if he would fall. The Englishman took him by the arm and kindly led him to a seat, then left him to bear his grief alone with God.

"Ann dead!" he cried; "gentle, patient, self-sacrificing Ann. Can she be dead? O, God! help me to bear this unexpected stroke."

Again there came visions of the past. The cool streams, shady dells, and wooded hills of New England rise up before him. Again the youthful pair in love's sweet bondage united; then desolate rovings from shore to shore; death of Harriet, and burial of little Roger; preaching, persecution, imprisonment; gloom and terror of the Let-ma-yoon, *the unshrinking hand;* a voice like music without, and a face like sunshine at the little door; the first sight of the puny babe; the blood-tracked march; the ministering angel of Oung-pen-la, she who had borne with him every grief, and who was the source of his every earthly joy; all come before him. Then, like a fast fading sunset-picture, he views the future that he had planned with her. Then it seemed glorious, now dark and uninviting. And it is yet four months ere he can behold the face of his little one, the only tie that now binds him to earth.

．　　　．　　　．　　　．　　　．　　　．　　　．

Mr. and Mrs. Wade arrived at Amherst about two months after the death of Mrs. Judson, and took charge of the mission. One evening, six weeks later, Mr. Wade was sitting at the window, his wife on the veranda with Maria. He saw a boat enter the harbor. "It is Brother Judson!" he exclaimed, and rushed down to the bank to meet him. With hearts too full for utterance the men grasped hands on the shore, after so long a separation and under such trying circumstances. Scarcely a word was spoken as they walked, arm in arm, up the path toward the house, the "old and new home" which Ann had built. Mekara met them under the mango trees, then came Mahdri and Manohara, weeping as they saw the lone widower. On the porch he shook hands with Mrs. Wade, who held his child, then started to take the little one in his arms. But she had long since forgotten him, and turned away with a cry of alarm, hiding her face on Mrs. Wade's breast. With a bursting heart he turned away. No one offered to follow, for he went toward the Hopia tree. On his knees in the long grass by the head-stone he prayed and wept. Then he stood under the mangoes where they had parted. Night came on, and yet the lone mourner wrestled with his grief, seeking to reconcile himself to the will of God.

.   .   .   .

The next evening when the mission family had gathered together, Mr. Judson heard in full the story of the happiness that had come to his faithful friends and adopted daughter. It in some measure relieved him of his own heavy burden to see them so happy.

After Mekara and Mahdri had each told their story, Manohara asked her mother if she knew what became of Asita. "Surely," thought she, "something evil must have happened to him for so much wickedness."

"Oh, yes," said Mahdri, "there is a link of my story left out. Several months after my conversion I returned to the Grove of Sorrow with Krishna Pal. The tracts he had circulated in the village had led several to a serious consideration of the Christian religion. Old Asita himself stumbled upon one on his way, one morning, to the mountain shrine. He read it and threw it down in disgust. But the Spirit of God wrought on him all the way to the little temple, and he became so much interested that he sought for the tract again on his return, and carried it with him to the forest. When we found him, six months later, he had given up his visits to the shrine, the devotees were compelled to shift for themselves, and he was earnestly praying for light. He was somewhat abashed and surprised to see me yet alive, but when Krishna opened to him the way of salvation he eagerly embraced Christ, and was baptized in the very spot where he had persuaded me to throw my precious child. We both prayed forgiveness of God for that murder, but I could never forgive myself, and it almost killed me when the teacher asked me one day, in Rangoon, if I had ever had a child.

"Asita then told me that my husband was not dead, as he had falsely reported, but had gone up the river. He sought to atone for the mischief he had done by going with me up the river in search of my husband, leaving Krishna to preach to the ascetics. We penetrated to Hudwar, at the feet of the Himalayas, but

could find no trace. I determined that I would never
despair of finding him, but would pray, labor, and wait
till God's good time. When we returned, the Grove of
Sorrow had been converted into a temple of rejoicing.
And wailing devotees were now lifting renewed souls to
God in those sweet words of Krishna that first attracted
me—

> ' O thou, my soul, forget no more,
> The Friend who all thy sorrows bore !'

"Oh! the power of God is wonderful, wonderful!
and his goodness beyond all comprehension!"

The whole company sat in mute thanksgiving as
Mahdri concluded her narrative. But there were other
things Manohara wished to have explained. Turning
to Mekara, she asked:

"Papa, why do you not claim your crown? The people love you, and would gladly place you on the throne
if you would only make yourself known."

"Why should I, my child? Where, in all the world,
is there a monarch now so happy as I? I would rather
be a door-keeper in the house of the Lord than to dwell
in the tents of wickedness. No, if my haughty nephew
can derive any pleasure from my inheritance, he is
welcome. I shall be a private soldier of the Cross, and
devote my life to the service of the King of kings. I
told my poor, down-trodden people when I left them
that when the light was found I would bring it to them.
I would rather bring them as sheaves to my Master's
feet than have them bow servile necks to me, and render that fear and allegiance which only to God is due.
I shall go soon to Tavoy, where I made many friends

21

while living a fisherman's life. There I will tell the 'Old, old Story' of the Cross, but tell it as a fisherman among men. My own story must never be told beyond this little circle. I am still Moung Ing, and never wish to be called by any other name."

It was now growing late, and the family retired to rest.

Mr. Judson could not rest from his labors. Gathering around him his books and papers, he once more busied himself in the translation of the Old Testament. Maria had, at last, consented to make his acquaintance, and often beguiled his sadness while in his lonely room. She was all that was left to him now, and tenderly did he bind her to his heart as a balm to the wound of her mother's loss. But even this was soon denied him. Day by day he saw her fading like a flower plucked from its parent stem. Then once more the soft tread, whispering voices, and mournful faces. Little Maria sleeps again on her mother's bosom.

Mr. and Mrs. Boardman arrived the same day to strengthen the missionary force. Mr. Boardman constructed the little coffin, another grave was opened beneath the Hopia tree, and the curtain closes over the last act of the sad tragedy of Amherst.

CHAPTER III.

—Tennyson.

THE mission at Amherst is now to be abandoned. There had been a misunderstanding between Mr. Crawford and Sir Archibald Campbell, the latter of whom had selected a site for the capital at Maulmain, twenty-five miles further north on the coast. Here he had established the royal troops, and thousands were flocking thither in preference to Amherst. Mr. and Mrs. Boardman removed to that place in a few days, while Mr. Judson prepared to remove the effects of the household as soon as possible. He still held public worship, however, and with the assistance of Moung Ing taught all who came to him.

One day Moung Schwa-ba, the native Christian who had accompanied him from Rangoon, entered, followed by a Karen.

"Teacher," he said, "here is a poor Karen who was formerly my servant in Rangoon. His people are despised and reviled by the Burmans, but he had heard of Christ and seeks knowledge. I told him I thought the gospel was intended for the low and vile, as well as the rich and proud. I found him by accident, he hav-

(323)

ing come to Amherst merely through curiosity. Will you instruct him?"

"Gladly, my brother," said Mr. Judson, and taking the timid inquirer by the hand, he sat down beside him and inquired to see if he had any conception of a God.

"Yes," said the Karen, "my people all believe in one God, but I never but once heard his name mentioned by Burman lips. I rowed the boat in which Prince Mekara left the kingdom, and he told me of his belief in a God. We know nothing definite. We have been waiting for the coming of the white foreigner with the Holy Book. Are you the one who was to come, and have you the Book of God?"

Mr. Judson was surprised, and rejoiced at what he heard. He then explained the nature of God to him, told him of Christ and the atonement for sin. But the latter was a new thought to him, and his mind could not comprehend it. In a God he believed, but who is this Christ? Mr. Judson talked with him long and earnestly, and when he arose to go gave him some tracts, with part of the Bible to read, inviting him to come again on the morrow.

As he went out the door Mr. Judson called him back and inquired:

"Did you not say you saw the prince when he was leaving Burmah?"

"I was with him, teacher."

"Will you promise to keep a secret?"

"I will."

"Mekara found God, and is now in this house."

"Prince Mekara here!" he said, with more animation than he had before shown. "May I see him?"

Mr. Judson stepped out of the room, and in a few moments Moung Ing entered. As soon as he saw the Karen he clasped his hand warmly.

"It is my old friend Ko Tha-Byu," he exclaimed. "Where have you been all these long years?"

"Wandering about, my lord, driven from post to post, waiting, with my brethren, the coming of the white man."

"Now," said Moung Ing, "the white man has come. Do you accept his religion?"

"His doctrine of a God I believe, but I cannot understand the atonement of Christ. He gave me some little books to read. I shall still seek for light."

Moung Ing then gave him a lengthy account of his own experience in obtaining salvation, and before he was through, the dull mind of the Karen began to grasp the truth.

"I see it better," he said.

Moung Ing forbore to press the matter rashly, but told him to read the books and return every day for instruction. This he promised to do; and before the missionaries left Amherst they had satisfactory evidence that the grace of God was manifest to him.

.   .   .   .

All things were now ready for the departure to Maulmain. Manohara had been busily engaged the whole day in packing the plunder for exportation. After sunset she walked out on the bank of the river to enjoy the cool air. As it was growing late, she turned her steps back toward the house. Coming through the shrubbery into the path, she suddenly confronted a man coming from the direction of the river. It was Robert Stuart.

"Mahree!" he cried, joyfully; "now you can greet me in the way I desired. I have come for my wife."

She held him off, as if not much concerned to see him.

"Have you been successful in your search?" she asked, simply.

"I have. I found Mr. Carey himself, who told me the contents of the casket. He rescued you from the Ganges just after your mother had thrown you into the water as a sacrifice. The little box contains a bracelet, which he took from your arm, inscribed with your name, 'MANOHARA.' Now, have I not won my prize?"

"Not yet," she said.

"What is now lacking?"

"The success of which you speak is not satisfactory. It leaves me as much a waif as ever—even more so. How do I know who my parents were, and the design of my mother in throwing me into the water? It is a very interesting story; but I cannot marry with simply the name 'Manohara.' I must know something of my parentage. I tell you now plainly, and once for all, unless you see my father and mother face to face, and obtain their consent, or ascertain that they are not living, I shall never be your wife. That is fixed."

"Mahree," he said, reproachfully, "you are a hard task-mistress. You exact entirely too much. If your parents are living, what right have they to command you, after having so mercilessly discarded you in infancy? And if dead, what pleasure will it be to learn it? Come; be reasonable, and say I have done enough."

"You have heard my terms," she said. "I shall revoke nothing I have said."

By this time they had approached the door of the veranda. Robert thought he had detected a slight spirit of fun in her manner, which he could not explain. Laying his hand on her arm, he detained her for a moment before entering the house. There was a deep seriousness in his eyes as he asked earnestly:

"Mahree, do you love me in reality?"

"I do," she said; "devotedly."

"Then why will you not marry me?"

"I will."

"When?" he asked, hopefully and eagerly.

"When you have complied with the conditions," she said saucily.

"I fear that will never be," he answered, with an expression of despair.

"Don't be so easily discouraged," she said. "Come in, and we will further discuss the matter."

The whole of the mission family was seated in the room, Moung Ing and his wife nearest the door. They all arose courteously as the young officer entered.

"Captain Stuart," said Mahree, at his side, "allow me to introduce to you my father, Prince Mekara, the eldest son of the great Min-dor-a-ge Praw: and this is his wife, Princess Mahdri, my mother."

The young man was thunder-struck, and so confused that he was speechless. Seeing his embarrassment, Mahree turned, and, burying her face in her hands, burst into uncontrollable laughter. Even the older members partook of her merriment.

"You naughty girl!" he cried; and seizing her in his arms before the whole company, he raised her head and, in spite of her protests, kissed her a half dozen times in succession.

Struggling vigorously, she escaped his grasp, and looking at him with an expression of abashed pleasure mingled with assumed anger, she exclaimed:

"How dare you, sir?" and rushed from the room, followed by Mahdri, who enjoyed immensely the turn affairs had taken.

Of course, the imaginative reader has already guessed the conclusion to this little drama. Suffice it to say that before the missionaries embarked for Maulmain, Robert Stuart and Manohara were united in marriage. Mr. Judson pronounced the solemn, impressive words that bound them together as one. On the next day they sailed for Calcutta, where Robert's command had been ordered, going by the way of Rangoon. As they were to lie at anchor here till evening, Robert said he must call on his friend Havelock, and insisted that his bride should accompany him to the camp. Hoisting a large umbrella to protect them from the heat, they passed through the city and out into Pagoda street.

"Why, Robert," said Manohara, "we are going wrong. This is the way I always saw the worshipers go to the great golden pagoda. There cannot possibly be anything else out here."

"Perhaps I have been here since you have, my dear," he replied. "Just be patient and we will be in camp in a few moments."

The magnificent form of the Shway-da-gong lifted its mountain-like mass, with its golden sides glittering before them. They entered the gorgeous enclosure, its brilliancy painful to the sight in the full blaze of the afternoon sun. All was still as death. Not a breath stirred the listless bells. The great gongs, for once, were silent.

The chaplets of flowers withered about the necks of their grinning idols. They passed around to the northern side, where the great shadow covered one of the idol temples. A sound of singing came from within. They stole softly into the vestibule and waited. There was a strange sight for Rangoon. A company of soldiers sat within, silent and attentive. At the farther end stood Lieutenant Henry Havelock, preaching the Gospel of Jesus Christ. His bible and hymn book lay, with his sword, on the stand before him. But the surroundings were remarkable. Every niche was filled, and the walls covered with images of Gautama, their legs crossed complacently, their hands resting tranquilly on their laps and their lips smiling approvingly on the scene. The temple had no windows, and the shade of the pagoda cut off the sunlight from the door. They had hit upon a novel plan for lighting the interior. Bringing lamps and lighting them, they set them in the laps of the idols to hold for them while they engaged in their worship. "At last these smiling images of 'The light of Asia' had reached their highest destiny." They contributed, in a small measure, to the kindling of that flame whose radiance reflects the Light of the World.

The young lieutenant is now thus beginning that brilliant career which is destined to work a mighty revolution in the civil and religious condition of all India. When the darkness of Hindu superstition shall begin to fade, he shall glow as a star of the first magnitude in the zenith, to be eclipsed only by the appearing of the Sun of Righteousness.

CHAPTER IV.

MESSRS. JUDSON and Wade having now settled at Maulmain, Mr. Boardman, becoming much interested in the Karens through the new convert, Ko Tha-Byu, decided to go in company with the latter, and establish a mission at Tavoy. Here Ko Tha-Byu was baptized and acting as interpreter to Mr. Boardman, they began work with the most flattering prospects. The Karens of the surrounding villages flocked in great crowds to the zayat to learn of God, and to hear read the Book which the "white man from the West" had brought.

In one of the neighboring villages lived a Karen prophet who had been gathering the people together for several years, and predicting the coming of the "white man with the Book of God," and urging them to pray for his coming. The Burmans, who were, of course, unfavorable to the invasion of foreigners, persecuted the old man for his prophecies, and threw him into prison. While here he met with an English officer who gave him a little book and exhorted him to read and follow

(330)

its precepts. But it was written in English and could not be read by the old man. Accordingly on his release, he buried it in the ground to keep it safe, and clothing himself in a yellow robe after the manner of a Buddhist priest, with staff in hand, he assumed charge of the sacred relic till some one should explain its contents. All the natives knew of the wonderful book left by a white man, and were anxious to have it interpreted. Hearing of Mr. Boardman's residence in Tavoy, several, in company with the self-elected priest. visited the zayat.

"Teacher," said the prophet, " there has long been a belief among our people that the Book of God should be restored to us by a white man from the West. Such a man left a book in my tent. Is it the Book of God?"

"I cannot tell," replied Mr. Boardman, " till I see the book. Go bring it hither."

He hastily departed to the village and dug up the book, returning with it in a short time. It was covered with a coat of pitch to protect it from moisture. This being removed, several folds of fine linen were found, enclosing a much worn prayer-book, with a few of the Psalms attached.

"No," said Mr. Boardman, "this is not the Book of God, but it is a good book and tells of him. I have brought with me the true Book."

He then produced a copy of the Bible and read a few passages.

The old prophet threw off his robe and laid aside his staff.

"My office is at an end," he said. "The Book of God has been found and our long waiting is over. Let us listen to its teachings."

The news spread rapidly and hundreds of eager natives came, desirous to hear the wonderful story of the Cross. Many who lived at a distance begged Mr. Boardman to visit their villages and preach to their people at home. This he promised to do, and in company with Ko Tha, who was beginning to be very useful in the work, he set out on the journey. It was a daring expedition, as it led through wild mountain passes and trackless jungles, the places which alone could afford refuge for the oppressed tribes of the reviled race. Mrs. Boardman wept to see her husband venturing upon such a journey. Ko Tha's wife, who remained with her, and who had recently been converted, offered such words of consolation as are characteristic of one who had undergone such a transition from darkness to light.

"Weep not, mamma; the teacher has gone on a message of compassion to my poor, perishing countrymen. They have never heard of the true God and of the love of his Son Jesus Christ, yes, Christ who died upon the cross to save sinners. They know nothing of the true religion, mamma; and when they die can not go to the golden country of the blessed. God will take care of the teacher; do not weep, mamma."

The missionaries were hospitably received at all the villages, and when their object was made known, the natives ran from door to door crying to every one they met.

"The white man from the West has come with the Book of God! The white man with the Book of God! Come hear him read and explain it!"

They seemed hungry for the Gospel, and bore away with delight the tracts and portions of Scripture distributed among them.

Ko Tha-Byu's heart was deeply touched by the longing of his perishing countrymen, and he resolved to devote his life to preaching the Gospel in the jungles. He was not educated, but he was deeply earnest, and understood from joyful experience the full meaning of salvation by grace. Accordingly, after their return to Tavoy, he was ordained to the full work of the ministry.

He went far into the mountain recesses to begin his labor. In a hovel on a wild mountain-slope he preached his first sermon. It was in the home of Sau-Quala, of whom we made mention before. Both the child of "Hope" and his mother were converted by the sermon, Quala remarking:

"Is not this the very thing for which we have been looking and waiting so long?"

The prophetic "hope" of the parents was at length realized. Quala now felt the Spirit of the Lord laid mightily upon him, impelling him to go with Ko Tha to bear the news to his people.

Thousands of Karens have been since converted through the labors of the two zealous missionaries, their success being so marvelous that they have been appropriately titled the "Karen Apostles."

The converts among the Karen were the most satisfactory of any the teachers had ever seen. They manifested a spirit of such meekness, docility, and earnestness as would put to shame many of their more enlightened brethren in civilized lands. Mr. Judson often spent months in the jungle preaching to them. The noble Boardman sacrificed his life in their midst. On his death-bed he had the joy of witnessing the solemn ordinance of baptism administered to thirty-four of his recent converts.

. . . .

After having established missions in Maulmain and around through the country, Mr. Judson traveled much from place to place. Since Ko Tha had gone with Mr. Boardman to Tavoy, Moung Ing and his wife were appointed to labor in Rangoon, and endeavor to re-establish the church there. Mr. Judson visited the valley of the Irrawaddy again, bringing with him a great quantity of tracts and extracts from the Bible, which was now wholly translated into Burmese.

A great interest had sprung up. The tracts formerly circulated, like leaven, had pervaded the whole empire. The king still opposed, but the people clamored for a knowledge of the true God, showing how essential God is to the soul in all nations. Mr. Judson writes from Rangoon to a friend:

"The great annual festival is just past, during which multitudes came from the remotest parts of the country to worship at the great Shway-da-gong pagoda in this place, where it is believed that several real hairs of Gautama are enshrined. During the festival I have given away nearly ten thousand tracts, giving to none but those who ask. I presume that there have been six thousand applications at the house. Some come two or three months' journey, from the borders of Siam and China. 'Sir, we hear that there is an eternal hell. We are afraid of it. Do give us a writing that will tell us how to escape it.'

"Others come from the frontiers of Kathay, a hundred miles north of Ava. 'Sir, we have seen a writing that tells about an eternal God. Are you the man that gives away such writings? If so, pray give us one, for we want to know the truth before we die.'

(335)

"Others come from the interior of the country, where the name of Jesus Christ is little known. 'Are you Jesus Christ's man? Give us a writing that tells of Jesus Christ.'"

A printing press was at work day and night, but it was unable to supply the wants of the craving multitude. Thus the Lord has blessed the labors of the two missionaries who landed there under such discouraging circumstances fifteen years before. The sufferings were great—the loss of wife and babes severe—yet the grand results compensate for all the sufferings of the past; and now is the cry:

"The harvest is plentiful, but the laborers few. God, send us more laborers into the field!"

CHAPTER V.

" Havelock's glorious Highlanders answer with conquering cheers,
  Forth from their holes and their hidings our women and children come out,
  Blessing the wholesome white faces of Havelock's good fusileers,
  Kissing the war-harden'd hand of the Highlander wet with their tears.
  Dance to the pibroch !—saved ! we are saved !—is it you? is it you?
  Saved by the valor of Havelock, saved by the blessing of Heaven !
  'Hold it for fifteen days !'   We have held it for eighty-seven !
  And ever aloft on the palace roof the old banner of England blew."
  —*Tennyson.*

THE reader's attention is now directed forward over
a period thirty-one years from the death of Mrs. Judson,
to the close of the year 1857, when we look upon the
final scene that opens the gates of the East to the King
of Glory.   In India all seems quiet, the hundreds of
millions of subjects bowing in meek submission to the
handful of foreigners, and thousands of the natives
serving as soldiers in the pay of the British.

Suddenly, like a spark of fire to a powder magazine,
there burst forth a' mutiny at whose atrocities the ears
of all nations were made to tingle with horror.   The
Sepoy armies learned that the cartridges furnished
them by the British for use in their rifles were greased
with beef's tallow.   To touch that product of the sacred
bullock was to lose caste.   Their rage knew no bounds.
The mutiny spread throughout the land.   All English
garrisons were furiously assaulted, and their inmates,
who could not escape, relentlessly butchered.   The
insurgents professed to restore the ancient Mogul
dynasty, and fought in the name of the King of Oude.

Missionaries were dragged about the streets of Delhi by Moslem fiends, who continually beat them over the heads and called on them, in derision, to preach Christ to them. Helpless women and children were foully murdered in their beds, their feet cut off and placed in rows around the walls, while their amputated hands and heads were piled in ghastly heaps in the middle of the floor, leaving the gory bodies weltering among the bed-clothes. Little children clinging to the bosoms of their mothers were thrust through by savage bayonets and left fastened there, mingling their frantic death agonies together; and old veterans were ruthlessly dragged from their rooms, where their captors, clutching their gray hair in one hand, smote off their heads with a sword in the other.

A vast horde of rebels surrounded Cawnpore, whose feeble garrison contained less than three hundred soldiers, with five hundred women and children, the families of officers, then besieged at Lucknow. The atrocious Nana Sahib led the insurgents in person. The garrison resisted bravely for more than seven months, until it seemed that they could not stand another day longer. At this point Nana Sahib, wearied with their long endurance, made them a seemingly generous offer, proposing to furnish them boats and a safe passage to Allahabad if they would lay down their arms. It seemed the last resort, as their store of provisions was about exhausted. They embraced the opportunity of escape, and went aboard the boats provided for them. But no sooner had all embarked than a masked fire was poured upon them, and the banks were both soon lined with mounted horsemen. All escape was cut off to the now helpless band, and they were compelled to die, without resistance, thus beset on every side. The water was soon red with the blood of the slain. Boats floated away empty or sank overladen with the dead and pierced with bullets. A few of the women and children were spared for a worse fate. In a few days they were brought out of their prison, before their treacherous protector, who had them immediately executed, and their bodies, many of them yet breathing, thrown into a well in the court-yard.

Like horrible scenes were enacted at Allahabad and Benares, but Colonel Neill rescued each place before matters had reached such a crisis as at Cawnpore.

The gallant General Henry Havelock, whose fame was now spoken of the world over, having heard of the seige of Cawnpore, hastened thither with his troops of Highlanders to the relief of the garrison, but arrived too late, the massacre of the women and children having taken place the day before. On the bank of the Ganges he defeated Nana Sahib, and then joining his army to that of Sir James Outram, who had just arrived, hastened to the relief of Lucknow.

Never before, since the memorable seige of Jerusalem, has earth witnessed such an action as that at Lucknow. Sir Henry Lawrence who had charge of the residency, had made some successful sallies upon the besiegers, but was finally slain and the troops compelled to retire into a smaller fort, where, under the command of Colonel Robert Stuart, they continued bravely to resist the foe. Many of the wives and families of the Highlanders had been left at Lucknow for protection. Manohara stood by her husband, the gallant Colonel, through all the seige, encouraging him by her hopeful words and heroic fortitude. It was, by no means, the first time they had braved death together, and they resolved to die rather than surrender the garrison to the tender mercies of the murderers of Cawnpore's innocents. But now it seemed that every hope was lost. Provisions were scarce, ammunition almost exhausted, and the strength of the soldiers failing before the ceaseless charges of the enemy which was renewed by daily re-inforcements.

The relief party made desperate efforts to reach the city as soon as possible, but found every foot of the way contested. Numerous engagements had been fought, and they were almost worn out with fatigue, and many of them weak from loss of blood. Beneath the walls of the Furred Buksh Havelock and Outram held a consultation.

"The brave troops have come through many difficulties to-day," said Outram. "I fear they will be unable to advance any further, much less meet successfully a fresh foe of more than ten times their strength. Had we not better go in camp till morning?"

But in every engagement Havelock's cry had ever been "Forward!" To his untiring persistency he owed his success.

"No, we must press forward this very night," he said. "Think, the garrison may, at this moment, be exposed to the final assault; the enemy may collect during the night in overwhelming masses; it is of much importance to let the garrison know that succor is at hand."

At last General Outram consented, and taking only two regiments, the Highlanders and the Sikhs, they pressed forward to the beleaguered city.

As the slender column entered the street, the houses on either side flashed with almost a solid sheet of flame, as the bullets whistled through the air, and rattled against the stones; while, to retard the progress of the rescuers, deep ditches had been cut across the streets. The housetops, and connecting arches were alive with men, and ablaze with flashes of fire and rolling smoke. Passing under one of these arches General Neill, the hero of Benares and Allahabad, fell from his horse, a corpse. His enraged followers turned aside, for a moment, in a useless endeavor to avenge his death by a volley among the countless throngs around and overhead. Only for a moment. "Forward!" in thunder tones came the stern command of Havelock. Even though his own brave son fell at his side, he did not halt, but rode calmly at the head of his rapidly decreasing ranks. It was not an hour for lamentation or revenge. At each crosssing were placed batteries that vomited forth a continual stream of fire and burning showers of lead and iron into the approaching ranks. Each street they entered seemed to enclose them between two walls of incessant, lurid flames. Around each corner drifted a storm of leaden messengers, like snow-flakes driven by the wind in a blizzard, covering the ground with writhing heaps of dead and dying. Thousands of hideous voices yelled in rage and defiance, the streets and walls rattled with the rain of balls, like hail on a roof. The smoke rose aloft, giving the city, as it stood in the night, more the appearance of a volcano than a residence of living beings. Havelock turned his face neither to the right nor to the left. If the bleeding column faltered, his clarion voice crying

"Forward!" heard above the din of battle, was sufficient to nerve them for yet another exertion. Now the
walls of the residency are reached, and the Highlanders
place the bagpipes to their lips to announce their victory.

A crisis was approaching within the garrison.

"Hold it for fifteen days. Never surrender, but let
every man die at his post!" had been the dying words
of the gallant Lawrence.

They had held it for fifteen days and thrice the time;
they had never surrendered; and it seemed that every
man was about to die at his post. The ablest of their
number had fallen, picked by sharp-shooters from a
lofty mosque overlooking the wall. Fever and cholera
were raging. They could not venture out to bury their
dead, even if they had had the time. The heat was
almost unbearable, and mingled with the odors of decaying flesh it was deathly in its effect. Mine after mine
had been sprung. Numerous rents had been made in
the wall. Even now an ominous "click, click" could
be heard close without. Kegs of powder are being
rolled into the opening made beneath. Only a touch
of fire now, and all is over. Every man was fully persuaded that within twenty-four hours their fate would
be sealed. Havelock was doubtless defeated, and they
must prepare to die "every man at his post." The
children cried, and the women prayed within.

From a commanding position Colonel Stuart watched
the designs of the enemy and issued orders to his men
in what way to thwart them. Thus many a scaling
ladder lifted toward the wall was dropped as its bearer
fell, pierced by a timely ball from within the barricade
Manohara was here, there, everywhere; bearing mes-

sages from her husband to different parts of the garrison, and bringing cups of hot coffee to the exhausted gunners. On one of her rounds she was accompanied by Jessie Brown, the wife of a corporal in Colonel Stuart's regiment. Poor Jessie had been feverish and excited during the whole siege, and, at times, delirious. To-night she was unusually restless. Returning she sank down with fatigue, and soon fell asleep, begging Manohara to call her when her "father should come home from the plowing." Manohara was herself weary and exhausted, and also fell into a slumber, despite the roar without. Suddenly she was awakened by a shrill, unearthly scream at her ear. Jessie stood in the middle of the floor, a wild look on her face, her hands behind her ears, and her eyes piercing out over the clouds of smoke as if listening.

"Dinna ye hear it? dinna ye hear it?" she screamed in delight. "Ay, I'm no dreamin'; its the slogan o' the Highlanders! We're saved, we're saved!"

Then falling upon her knees, with streaming eyes and fervent voice, she thanked God for his deliverance. The eager women within ran anxiously to the spot to listen, but no one could hear aught save the roar of cannon. She now darted away to the line of soldiers.

"Courage! Courage!" she cried. "Hark! to the slogan—to the MacGregor, the grandest of them a'. Here's help at last!"

The soldiers stood as if electrified. With poised guns ready to fire, they paused to listen. Only the rattle of musketry. In bitter disappointment they turned to their duty. The women set up a pitiful wail as the Colonel shook his head in answer to their inquiries

whether he heard anything. The poor, half-frantic
Jessie sank to the ground as in a swoon. After a few
moments of anxious suspense she sprang to her feet
and cried with a piercing voice heard to the end of the
line.

"Will ye no believe it noo? The slogan has ceased
indeed, but the Campbells are comin'! D'ye hear?
D'ye hear?"

Now indeed was heard a sound as sweet to the besieged
garrison as the music of angelic choirs, as, above the
din of battle, rose the shrill notes of the Scottish
pibroch, now wild and harsh as if threatening vengeance
upon the foe, then softly promising deliverence to their
friends. With one accord, all fell on their knees, forgetting their loaded guns, to thank God for his mercies.

. With a mighty shout the Highlanders burst through
the barricades headed by Havelock. Cheers answered
from within. Havelock and Stuart rushed into each
other's arms, while the Highlanders clasped their wives
and children to their breasts. In the midst of all
Havelock was heard to exclaim, "Not unto us, O Lord!
not unto us, but unto Thy name give glory!"

The garrison now raised the shout, "God save the
Queen;" to which the pibrochs replied with the strain,
"Should auld acquaintance be forgot?"

Joy reigned in every bosom. A rich banquet was
given the famished garrison, in which the officers drank
to Jessie's health and the Highlanders marched around
the table playing the familiar and soul-stirring air of
"Auld Lang Syne."

CHAPTER VI.

* * * * *

THE RESCUE of Lucknow practically ended the war of
the rebellion, as news now came of the capture of the
other important points; but the rebels were not wholly
conquered until Sir Colin Campbell arrived with re-
inforcements, and struck the decisive blow. The salvation of the garrison had been bought at a terrible cost.
One-third of the brave rescuers lay dead in the streets,
their bodies trampled beneath the feet of the raging
mob. But more than all, their heroic commander,
Havelock, now lies at the point of death. The excessive fatigues and anxieties of his numerous engagements, together with the climate, so unfavorable to great
activity, brought on dysentery, which prostrated him
with the first attack. He was dying at the zenith of
his fame. The Queen of England recognized his bravery,
and rewarded it with the highest honor. He was
removed from the residency to the camp of Sir Colin
Campbell, who now, by the authority of the Queen,
addressed him as Sir Henry. Though called to go at
the time when the laurels were just within his grasp,

the good man was happy. He had fought a good fight,
he had kept the faith.   For the success of every battle
he had given God the glory.   After every marvelous
escape from death he had assembled his troops and
caused them to kneel while he offered up thanks to the
Lord of Hosts.   To Sir James Outram, who stood by
him, he said:

"For forty years I have so ruled my life that when
death came I might face it without fear."

He was happy, too, because his wife and little ones
were safe from the cruelties to which hundreds of others
had been subjected.   He had already established them
in Germany on the Rhine, where he expected his children to be educated.   But his wife was the daughter
of that great light of the Serampore Mission, Dr. Marshman, and would have bravely remained at his side if
he had consented.   Now, too, the widow would be provided for.   He could not enjoy the Queen's bounty, but
the thousand pounds a year would still go to her and
the children.   He was happy, also, because the great
war was over, and his beloved Stuart would take his
place in restoring peace and quiet to the distracted land.

Robert and Manohara were by his side till the last.
She held his throbbing head and bathed his feverish
brow as tenderly as his own wife could have done.   In
his last moments he thanked God for the waif of the
Ganges that had been brought to the "white mamma"
and trained to be a Christian soldier's wife.

Two older sons had engaged with him in the battle.
One fell in the streets of Lucknow; the other, with a
broken arm, stood beside the sick bed.   The end was
near.

First Lesson in Idolatry.

"So be it," said the sufferer; "I am ready."

Then, seeing his sorrowful son standing near, he called to him cheerfully:

"Come, come, my son, and see how a Christian can die!"

Then, with his son holding one hand and Colonel Stuart the other, he quietly breathed his last.

.   .   .   .

We are now called upon to witness a great and happy change in the government of India. It was now transferred from the East India Company to the English Crown, and Queen Victoria was proclaimed Empress of India. Strong garrisons were firmly established in all the principal cities, and peace and order restored. The new government, instead of throwing obstacles in the way of mission work, now offered encouragement. Great attention was now given to religion and education, for it has been proven that these are the most potent factors in successful ruling. The wholesale suicides at Hurdwar and Benares, the drowning of infants in the Ganges, and the suttee of widows were strictly forbidden. General Robert Stuart was stationed at Benares with his forces to prevent any violation of these restrictions. The law was hard to enforce on account of the superstitions of the people, but they gradually submitted. Many a poor child did Manohara herself preserve from the crocodile's jaws She told the deluded mothers of her own narrow escape, and pointed them to Christ, the Atonement for sin.

Instead of missionary progress being impeded by the loss of life and property by the war, it was greatly advanced.

The story of sufferings and persecutions touched a chord of sympathy in the hearts of English and American Christians, and they responded warmly to the appeals for aid. New forces were sent, colleges and churches erected, publication houses established, and a wonderful impetus imparted to the instruction of the natives. The English language is the language of the conquerors, and all wish to learn it. With it goes a knowledge of God.

How sublime are the wonderful workings of Jehovah! When the storm raged in Burmah, we cried out in despair:

"Alas! alas! only two missionaries, and they in prison. Our cause is hopelessly lost!"

But that very persecution was the means of bringing the persecuted teachers into the sympathies of indolent Christians throughout the world, who now rallied to their assistance, and of bringing them in closer contact with the obtuse-minded and proud-hearted officials, who would never have known them otherwise. Now the clouds have rolled away, the Sun of Righteousness beameth on the darkened country of the Golden Face, and tens of thousands praise the Jehovah of the despised Karens.

When the raging blast of the rebellion swept with such terrific fury over India, it threatened to annihilate the germs of civilization, and leave the blood-soaked soil free once more, to sprout the gory dynasty of the decaying Mogul glory. But the poetic days, when the glittering splendor of the Rajahs exulted over the cries of the slain, had passed. The hand of God had planted the seeds of the truth, even turning the opposition of stubborn rulers into praise and thanksgiving.

"Oh, the depths of the riches, both of. the knowledge and wisdom of God; how unsearchable are His judgments and His ways past tracing out!"

. . . .

Here, thinking my work was completed, I laid aside my pen and, much wearied, fell asleep, when there occurred to me such a vision, that I must tell it to the reader, for its scenes are true.

Methought, by a swift conveyance of modern invention, I was transported through the air and over intervening seas, until I stood on the topmost crags of the Himalayan peaks. The thin air was clear and pure, as I looked with rapturous gaze upon the luxuriant plains and embowered cities in the South, stretching from the base of my lofty pedestal even to the blue line, where I knew sparkled the waters of the Bay of Bengal. Slowly oozing from the snows beneath my feet, and trickling like icy pearl-drops down the crags, I saw the fountain of the Ganges. Following the streamlets as they increased, I beheld the mighty tide rushing through the gates of Hurdwar and spreading out, a placid stream, rolling along the plain. Looking to the southeast I saw the Irrawaddy traversing its fertile valley, and, far to my left, the great Yangtse Kiang of China. The aspect of Burmah had changed; once more she had made war with England and had been forced to surrender large tracts of her territory. These the people of God had appropriated at once. The government of the Burman monarch had grown smaller and smaller, until it scarcely was felt beyond the limits of the Golden City; while foreigners, bearing the seeds of the Gospel, are penetrating every jungle and settling in every city and village. The white-leaved tracts and Bibles are circulating in every direction. King Thirrawaddy, sitting on the throne of his deposed brother, says to a teacher, "Come to the Golden City, and I will build you a zayat to preach in." Prince Mekara, or Moung Ing, heeding not the political strifes of his covetous nephews, is leading the Lord's hosts to possess the land, and soon the whole will be ceded, not to Victoria, but to Prince Immanuel.

In India, too, a mighty revolution has taken place. Calcutta, Madras, Serampore, Benares, Delhi and Agra are becoming great centers for soldiers of the Cross, and Allahabad is becoming more of what its name implies, "The City of God." From Bombay, stretching across to Calcutta, and touching all intervening cities of importance, I see a huge black line, with numerous branches intersecting it in various directions. "Something new," thought I. "What can it be ?" Then I heard a shrill whistle—strange sound in that hitherto unprogressive land—and waking the echoes in the ruined temples and crumbling palaces; a long line of white smoke; a thundering tread, that caused the sandy ground to tremble beneath; a glimpse of rapidly revolving wheels—and the stranger was gone. But in its wake were left, at various stations, articles of merchandise, books, tracts and missionaries.

Then I noticed a change in the aspect of the Ganges. Dead bodies no longer floated on her bosom, but the white sails of commerce glided from port to port.

Benares is wonderfully changed. It is Sabbath morning. A great crowd is standing on the bathing ghaut at the river. In the water is a pale-faced foreign teacher, surrounded by a number of natives with meek, tranquil faces. On the bank stands another teacher, reading aloud from a sacred book—but not the Shaster. One by one, the man in the water administers the sacred rite of baptism to each new convert. Then they come out and a sound wakes the air from a thousand voices, but no gongs are heard. It is Jehovah's praise they sing. The thin air around me seems an electric medium, through which every sound is borne to my ears.

Now from among the golden-spired temples on the cliffs there peals a sound that arouses my curiosity more than ever. Can it be the pagoda bells ? No, the air is perfectly still, and then it is too deep and full for that. Is it the gong in the temple? No, it is too soft and melodious for that. Now another and another, here and there, they resound in every part of the city. The pigeons circle about the spires in alarm. The grinning monkey-gods leap upon the roof of their dwelling and look around with a quizzical expression.

The crowd at the river now begins to approach in the direction of the sounds, and I understand the mystery— church bells; strange, and yet how sweet their music ! Now my ears are ringing with vibrations, so that I can scarcely distinguish one sound from another. Grad- ually I grow more accustomed to them and can trace each to its source. From Bombay they come, joining others along the line of the railroad; from the Punjab; from the Deccan; from Hurdwar throughout the valley to Calcutta. Then from my left, I hear something. Is it an echo from the rocks? No, up from Rangoon, Burmah, the music floats. Maulmain joins the chorus;

then Tavoy, Prome, and even Ava. Arracan resounds along the seashore; then a fainter sound; from away down in Siam it comes stealing. Over my shoulder floats a timid strain. I listen closely. Thank God! Old China is speaking. Revelling in these delightful sounds I stood musingly gazing down upon Benares, the Holy City. It seemed that I must be in heaven listening to the music of angelic voices, so sweet was the sensation of my soul.

The music ceases, a feeling of sadness follows; for I fear the spell will be broken and the vision lost. But, no. By a swift transition from light to darkness, and night to day, Monday morning dawns and the scene remains the same. The bathing ghauts are thronged as usual. Near the outskirts of the city a mother timidly shrinks behind a wall on the river bank, holding a child in her arms. She glances cautiously around, for the deed she contemplates is now considered a crime instead of a religious duty as formerly. Yet she cannot give up the old faith, and the Brahmins have encouraged her to perform her duty. Laying the precious burden on the ground, she kneels and earnestly prays to Vishnu that the soul of her dear one may be preserved and born again free from the curse of womanhood. Then, with a bursting heart, she stands and clasps her babe to her bosom for the last time. The cloak is wrapped about the little form and all is now ready for the sacrifice. She starts and turns in alarm, for a hand is laid gently on her shoulder and a sweet voice bids her listen for a moment. Manohara, suspecting the woman's purpose, has followed her. She tells the mother her own story of rescue from Ganga's

23

arms, and points her to Christ the Sacrifice for sin.   The other listens eagerly, then follows her back to the zenana, her child in her arms.   I look at the zenanas of the city.   They are no longer harems but homes, joyful with the laughter of merry children.   The women are no longer slaves, but true wives and mothers.   My own reason answers the question.   "Why is this?"   The Gospel has converted the men and made them sympathetic husbands and fathers.   Aided by the same means Manohara's influence has elevated the women to their true sphere, and girls are no more a curse, nor widows condemned to shame.

What is that massive structure outside the gate looking so neglected and lonely?   Ah! I see now the stone wheels, red with human blood.   But it moves no more. The Gospel has chained its wheels, and the smile of Juggernaut is a burlesque of the past.   Robert Stuart has cut the great cable with his sword.   My soul expands with delight as I see the great cities illumined by the Gospel; but I shudder to see the black pall that still hangs over the country and the inland towns. From every direction come the earnest cries, "Send us light, for we wander in darkness!"   And the answer comes from the toiling missionaries, "Only be patient. The harvest is great, but the laborers few.   We are praying God to send us more candle-sticks to bear the light.   Lord, open up the hearts of Thy people to behold the darkness around us, and send them to our relief!"

My soul burns within me.   Oh! that I had a thousand tongues to tell the "Story of Jesus and His love" to these perishing ones!   Will my countrymen never awake to their duty?   Arise, ye that slumber!   Ye Soldiers of the Cross, who have enlisted under the banner of Prince Immanuel, see ye not the kingdom of your Master occupied by Satan's barbaric hosts? Behold, the dawn approacheth. When the golden hue of the Millenial morn shall illuminate the Oriental hill-tops, and the effulgent beams of the Sun of Righteousness shall reveal the iniquity of the dark valleys, will He find you sleeping? Oh, awake! awake!

With that methought a cloud skirted the mountain side, shutting off the scene below; and bidding farewell to the CHILDREN OF THE GANGES, I awoke in my own room.

Important Missionary Publications.

AUTOBIOGRAPHY OF JOHN G. PATON. Missionary to the New Hebrides. Introductory note by Arthur T. Pierson, D.D. 2 vols., 12mo., portrait and map, in neat box, $3.00.

One of the most remarkable biographies of modern times.

"I have just laid down the most robust and the most fascinating piece of autobiography that I have met with in many a day. . . . . It is the story of the wonderful work wrought by John G. Paton, the famous missionary to the New Hebrides; he was made of the same stuff with Livingstone."—T. L. CUYLER.

"It stands with such books as those Dr. Livingstone gave the world, and shows to men that the heroes of the cross are not merely to be sought in past ages."—*Christian Intelligencer.*

THE LIFE OF JOHN KENNETH MACKENZIE. Medical Missionary to China; with the story of the First Chinese Hospital by Mrs. Bryson, author of "Child Life in Chinese Homes," etc. 12mo., cloth, 400 pages, price $1.50 with portrait in photogravure.

"The story of a singularly beautiful life, sympathetically and ably written. . . . . A really helpful, elevating book."—*London Missionary Chronicle.*

"The volume records much that is fresh and interesting bearing on Chinese customs and manners as seen and vividly described by a missionary who had ample opportunities of studying them under most varied circumstances and conditions."—*Scotsman.*

THE GREATEST WORK IN THE WORLD. The Evangelization of all Peoples in the Present Century. By Rev. Arthur T. Pierson, D.D. 12mo., leatherette, gilt top, 35c.

The subject itself is an inspiration, but this latest production of Dr. Pierson thrills with the life which the Master Himself has imparted to it. It will be a welcome addition to Missionary literature.

THE CRISIS OF MISSIONS. By Rev. Arthur T. Pierson, D.D. Cloth, $1.25; paper, 35c.

"We do not hesitate to say that this book is the most purposeful, earnest and intelligent review of the mission work and field which has ever been given to the Church."—*Christian Statesman.*

MEDICAL MISSIONS. Their Place and Power. By John Lowe, F. R. C. S. E., Secretary of the Edinburgh Medical Mission Society. 12mo., 308 pages, cloth, $1.50.

"This book contains an exhaustive account of the benefits that may, and in point of fact do, accrue from the use of the medical art as a Christian agency. Mr. Lowe is eminently qualified to instruct us in this matter, having himself been so long engaged in the same field."—*From Introduction by Sir William Muir.*

ONCE HINDU: NOW CHRISTIAN. The early life of Baba Padmanji. Translated from the Marathi. Edited by J. Murray Mitchell, M. A., LL.D. 12mo., 155 pages, with appendix. Cloth, 75c.

"A more instructive or more interesting narrative of a human soul, once held firmly in the grip of oriental superstition, idolatry and caste, gradually emerging into the light, liberty and peace of a regenerate child of God, does not often come to hand."—*Missionary Herald.*

AN INTENSE LIFE. By George F. Herrick. A sketch of the life and work of Rev. Andrew T Pratt, M.D., Missionary of the A. B. C. F. M., in Turkey, 1852-1872. 16mo., cloth, 50c.

Important Missionary Publications

(*Continued.*)

EVERY-DAY LIFE IN SOUTH INDIA, or, the Story of Coopooswamey. An Autobiography. With fine engravings by E. Whymper. 12mo., cloth, $1 00.

THE CHILDREN OF INDIA. Written for children by one of their friends. Illustrations and map. Small 4to , cloth, $1.25.

"These are good books for the Sunday-School Library, and will help young people in missionary societies who desire to have an intelligent idea of the people in India whom they are sending their money and their missionaries to convert."—*Missionary Herald*

HINDUISM, PAST AND PRESENT. With an account of recent Hindu reformers, and a brief comparison between Hinduism and Christianity. By J. Murray Mitchell, M.A., LLD. 12mo., cloth, $1.60.

"A praiseworthy attempt to present a popular view of a vast and important subject."—*Saturday Review*.

GOSPEL ETHNOLOGY. With illustrations. By S. R. Paterson, F. G. S. 12mo, cloth., $1.00.

" The first attempt to treat this subject from a thorough-going scientific standpoint. A very powerful argument for the truth of Christianity."—*English Churchman*.

"A book to refer to for information not easily to be obtained otherwise.—*Church Missionary Intelligencer*.

NATIVE LIFE IN SOUTH INDIA. Being sketches of the social and religious characteristics of the Hindus. By the Rev. Henry Rice. With many illustrations from native sketches. 12mo., cloth boards, $1.00.

"Those who have heard Mr. Rice's missionary addresses will be prepared to hear that this is a fascinating book."—*Life and Work*.

CHRISTIAN PROGRESS IN CHINA. Gleanings from the writings and speeches of many workers. By Arnold Foster, B.A., London Missionary, Hankow. With map of China. 12mo., cloth, $1.00.

AMONG THE MONGOLS. By Rev. James Gilmour, M.A., London Mission, Peking. Numerous engravings from photographs and native sketches. 12mo., gilt edges, cloth, $1.00.

"The newness and value of the book consists solely in its Defoe quality, that when you have read it you know, and will never forget, all Mr. Gilmour knows and tells of how Mongols live."—*Spectator*.

EVERY-DAY LIFE IN CHINA. or, Scenes along River and Road in the Celestial Empire. By Edwin J. Dukes. Illustrations from the author's sketches. 12mo., with embellished cover, $2.00.

That China is a mysterious problem to all who interest themselves in its affairs is the only excuse for offering another book on the subject.

NEW YORK. :: **Fleming H. Revell Company** :: CHICAGO.

MISSIONARY ANNALS.

I.
MEMOIR OF ROBERT MOFFAT.
BY M. L. WILDER.

II.
LIFE OF ADONIRAM JUDSON,
BY JULIA H. JOHNSTON.

III.
WOMAN AND THE GOSPEL IN PERSIA.
BY REV. THOMAS LAURIE, D. D.

IV.
LIFE OF REV. JUSTIN PERKINS, D. D.
BY REV. HENRY MARTYN PERKINS.

V.
DAVID LIVINGSTONE,
BY MRS. J. H. WORCESTER, JR.

VI.
HENRY MARTIN AND SAML. J. MILLS.
BY MRS. S. J. RHEA AND ELIZABETH G. STRYKER.

VII.
WILLIAM CAREY,
BY MARY E. FARWELL.

VIII.
MADAGASCAR.
BY BELLE MC PHERSON CAMPBELL.

IX.
THE LIFE OF ALEXANDER DUFF.
BY ELIZABETH B. VERMILYE.

Price per volume: Cloth 30c., Paper 18c.

Sent Postpaid on Receipt of Price.

FLEMING H. REVELL COMPANY,

CHICAGO, | NEW YORK,
148 & 150 MADISON STREET. | 30 UNION SQUARE E.

Publishers Evangelical Literature.

9 783337 088880